DEADLY
Affections

TRACEE
LYDIA
GARNER

DEADLY AFFECTIONS
Copyright © 2017 by Tracee Lydia Garner
www.Teegarner.com

Published by Tracee Lydia Garner
ISBN: 978-0-9981099-1-6

This is a work of fiction. Names, characters, places and incidents are either the product of the author's imagination or are used fictitiously, and any resemblance to actual persons, living or dead, business establishments, events or locales is entirely coincidental.

Printed in the USA.

Cover Design and Interior Format
© KILLION
THE
GROUP, INC.

ALSO BY TRACEE LYDIA GARNER

FICTION

Family Affairs (All That & Then Some anthology)
Come What May (Jameson Family Book One/Tish's Story)
The One Who Holds My Heart
(Jameson Family Book Two/Dean's Story)
Love Unchosen
Anchored Hearts (Book One/Cole Parker's Story)
Deadly Affections (Book Two/Dexter Parker's Story)

NONFICTION

Pack Light: Thoughts for the Journey

ACKNOWLEDMENTS

Oh, the Lord is good to me
And so I thank the Lord,
For giving me the things I need,
The sun and the rain and the apple seed,
Oh, the Lord is good to me.

—Johnny Appleseed Prayer
(as told to me by Jackson Julius Garner)

CHAPTER ONE:
TAKEN

IN THE DARKEST ROOM SHE could imagine, Leedra Henderson was a moment away from screaming at the top of her lungs. The only reason she hadn't was her companion: small, cute and, as far as she could tell, just as scared as she was.

Leedra rolled to a fetal position. Sheer force of will was preventing her from surrendering to the familiar feeling of a concussion, threatening to carry her off into a deep sleep. She sat up slowly, one hand on her head and the other steadying her body as she pushed herself up from the cold concrete floor. She was racking her brain, trying to remember what had happened. A strong hand, a blunt object, a thudding pain at the back of her head. Trying to guess what that object had been, she hoped fervently that it hadn't been a loaded gun.

She caught her breath and thought again about screaming, but she had to think first. She wasn't sure any help was nearby to hear her, even if any bad guys were gone. She knew that if they were in fact present, screaming might just mean another clunk on the head. She needed to avoid that at all costs.

She'd been happy earlier that day, getting ready to start her life anew. She'd been en route to the house of her new boss for a meeting to discuss her new job at the Anchored Empowerment Center, a non-profit organization serving women and their children who had been battered and abused. The Center helped to make new lives happen for the women and children they served. She was so excited about being able to offer others the same chance for rescue that she herself had received years ago.

Leedra's mind drifted again, and she touched the side of her head to find a growing lump. She skimmed the raised flesh gingerly and was happy that at least no blood oozed from the sore. Slowly but surely, her mind was clearing.

"Hello?" she called softly. "Honey? Honey, are you there? Sweetie, I'm here to help you. You can trust me. Are you doing okay?"

Leedra sat straighter, hearing a shuffling just feet from her in the murky darkness. "Honey, please answer me and let me know you are okay. I'm not here to hurt you, I promise." Leedra waited patiently, and eventually she felt the girl's small clammy hand touch her leg. Leedra grabbed the hand and gave it a reassuring squeeze.

"Hello, hi there. Are you okay?" Her vision blurry, thanks to her glasses having been knocked off, Leedra leaned down to look closer at the girl's face. Adjusting to the dark, she could make out large, pretty brown eyes and thick eyelashes fanning out for days. The child's eyes were as wide as her own and just as scared.

"I'm scared," came the little voice.

"I know, sweetie. Me, too."

"What are you doing here?"

"Me?" Leedra asked, surprised. "What are *you* doing here?"

She could feel the girl shrug in response. "Well," she continued, "*I* just happened to be in my car minding my own business, and I saw you, and I saw that white van, and I saw them jump out and grab you, and I felt like I was . . . in another world."

Having an out-of-body experience, to be precise, but that would probably be a little too much for a small child.

She said, "I was like, uh oh, what's going on?"

"So you came to help me?"

"Yes, dear." Leedra assured.

"Thank you."

Leedra was silent. Having focused on making the day's earlier events seem more like a funny adventure for her companion's benefit, she was taken aback by the child's manners.

"You are welcome, my friend. Did you recognize either of the men? The child shook her head. "What do they want?"

To terrorize poor little innocent children for some reason, Leedra thought silently. Aloud, she said, "I don't know, but you're going to be all right. You can trust me, okay?"

The tiny hand moved in Leedra's own as if making itself more comfortable, letting her know that she was now a trusted party. Leedra squeezed it, trying to push back the memory of a time when there were no caring adults to hold and comfort her.

"So, let me tell you what: I'm so glad that there aren't any thunderstorms here! If there were a thunderstorm while we were stuck in this little bitty room, I—well I'm telling you, I would not be your strong buddy right now. I'd be that puddle on the floor over there." She didn't know where in the world the thunderstorm narrative came from; she only knew that she was trying to make small talk with a kid, and she was improvising. Divulging her own fears would, she hoped, give them some common ground and take her own mind off their present dismal state.

"What are you doing?" the girl asked as Leedra stood. A sudden new pain shot through her leg, so strong that she almost collapsed to the floor again. Touching her thigh, she felt another wound: a deep flesh wound, sticky with what had to be blood.

Thankfully, the room finally stopped tilting. Restless but stable, her hands felt around the room's cold walls, searching almost blindly for cracks, crevices and maybe, God willing, an opening of some sort that could provide an exit from their nightmare.

"I'm just trying to—uh . . ." Leedra's fingertips felt a ledge and she stretched herself as far as she could. The tips of her toes lifted her up a few more inches so she could peer over the top. Nothing but more blackness greeted her. Continuing to grope around while favoring her injured leg, arms extended to their fullest reach, her heart leapt when she felt a small window. Through the dusty, dirty pane of glass, a weak sliver of light crept in. Someone had taken the time to coat the glass with shoe polish, black paint or some other dark, slick grease. The goopy residue now coated her fingers, particles of it drying and flaking away with each swipe of her hand against her clothes.

Ultimately, the window didn't budge against her straining, pushing fingers. Without something to stand on and a heavy object, they did they stand a chance of getting through it. Leedra sighed as she brought herself back to her normal height and her feet back to flat. After just this mild exertion, she felt emotionally exhausted.

She sat down again and struck up conversation once more with the girl. "Do you remember where you live? Like, do you know your address?"

Leedra didn't know why she asked that question. She didn't really need to know where the child lived. She didn't remember how far they had driven, but it had been day when she left, so presumably quite a few hours had passed.

The smart thing to do, obviously, would be to seek out the nearest authority facility as soon as they got out of this mess. A police station or fire station would do, or just any official-looking person wearing a state-issued uniform.

Unfortunately, Leedra couldn't risk that.

For any normal person, these authorities would be the most logical people to seek—but she wasn't any normal person. If there was one thing Leedra Henderson avoided, it was contact with the law. She'd have to find a way to get the child to safety, but she'd have to do so anonymously. If—*when* they got out, she corrected herself staunchly—her mission was clear: return the child anonymously to a safe space and proceed to run far, far away.

"I live at my grandma›s house. We moved after my mom died. My dad grew up there."

Leedra looked up, so lost in forming her own plan of action that she'd forgotten the question she'd posed. "Oh, well . . . um . . . th-that must be a special place."

"It was. Then it burned down a few years ago. Then my Daddy and my Uncle Cole rebuilt it. They changed it around. It looks different now, and it's much nicer. We have a huge kitchen, and I got my own room with bunk beds so I can have sleepovers. We also have a library."

"A library? That sounds wonderful, honey. Does, uh, your daddy let you have lots of sleepovers?"

"Only with my cousin. Actually, she's sorta my aunt."

"Huh?" Leedra said, confused—but she quickly silenced the girl before she could respond. Distant footsteps were coming down the hall. The child, picking up the unspoken alert, sat up and stopped talking completely. Leedra's eyes were riveted to the dim outline of the door. Leedra grabbed the child to her chest, willing her pounding heart to calm and her nerves to steady.

The figure of a man looked in. Leedra just had time to notice the gun in his hand before a blinding light seemed to burst from behind him, stabbing painfully into her occipital lobe and forcing her to look away. The next instant, the door slammed shut and the light disappeared.

Thankfully, the child was still sitting in her lap.

Adjusting her eyes to the dimness once more, Leedra tried to salvage some consequential impression of the man. Had he uttered a grunt, a comment, even just heavy breathing? Did he have an accent, perhaps? Unfortunately, he made no sound during their split-second encounter. A smell, then: smoke, liquor? Nothing. She wouldn't be able to identify him to anyone. Disappointment clouded her relief.

Perhaps the captors hadn't expected her to be there with the little girl, which was good. Her presence complicated matters. Then again, Leedra herself hadn't counted on being there either. She had been on her way to a new job and new life, for heaven's sake. When that white van had pulled up just feet from her car, with a man leaping out and snatching up a child, Leedra hadn't thought twice. She'd been discovered by the kidnappers and then been thrown into the dungeon with their other loot. That gut reaction had landed her smack-dab in her current predicament.

The girl, sensing that danger had temporarily passed, began talking quietly again. Leedra listened with half an ear, the other part of her brain churning. She contemplated whether screaming would get them anywhere, then wondered how she might be more prepared if anyone entered again. Leedra nodded absently as the child looked at her expectantly. Kira Parker. Her name was Kira Parker; she was eight years old.

"Guess what? My daddy was in foster care just like my cousin was until her brother found her. Well, actually my Aunt Allontis found her."

"Allontis?" Leedra's heart took a dive and then surged. She mostly had a hard time following Kira's childish narrative—an uncle finding his little sister?—but that unique name made her ears prick up.

A few years ago, before she'd returned to the United States, she would check the *Washington Post's* website regularly to keep up with news, just to stay in touch with events back home and to remind herself of the place she wanted to return to some day. Memories jangled in her mind of a news story she'd followed: lots of scandalous coverage of some Maryland senator's awful embezzlement schemes and an illicit affair with a minor that had produced an illegitimate child. Leedra had learned some extra details about the story, not from the *Post's* coverage but from email exchanges with her distant friend Allontis Baxter. While Allontis's name had barely been mentioned in the press, that of one Cole Parker had been a main feature. Cole Parker, who Kira had just said was her Uncle.

Thoughtful but cautious, she asked aloud to be sure. "Is your aunt's name Allontis Baxter?"

"Yes, well, used to be. We call her Aunt Lonnie now - she married Cole. She's a Parker now, like me."

"Oh, how nice," Leedra breathed, trying to sound nonchalant.

"Do you know her?"

"I might. Um . . . is your father's name Dexter? Did the Parker family adopt him like your Uncle Cole? How old is your daddy, sweetie?"

Leedra tried to slow her tumble of questions, but this could be huge. If Kira's father really did turn out to be Dexter Johnson, the boy she knew from foster care as a child, this would turn out to be the most amazing coincidence Leedra had ever known. The Dexter she knew so long ago had been brought to her foster family after she'd been there just a few months herself. There had been other children there: two girls she'd called her sisters, plus her own biological sister. The old man that lived there had left the boys mostly alone. It was

Leedra and the other three girls he'd been more interested in.

Leedra shook her head, annoyed that in her reverie she might have missed important answers from Kira. Right then was definitely not the time to relive her childhood. It was better off forgotten, although she could never forget. Yet, she had always wondered what happened to Dexter Johnson. That little boy had made her time in foster care a little easier.

Leedra took a deep breath and wiped her eyes. She'd shed no tears, but her eyes hurt from straining to see everything. She shook her head to clear her thinking. There was no way that the man she knew then could somehow also be this child's father. That was too eerie a thought. Although she was curious about him, she didn't want to be connected to anyone who might remind her of that painful time. In any case, if they did see one another, she didn't even have to admit to being that little girl. He might not even remember her, and it was best for everyone if it stayed that way.

Her mission right then was to ensure the child currently in her care made it home safely.

Kira had fallen asleep on her lap and Leedra caressed her forehead tenderly. They were strangers, but the fact that the child could relax enough to sleep in her care must mean that some level of trust had been established.

"I'm gonna get you home," Leedra whispered. "I promise."

Leedra decided to let the child sleep a little longer while she worked out a plan to get them both back to their lives. She continued to talk in a whisper to herself. "If Dexter Johnson is your father, you're the luckiest little girl in the world. He's probably going crazy wondering where you are."

Her mind was made up. If she had escaped the tragedies of her childhood, albeit with many battle scars and lots of baggage, then surely she could take on a couple of punks who preyed on the weak, small and innocent, for whatever sick reason they were doing it. She hadn't returned to Virginia, the state she longed to make her home, only to fall at the first hurdle. She wanted a life, and this incident was just a bump in the road. Determined to get on with it, she would have to act now. "I know you're with us, Lord. Help us through. Protect us," she whispered.

After her short prayer, Leedra roused Kira from her sleep and told her about her plan to return Kira to her family, unharmed. Once the little girl seemed fully awake and understood her role, Leedra prayed all the harder that her plan would work.

CHAPTER TWO:
JUST ACT NORMAL

DEXTER PARKER COULD FEEL HIS day heading right down the drain. As he went about supervising the busy hall of INOVA Hospital's emergency ward, his heart sank and his world crumbled just a little. This was the case when he saw the trauma patients roll through the doors at his ER department. Every time, he was transported back to three years prior, when his own wife had rolled through those same doors.

Having patients die wasn't uncommon; he just hoped it didn't have to occur on his watch, and certainly not right in front of him. He asked God everyday to guide his hands and strengthen his mind to make the right decisions and save the lives brought through the doors of the hospital. Ultimately, though, he knew that even as the head of the ER department, he was simply supporting the work of a much higher power. He'd always known that.

He was continuing with his usual rounds when the head nurse called to him. He listened, expecting details of another emergency case, until the name of his daughter, Kira and the word 'taken', left her lips. Whatever she said next, the nurse might as well have vanished. He left her behind as he took long strides down the corridor. She followed, breaking into a small run to keep up. Abruptly, he turned to her. "Get my brother on the phone. Now, right now," Dexter snapped, taking off again at a full run this time.

In a matter of minutes, he had his coat and wallet and was in his truck. The nurse had followed him and was standing at the passenger window. Through the glass he could see her lips moving, the palms of her hands pounding, pleading with him to stop a minute. His hands shook as he gripped the steering wheel and willed himself to calm down and focus, then jabbed the button to lower the window. Listening to the nurse as if through static, his hand let go of the wheel to grip the shift, his eyes already checking the rearview mirror, primed and ready to speed away to his nearby home. He was numbly thankful that he hadn't parked in the multi-storied garage today.

"The *police*, Doctor," the nurse was saying. "The police are on their way here to you. They said for you to stay put. Please!"

"What about my brother?" Dexter blinked again.

"He's coming too. He's on the phone now. He's on his way."

Dexter nodded to the panicked nurse and cut the engine. Stepping from the vehicle, he made his way back into the hospital and down the hall to his office. It wasn't overly private, but at least it would be moderately closed off from the many prying eyes that had followed him as he exited moments ago.

The nurse, still at his side, handed him the phone and he put it to his ear. He listened to his brother calmly intone instructions for Dexter to follow until he could get there.

Dexter could make sense of medicine. That much he knew. That much he was comfortable with. Other things were so much harder: striving to heal people's psychological pain and the injuries brought on by, more often than not, man's own brutal hand; poor self care; bad habits or lack of access to proper medicine administration. Of everything recent in his life, there was so much Dexter couldn't figure out. He'd never understand why his wife had to die the way she did, so tragically in a car accident. After living through that horrible experience, he simply couldn't fathom losing the one and only person he had left to continue living for: his eight-year-old daughter, Kira. She was the only thing that mattered to him, that kept him going and kept him sane. She needed a daddy, he knew that. But if he left the earth, Cole and his wife Allontis would likely do a better job than he. He needed his brother because Cole Parker would know what to do in a situation like this—because right then, Dexter couldn't seem to formulate conscious thoughts and complete sentences of his own. His brain was scrambled.

When Cole arrived, less than ten minutes later, two uniformed officers were with him. In Dexter's office, they gave the brothers a brief rundown of the information they had. They emphasized that they were moving so quickly on the case because of several child predators rumored to be in the area. Dexter bristled at that comment and at the number of times the cops seemed to ask for the same information over and over. Glancing over at his brother, pleading silently for calm and help, Dexter knew Cole would be able to tell he was on the verge of snapping at the officers' apparent insensitivity about the whole matter.

"The teacher said she didn't come to class this morning. The girls she normally walks with said she went back home because she forgot something. I know she didn't come back to the house because I was there the entire time."

"Someone took her, obviously."

"In between telling the girls she had to run home and her actually getting back home?" Dexter asked, incredulous.

Cole nodded, pulling a file from his coat pocket. Dexter was surprised to see numerous pictures of Kira that Cole laid side by side on the metal desk. "Send me some of the photos on your phone and then take some shots of these," he said evenly. "Send photos of her on her own, not with you or in a group—that's why I brought these school pictures. Once you've done that, we can distribute them to the media. Oh, and write down her eye color, height, weight and date of birth. Now, what was she wearing this morning? Her purple sparkle sweater and—"

"The blue Keds." Dexter nodded mechanically. He was trying to absorb everything, the magnitude of the situation, while numbly continuing to follow his brother's lead.

"I'm waiting for a full list of media contacts. I have a partial list compiled already. We should also send the stuff to the Center for Missing and Exploited Children."

Dumbly, Dexter nodded again. He looked down at the photos and tapped at Cole's phone with shaky hands. He grew immediately annoyed at himself for what he felt was a clear display of weakness. At the same time, his heart was caught and pulled painfully by his little girl's beautiful eyes as she gazed up at him from the photos. All the photos were fairly recent, each showcasing the same toothy smile. Those eyes were either telling him that she was all right or pleading that he save her. Dexter wasn't sure.

He managed to get a few shots of the hard-copy photos before he fumbled and dropped the phone. Defeated, his eyes met Cole's. "I can't lose her, okay?" His voice was distant, barely above a whisper even to his own ears.

"We will find her." Cole's hand rested on Dexter's shoulder momentarily, before his phone buzzed with an incoming call and he reached to pick it up.

Dexter sat down heavily, but straightened when the uniformed men came back into the room. After additional details were exchanged, Cole gave orders, as if he were in charge. Normally, Dexter would have hated that. In this situation, though, he was actually thankful.

Dexter answered yet more questions, some of them seeming painfully redundant Hours passed and Dexter still had no answers and no child.

Cole returned to Dexter's side, holding the phone out to him. "It's Lonnie—she wants to talk to you," Cole said at Dexter's questioning gaze.

Dexter shook his head and turned slightly away. He couldn't possibly talk to Cole's wife, Allontis, at this particular moment. He could barely talk to the police. He shook his head again. "I can't. I'll stress her out. That's not good for the baby."

"I know that. But not hearing your voice, not getting confirmation that you're still breathing—*that* will stress her out more. Please just try, okay? Hold it together for a few more minutes."

Dexter returned a look of agony. He was holding it together, just about, but it wasn't going to last much longer.

He took the phone with a sigh and stood, moving to a quieter part of the office. Keeping his eyes on what everyone else in the room was doing, he barely listened to her voice. He could tell she was on the verge of tears. "I'm all right," he told her before she could ask.

"Are you sure?"

"Yeah."

"Okay."

He nodded when she asked him questions, forgetting she couldn't hear him nod and not sure whether it was the correct response anyway.

He held out hope. After everything he'd been through in the last few years, his world couldn't just crumble to nothing like this. Not now. He prayed for strength to help him through this ordeal and made up an excuse to end his conversation with Lonnie. Steeling himself, he turned to rejoin the men and focus on finding out what could have happened to his daughter.

CHAPTER THREE:
FLASHBACKS

LEEDRA HENDERSON WAS BACK ON point, but still nervous. Her miraculous escape from the would-be kidnappers with Kira last week had left her shaken and watchful, seeing danger around every corner.

Even now, she couldn't remember exactly how she had gotten them both out safely. She supposed that sheer adrenaline had allowed her to power through the horrible pain from the stab wound in her leg and the bump on her head. She remembered pushing a man aside, dodging, running with all her strength, leaping into her car and gunning the engine to get them away to safety, all while somehow keeping hold of Kira's arm. The only thing she remembered clearly was dropping the terrified child off at the police station, watching her, from afar, speak with an uniformed adult and when she was certain the child was safe, she'd walked away quickly before anyone could identify her. A part of her mind went back to consider whether their kidnappers had truly fought back, or had they let her and the child go because she'd showed such determination? She couldn't be sure and not knowing with certainty, niggled her. Leedra shook her head in frustration. She was safe.

After contacting her new boss to use the excuse of a delay in her travel plans as the reason why she had missed their first meeting, Leedra had bought herself only a few days to try to recover and piece together some composure. Not wanting to reveal any more than she had to, she had assured her boss that she could still begin her new position on Monday. Now here she was, with the backdrop of the recent trauma adding to her usual first-day nerves.

She walked down the hall from her temporary office at the Anchored Empowerment Center, taking long deep inhales through her nose and exhaling through her mouth. The breathing technique was only moderately helpful. Her instinctive thoughts of the moment were still along the lines of: run, hide and quit. Quit this job she'd barely started.

The chatter she'd heard coming from the room as she walked down the corridor silenced when she entered. Everyone was seated; all eyes turned to look at her. She smiled tightly. If this initial reaction was less than receptive, that was okay. She had expected as much. She was an outsider. She didn't know these people and they didn't know her, yet somehow they were supposed to … what … work with her immediately? Trust her? Suddenly she empathized with first-time substitute teachers across America.

Mentally, she gave them a pass for the cold reception. Their regular leader was absent; they didn't know what they were signing up for, and they certainly didn't know her. She had work to do—but then again, a challenge was exactly what she needed right now. Anything would suffice to take her mind off the week she'd had.

"Good morning, everyone." Leedra lifted her chin and squared her shoulders, walking briskly to the front of the room. "I'm Leedra Henderson, and I'm the acting director for the Anchored Empowerment Center." She took a moment for pleasantries, smiling warmly and shaking everyone's hand as she passed by.

Turning, she noticed the blackboard behind her and gave a start. The dusty green board looked primitive, an antique. It reminded her of why Allontis had brought her to the organization in the first place: to bring it into the current century and overhaul everything, including the dilapidated equipment she'd be using to start her job.

"It's just a chalkboard," a sardonic male voice said at her back. She didn't turn around, but she did note the breeze of chuckles that swept around the table.

"Of course it is." She shrugged both things off: her surprise and the sarcastic comment. "I just thought all those had gone out with the eight-track."

She got a louder, more generous laugh at this clever retort and turned around to grace everyone with another, more genuine smile. She looked down at the papers before her, giving herself an internal pat on the back. An older woman seated near her gave Leedra an encouraging smile. That was all Leedra needed: a kind and caring face amidst so much that was unknown and unfriendly. She smiled back. She could do this. She immediately started to relax—not much, but a teeny bit. Enough.

"I just need—uh—chalk!" she declared, more confident now. She spotted a small basket in the corner containing pitiful slivers of chalk. "Here we go."

Leedra wrote her name on the board. She heard the door open and close behind her as she did so. When she finished writing, she set down the chalk to dust off her hands. As she turned back to face the group, her eyes landed on the newcomer: the man she had fervently hoped not to see there, today or ever.

"Sorry I'm late," the man said by way of introduction, addressing her and everyone else apologetically.

Her eyes met his and a thousand years seemed to pass between them. She wanted to hide, but she simply turned and sank into her seat. She was suddenly exhausted, although the meeting had only just begun.

"Yes, of course, Mr. . . . uh . . . ?"

"Parker," Dexter supplied.

"Great," Leedra continued, a little breathlessly. "We were just getting started. I'm Leedra Henderson." She almost reached to shake his hand, but thought better of it.

"Let's see . . . let's go around the room and everyone please tell us your name and your connection to the Center. Please also share any other personal ties you have to Allontis and her wonderful family."

The meeting began and Leedra ensured she was attentive as everyone spoke. She was prepared: she already had everyone's bio printed out and she'd been able to find pictures of just about everyone online.

She had to impress the people before her as their leader, albeit temporary, and she was determined to do a good job.

As people introduced themselves, Leedra made a small diagram in her notebook to help her remember everyone, drawing an oval for the table and putting names and professions at each setting. She glanced at her chart when it was completed, taking in the variety of characters in her new group. There was Ella Dupont, a pediatric nurse by day who also worked part-time at the county's local teen center. She was rather quiet, but she also candidly shared a tale about her time at the Center that endeared her to Leedra straight away. Cason Carlton was next, a local banker. He was tapped to be the Treasurer for the Board. She made a note of that. Then there were two women, wives of local football stars, each representing the DC area's local teams. She smiled to herself as the two women made their intros. She planned to ensure no one was there solely to promote an agenda, football-related or otherwise. She wasn't trying to be a cynic so early on, but she did want to be sure of everyone's motives. If they weren't aboveboard, Leedra wanted to know. She planned to have personal interviews with everyone in the group soon, to give herself more to go on.

Continuing around the table, Lucient Douglass introduced himself. "Attorney at Law," he emphasized proudly. He winked broadly at her, to which she returned nothing but a cool stare. His good looks and three-piece suit weren't lost on her, but she was sure to signal through her neutral face that she was not here for anything other than official business, taking care of the staff and, most importantly, the women and children the Center was created to serve. She would obviously have to be on her guard with this one.

The more Lucient talked about his profession, the more painfully obvious it was that he was attempting to impress the crowd, going on at length about his schooling and professional experience. He gave her a final wink when he finished. Ugh. Leedra was relieved to shift her focus to the person next to him: Cathy Sampson, a slender woman with expensive taste made evident by her accoutrements. Allontis had mentioned to her that Cathy was a godsend to the

Center. She was a retired director of legal policy, no doubt adept at ensuring that the laws protecting vulnerable women were kept front and center in their advocacy work. Cathy had also assisted numerous women at the shelter with restraining and protective orders to keep their abusers away for as long as possible. Leedra thanked her.

Finally, there was Dexter Parker. Here was a man she could hardly look away from, try as she might. One look since he'd entered the room and she knew this was going to be difficult. She focused on what he said.

"Like Nurse Dupont," Dexter began, "I work at INOVA hospital, in the ER department."

Leedra listened to his deep voice. He spoke as if he were simply reading something from a card: smooth, yet automatic, with little inflection in his tone, as if he said these lines often. Truth be told, she had hoped that he wouldn't be coming to the meeting. In the last few days of teleconferences, Allontis had mentioned only that he "might come," but that his extended family had recently been through an ordeal so nothing was certain. Leedra didn't request any more details about the ordeal, but had understood that Dexter might no longer want to be involved in the development of the Center's new Board. Evidently, he did after all.

Leedra smiled encouragingly. Little did he know there wasn't much need for introductions. She already knew who he was, not only from the time she'd spent in captivity with his daughter just a few days ago, but because, to her surprise, he was indeed the same man she had known in that hellish foster home over twenty-five years ago. Now she could only hope that her new look and the time that had elapsed since then was enough to disguise her real identity.

Dexter looked up at everyone, then at her, as if he wasn't even sure where he was. She smiled her thanks for his introduction and stood up, ready to begin the meeting's next segment.

"Excuse me Ms. uh …?"

Leedra turned back in surprise. Dexter had more to say. She watched as his eyes shifted first to her name on the blackboard and then back to her, with a question in his eyes. "Henderson?" he repeated doubtfully.

"Yes. Leedra Henderson."

Leedra grew somewhat disconcerted. It was as if he didn't believe the name she had written on the board was her own—as if it contradicted something else he knew. Her hands grew sweaty with nerves from his scrutiny, and she resisted the urge to wipe them on the sides of her wrap dress. She could feel his eyes boring into her.

"I'm Allontis's brother-in-law," Dexter offered.

"Yes, of course." Leedra found her voice and managed another weak smile. "I think everyone knows that."

There was a faint chuckle from all attending.

After all, she hadn't been one hundred percent sure that Dexter wouldn't recognize her all these years later, but she'd hoped he wouldn't. The fact that he was repeating her name clearly showed he smelled a rat, and the way he narrowed his eyes, but then he seemed to notice her alarm and looked away.

"Again, I apologize for being late, everyone," Dexter continued, concluding his introduction. "I oversee the work of the Center's physician, and together we make recommendations for treatment. I also do the medication management for the residents. I've been here for four years. Uh . . . is there anything else you need to know?"

"No, nope," Leedra shook her head emphatically. "Thank you, Dr. Parker—"

"Dexter." He corrected her aloud. "Please call me Dexter . . . uh, everyone. Thanks."

Leedra nodded and turned back to the dusty board. She grabbed the chalk again and did whatever she could to busy herself: anything to get her eyes off that familiar face. She felt only moderately better after he put a stop to the way he was looking at her, and made an effort to ensure he was telling the whole group that they should refer to him informally, not just her. If anyone suspected that they might know each other—or worse—guessed that there might be anything between them, she'd have a new set of problems on her hands. She simply did not need any more.

"All right, thank you everyone," Leedra said, ready to move on.

"Thanks so much for those preliminaries and taking time out of your busy day to attend this meeting. First, what a wonderful and diverse group of people we've got. Allontis tells me that each of you has helped her to accomplish something spectacular here. Next, we are going to cover exactly what she is asking of you. As you are aware, we have received a substantial amount of new grant funding in the last year. The grant writer that Allontis hired did a phenomenal job and we've secured $1.5 million, largely through new initiatives from the Office of Violence Against Women, the local NFL Wives Club and some other fundraising efforts."

"More money, more problems!" Lucient interjected.

Leedra smiled tightly. Apparently, Chronic-Interrupt-Us, her new nickname for him, would not only be the one guy at the table ooz-ing braggadocio, he would also be her resident funny man. Oh boy. Undeterred, Leedra kept talking.

"That's one way to look it Mr. Lushhh-cen . . . " - Leedra looked swiftly down at her notes and gave up. "Mr. Douglass, the way I see it, these are not problems at all. They are in fact opportunities to make the Center great and take it to next level, and we're going to do just that." Nicely handled.

"Obviously, you were all tapped as influential supporters of the orga-nization over the last few years," Leedra continued. "I have prepared a board description and outlined various duties and commitments, detailing what your service will mean: term limits, voting processes and so on. I'm here to guide you into board leadership, ensuring we are in compliance with the Center's rules and regulations and of course with our funders. Now I'll entertain questions. Anybody?"

"Are you going to tell us anything about your own background and qualifications?" Lucient said quickly.

"Of course. Uh . . . my bio . . ." Leedra noticed one of the NFL wives reach over swiftly flip the paper in front of Lucient. "I think Allontis e-mailed it to you all."

"Of course she did, darling, but go ahead," said Cathy.

Leedra was grateful for this show of solidarity, her she noted the look of annoyance Lucient cast toward the woman who'd assisted him and thus embarrassing him in the process.

"Briefly, I was in charge of the largest Mercy Ship in the world. There are currently two of these ships out at sea. They help men, women and children in poor countries all across the world, but focus predominantly on the African continent. There are so many needs, obviously, but volunteer doctors and nurses did hundreds of cleft palate repairs, dental decay, breach babies and numerous other common illnesses complicated by poverty, years of neglect and simple inability to access medical attention. I . . . uh lived in Virginia as a child. Um, full disclosure: Allontis and I ended up in a few classes together pursuing our advanced degrees. I completed my course work through distance learning while abroad and thanks to technology that included Skype and Face Time, we forged a connection. We lost touch over the years but early on she would share her many hopes and aspirations for the Center. I have, uh, been a supporter of the Center since its inception. Like all of you, I value it deeply and of course I would like it to succeed, grow and become an example for other facilities. We can do some really wonderful things here."

"You got my vote already!" Cathy exclaimed, and everyone else murmured agreement, including Dexter, who'd been largely silent.

Leedra nodded and thanked them. "After individual meetings, we will have a board retreat in a few weeks. I'd like to get the meetings done this week."

"But it's already Thursday." Lucient was naturally the first to point this out.

"Would you like to go first, Mr. Douglass?"

"Sure."

Her nerves slowly left her as the meeting progressed, even with the chatty attorney interjecting his thoughts and snarky comments at even turn. For the time being, she would have to tolerate him.

As the meeting drew to a close, Leedra found herself wondering why the good-looking Dr. Parker hadn't had more to say. She knew, better than he could have suspected, that he'd been through a lot in the last few weeks. She found herself wishing they were friends now, so he might open up more to her about the terrible experience he had undoubtedly gone through when his daughter was missing.

She shook her head, silently chastising herself for the direction of her thoughts and resolving to get her mind back on task. As she was writing herself some notes, there was a knock at the door. Marcie, Allontis's right-hand woman, entered with the receptionist, helping to push a cart of food. The two women quickly set up the team's lunch: sandwiches, pasta salad, fruit salad, chips and beverages, just as Leedra had ordered. When the young receptionist left, Marcie greeted everyone personally, staying to chat briefly with those she obviously knew. Leedra pretended not to notice when Marcie spoke at length to Dexter before leaning close to him and whispering something Leedra didn't catch. She patted his arm in parting.

Leedra glanced again at the food to ensure everything they needed was there. Marcie exited, giving her a quick thumbs-up on the way out.

"All right, lunch is here. Let's take twenty: restroom break, get your food, then we can wrap up," Leedra said. "Please sign up for a time to meet with me. I'll pass this around." She waved her sign-up sheet for all to see and gave it to the woman sitting to her right, deliberately avoiding Dexter.

People started to move, the room's atmosphere relaxing into gentle breakroom hubbub. Remaining seated, Leedra pretended to be engrossed in her notes. She'd noticed that Dexter hadn't left the room, but was startled when she finally looked up to see that just the two of them were left.

CHAPTER FOUR:
FAMILIAR STRANGERS

AFTER THREE PAINFULLY LONG AND crazy days, Dexter had finally been reunited with his daughter. The terror he'd felt at the prospect of losing her was replaced only by the elation that overwhelmed him when she was back in his arms. Now, back to his real life and at the Anchored board meeting. He set his phone on the table, just in case another disaster lurked just around the corner. In his gut, though, he was certain that at this moment his daughter was safe. Both Allontis and Cole were looking after her with vigilance. He was beyond thankful that his daughter had been returned to him safe and sound.

Another week had passed since the day the police had brought Kira home. Seeing as no one had offered any answers about who or what could have provoked someone to take his daughter and—stranger yet—to return her once again. He tried to put the kidnapping out of his mind for now. He knew that as soon as he left the building, it would absorb his thoughts, again.

At the moment, the other thing he couldn't fathom was why he found himself constantly staring at the woman who'd said her name was Leedra Henderson—and why, for some reason, he didn't believe her.

It wasn't often that Dexter was rendered speechless, but for the better part of the meeting, starting from when he'd walked in with a heavy mind and a bruised and slowly-healing heart, he was yanked quickly and unwillingly back to the present. He wasn't much of a talker at the best of times. The real reason for the loss of his voice today was that he was sure he recognized the woman before him. For the better part of an hour, Dexter had sat mutely and argued with himself that such thoughts were impossible.

Long ago, if she was who he thought, they'd been two of the unfortunate souls placed with the same terrible foster family. While both of them had had awful experiences, he knew that the abuse she and the other girls had suffered was truly horrifying.

"Seriously, Dr. Parker, what on earth are you doing here, dear? Look at you. You can't even concentrate."

Caught off guard, Dexter tore his eyes away from Leedra to concentrate on the woman to his right. First he looked down at the frail hand resting on his sleeve. Reflexively, he covered the older woman's hand with his own. He stared at her blankly, with no idea of exactly what she'd said to him. Regardless, he decided to give her the same spiel he'd been giving everyone that had heard about his family's recent issues. That would likely work.

"Uh, everything's fine, Ms. Sampson." Patting her hand again before she removed it, Dexter sat forward in his chair and spoke louder as he addressed those that had returned to the room: "I appreciate your prayers and I know that, uh, you've all been worried and concerned about my daughter. I realize that Allontis solicited your prayers via texts and e-mails, and they have been much appreciated. And I'm thankful for the privacy you allowed me around what's been going on in my life right now."

"Of course we understand honey, this is a private matter. That precious girl of yours is so wonderful. God protected her and we thank Him. I just want you to take some time for yourself. You work too hard."

"Yeah, always," Dexter agreed and the woman smiled warmly before she turned to join the others and fix her lunch.

When he turned around, Leedra had left.

Almost everyone had reconvened by this time. Though they looked like they wanted to ask him questions, none did. He counted to ten and when it looked like everyone would be considerate enough to mind their own business, even though he knew curiosity was killing them, he strode to the door. He slipped out of the conference room and down the hall to where he knew Allontis's office would be and where he hoped to find the interim director's temporary digs as well.

Back in his twenties, Dexter could remember helping Allontis move into this building, so he knew the Anchored Empowerment Center's layout like the back of his hand. Leedra looked up when he entered her office and stood before her desk.

"Hello, Doctor. Can I help you?"

"How are you?"

"I'm great. It's nice to finally meet you. Allontis had mentioned that maybe you'd come, but she wasn't sure."

A pause.

"Is there something I can help you with?" Leedra asked.

Dexter decided to cut to the chase. "When you used to live here, in this area, as a child, how old were you?"

The way she kept looking toward the door was enough to let him know he was on to something. Here in her office, alone, without all the other onlookers, he had hoped that he would have the opportunity to talk with her more openly, but it was painfully clear how nervous she was about the very fact that it was just the two of them and that they were in such close quarters.

"What? Why all these questions?"

"I only asked you two."

"Oh. Well, I guess I was about, uh—"

"Eight?"

Leedra looked at him sharply. "Sounds about right."

"Evie," he whispered.

"What? I mean, uh, who is that?"

"You."

"Sorry?" she stuttered.

"Evie Carter. Please don't tell me you're not her."

"Just a moment, please. Stop right there."

Leedra stood and Dexter watched as she walked slowly to the door.

If he didn't know better, he'd have sworn she tried to cover a limp he didn't notice before. Unbidden, a feeling of concern began to prick at his heart. When she returned from closing the door, he gazed searchingly into her eyes. His emotions fought within him. Even if she was about to tell him the truth, part of him was annoyed that she felt like she couldn't tell him of her return sooner. That made him wary: he wouldn't trust someone like that. Perhaps he was being unreasonable, even stuck in a time warp. The Evie he knew so long ago had trusted him. And this person, he didn't truly know her at all yet he she was having an impact on his every thought.

Dexter felt like he was losing his mind, and, considering what he'd already been through, this feeling annoyed him tremendously. His heart was trying to tell him something that his mind refused to believe.

"I'm sorry." He stood up abruptly and paced before her. His hand rubbed his neck, trying to ease the tension building there. "I've, uh, been through a lot these last couple of weeks. I'm just going a little cray-cray." He laughed gruffly, if you could call it a laugh; it was more like he cleared his throat and stifled a yell at the same time. "I just, uh ..."

When he turned around to face her, he saw what he thought were tears in her eyes. He stilled, looking at her, in that instant recognizing the truth. He was silent as his hands gripped the back of the chair. He waited for her to move across the room.

"Look, I . . . I am not her, not anymore," she said softly. "My name is Leedra Henderson."

She took a deep breath before continuing, this time lowering her voice. "I'm her, but I'm not *her* anymore—you understand? I don't want you to think that your mind is playing tricks on you. You're right: you're not crazy. You've just been through a lot. I'm not going to lie to you. Perhaps you being at this meeting in the first place is, uh ..."

"Where have you been?" Dexter said, interrupting her. He took a seat. He knew she had deliberately avoided confirming his suspicion. He tried to understand her reasoning, or perhaps her need, to be someone else, but for now he couldn't. The confusion and the second-guessing had momentarily left him, replaced only with happy relief that she wasn't actively pretending *not* to be the person he knew she was. She just hadn't admitted the truth quite yet; he knew it was there, very near the surface. He longed to sit down while the revelations dawned on him and his brain worked overtime to process what his heart already knew. He was silent as he took it all in. All of her, standing before his very eyes, alive and well.

Leedra still didn't answer his question but walked around the desk. Dexter could see that she had briefly considered taking the chair next to him but chose to stand instead.

"Yes, I'm Evie Carter. But," she rushed on, "I created a new identity."

Leedra sat down and Dexter noticed her hand move to rub her leg.

"What happened to your leg?"

"Just an old sports injury," she said quickly.

"Why did you have to get a new identity?"

"Look, everyone at the meeting will be wondering where I am, where we are. I need to get back to the conference room now."

"Just waitplease?"

"I can't," she hissed.

Dexter was taken aback, but he said nothing. He simply put his hands up in mock surrender.

"Why?"

"It doesn't matter."

"It matters to me," he said quietly. He looked at her and noticed her unshed tears. He wondered if she knew how sad losing touch with her had made him. He tried to dismiss that time, to tell himself that it was too long ago and too far away to reminisce about, but he hadn't ever really forgotten her. "I always wondered what happened to that little girl. I prayed she was all right, even when I thought for sure she was dead. I prayed it wasn't true."

"You're talking about me in the third person."

"Isn't that what you want?" he retorted coldly. "For me to forget— to play along with your act that you're someone else now? You can change your name, but you have the same mannerisms. I couldn't forget you. You say you used to live here as a child and you're adopted?" he emphasized. "How could I forget the person that I shared hell with? You think I'm like that?"

"Stop it, please."

"No, you stop it." Dexter returned.

"No, *you* stop. That time for me *was* hell. You were just another one of the residents but I was being abused, me and the other girls— always the girls. Don't be mad at me for wanting to forget that time in my life, along with everything and everyone who was there. I *want* to forget it. I am here to do a job, nothing more. I'm sorry, we don't know each other any more. You are a part of my history, not my present, and that's the way I want it to stay. Please try to forget all about me."

Dexter was silent, seated, stunned by her words. She snatched up her papers and her phone and hurried out of the office, but not before he saw the tears that ran down her face.

Standing, he looked around the old familiar office. Some of Allontis's family pictures still stood on her shelf. That made sense. Allontis had been prescribed bed rest only in the recent months of her pregnancy, and the photos standing there on the credenza were a tangible reminder that Leedra's job here was only temporary.

He gazed at a family photo that featured his adoptive parents, Georgia and David, who were now deceased. They were standing behind a teenage version of himself. Cole and the other three boys who made up Dexter's mosaic family stood alongside them. Kira featured in the cluster of photos, too, next to them in a frame of her own. One space over from her, his nephew, Jacoby, grinned a gummy baby grin. Then came Cole and Hannah in a photo together. Long lost sister and brother. *Lost and found.*

As he turned around, ready to leave, his eyes fell on the datebook sitting on the edge of the desk. Yellowed edges of what looked like newspaper clippings peeked out from the cover flap. Curiosity trumping discretion, he leaned forward and tugged on it just a little. All of a sudden, photos of the very same little girls he'd just discussed with Leedra were staring back at him.

Dexter would never forget those little faces and it pained him to think that Leedra wanted him to. It couldn't be true. Seeing her, and now these pages so carefully preserved in her personal files, he began to realize that perhaps she was here at the women's shelter for a reason other than her new job. Perhaps the less people knew about her, the better she could investigate. Taking a deep breath, Dexter shoved the papers back into the datebook and left the office, flipping the light switch as he pulled the door shut behind him. The door was closed, but was the past reopened?

CHAPTER FIVE:
CHECK, PLEASE!

Dexter's coming to the meeting after all. Don't let people jabber on too much about the kidnapping. Act normal, noooo mention of any issues so people won't start bugging him about personal family stuff. Okay? TTYL.

LEEDRA PRESSED HER THUMB OVER the highlighted text message until the red "delete" option appeared. She was kicking herself. And what in the world did T T Y L, mean? *Tell. Them. You're. Lying?* She hated texting. Despite the annoyance over her inability to know the meanings of all the short hand, she was angry with herself all over again. If only she'd read her texts from her boss Allontis in a timely manner, she'd have known how best to conduct herself when Dexter Parker had shown up.

Text messaging wasn't something she was used to. People didn't text her in the days when she was out at sea. Out there, everyone's sole mode of communication was the loud crackling walkie-talkies they each carried at their hips. Even those primitive things were switched off when they were off duty, in which case the only goal was to find a dark corner of a cabin and get a few hours of much-needed sleep. It was either that or a state of constant sleep-deprivation, what with all the time changes.

Still sad about how things had gone between her and Dexter the other day, Leedra tried in vain to forget every single thing about the man. Each time she tried to put him out of her mind, though, there he was, zooming back at full throttle. She was a fool and it hurt to lie to him, not just about the major secret, but also about how she had felt about him in her past. Truth be told, he was her only saving grace at that time in her life, and if it weren't for him, she might have died too.

She bitterly regretted saying the things she had, but it was over now and all she could do was move on. The only action she could take was to avoid him. In the hopefully rare event where they would have to see each other, she would stay on neutral topics concerning the Center. She would stick to the notion that she did not care about him at all, that her past was just that—gone, buried—and that she was there only for the job and to start her life anew. She was holding herself to those goals. They were her only defense.

Looking out of her car window, she wished that she could put today's particular meeting off just a little longer. It wasn't a good thing to put off meeting your boss face to face. Skype and Face Time could only work for so long and were invented for when people were far away from each other. Distance was no longer an issue.

It wasn't that Leedra was so scared of seeing her boss, face to face. It had more to do with the fact that the last time Leedra had pulled her small Toyota Camry up along the curb on the very same street where Allontis Parker lived, things had gone horribly awry.

Trying to erase that awful day from her mind, Leedra looked up at the house in front of her and the neighborhood overall. It seemed nice enough, obviously, several steps removed from the people and the life she'd endured as a child.

Leedra glanced over her shoulder and did a quick scan of the quiet street, resolving not to find any other children being kidnapped this time. Of all the coincidences in the world, she still couldn't believe what had transpired less than a month ago: that the child she had saved was the daughter of her old foster brother. Despite that strange and unforeseeable detour, she chose to take a moment and list her positives. For one, she was doing well at work. It was almost time for the board retreat, and for the most part, things were good. Everyone was in place and agreeable. Her personal interviews with the board members were almost complete, and although Dexter now knew her real identity, he thankfully hadn't told anyone—as far as she was aware. She swiftly checked her face in the mirror, making sure she was presentable for her appointment with Allontis in just a few minutes.

This was her first face-to-face meeting with Allontis in a professional context, and while they had chatted and e-mailed almost everyday, Leedra was still peeved about how long it had taken for them to meet in person. The time lapse wasn't ideal: she could only make excuses for so long. So far, no one at the Center knew that the delay had been caused by the kidnapping of Kira Parker.

Leedra had checked the TV news and local papers every single day, but no new developments in the Kira Parker case were broadcast. The only thing reported was that she had been one of three children stopped and grabbed by a mysterious van. Still no witnesses and no suspects. Nice to know that not much had changed in society's ability to find criminals and bring them to justice, she thought cynically to herself.

The reports she'd read only noted what anonymous statements she'd made to them. They had no new developments and appeared to have given up. Having used a pay phone and now under a different name, Leedra was confident no one would ever know she'd actually been the hero of the hour. She didn't want that kind of attention.

At least Dexter is not here. That was the next thought that sent her stomach simmering to a low roll. There had been only two meetings with the board where she had had to see him, plus some coordination through phone and email. Other than those brief connections, he hadn't said much else to her.

Steeling her resolve, Leedra cut the car's engine. She checked all her mirrors and was thankful to see no school buses and especially no oversized white vans in the vicinity. As she moved to get her bag, she froze when a white SUV drove by, immediately on the alert for dangerous criminals. With relief, she dismissed the fear when she noted that it was just a smaller compact.

Leedra walked up the driveway to Allontis's side door, avoiding the front entrance, as Allontis had instructed. She tapped lightly. After a moment, the door was opened by a man who she immediately recognized as Allontis's husband, Cole, thanks to the pictures lining Allontis's office credenza.

"Uh, hello. I'm Leedra. Here to meet with Allontis."

"How are you?" Cole said, moving back and motioning for her to enter.

Leedra was surprised by how warm and firm his hand was as he shook hers briefly. "Uh, fine. Thanks." She put her hand quickly back down and held the old-fashioned briefcase she had bought just a few days ago in a death grip. She could almost feel Cole's warm, friendly and encouraging smile disarming her. Leedra took a deep breath. She hadn't been prepared for the friendliness of Allontis's husband, nor for the comforts of home greeting her in the form of heavenly, savory smells and a spread on the kitchen counter that looked fit for a king. Dragging her eyes away from a kitchen island that was long enough to play table tennis on, she noted that Cole was tall and his eyes were kind. Giving him a once-over, she couldn't help but compare Cole to Dexter. The two didn't look anything alike of course, as they were only brothers by adoption, but their manners shared many similarities. Once Cole shut the door, he caught her off guard by enfolding her in a brief hug before offering to take her coat.

"Thank you."

"Allontis is in our room. She's been on bed rest for a while now and hates it."

Leedra nodded, unsure what to say.

"I'll bring lunch up for you guys in just a bit. Do you have any dietary restrictions?"

"Oh, you don't have to do that on my account. I wasn't going to stay long," Leedra said in a rush.

"It's a working lunch, huh?" Cole said skeptically.

"Uh, sure."

"We feed people here," Cole said and smiled.

"Uh, okay. Well, I like just about anything."

She looked at all the food in front of them and while her mouth watered imagining what they would have for lunch, she really didn't want to stay longer than absolutely necessary. She almost asked whether Dexter and Kira visited the house often, but she kept quiet and decided against asking about him at all. If she was patient, Leedra hoped that Allontis might volunteer Dexter's visiting habits. That would help her plan her own visits more carefully. If no one mentioned him, she might eventually find a way to broach the subject of the handsome doctor in a casual way.

Cole was smiling expectantly at her, and Leedra hoped he hadn't said something she'd missed during her momentary reverie. "What?" she blurted, a little too curtly, in an attempt to mask her own inattention.

"Her room is toward the back of the house, last door on the left."

"Right. Thanks." Leedra averted her eyes from his gaze, moving quietly to the back of the house. She knocked on the door, partly ajar, before slipping inside.

To her surprise, the single bed at the side of the room was made up and unoccupied. Leedra's gaze panned the room—surprisingly large,—and her eyes fell on Allontis, sitting up in a blue-and-yellow patterned high-backed armchair in the smaller alcove.

"Hey, um, hello, Allontis."

"My goodness. Hi there! Please come in. How are you?" Allontis tried to stand, but Leedra hurried over to stop her.

"Please, don't get up. Your husband said you were on bed rest. What are you doing out of bed?"

"Not very professional, is it? This muumuu is bad enough." Allontis gestured to her loose-fitting outfit with a wry smile.

"It's pretty and you look great."

Leedra moved closer. Although she wasn't looking for a hug, she now assumed the whole family were just huggers, so she set down her briefcase and did her best to lean into Allontis's outstretched arms. Embracing her was made more difficult by the seated position and the belly. It was hard to tell exactly how much of it there was underneath the voluminous folds of the caftan. Leedra patted Allontis awkwardly on the shoulder before backing away from her boss and friend to take a seat in the adjacent high-backed chair, her briefcase at her feet.

"I see we'll have to work on the hugs." Allontis smiled but Leedra returned her look with some sadness.

"I'm just not used to uh, embracing other I guess," Leedra said by way of explanation.

"You obviously haven't been hugged by Dexter. He would cure you of that."

Leedra tried to smile.

"By the way, Dexter told me you were in foster care together. I didn't know that. You said you grew up around here, but you never really said where."

Leedra nodded. "I barely remember him," she lied. "I was there just a few years. We all got sent our separate ways by the adoption agency."

"You mean your first home was shut down?"

"Yeah . . . something like that. We were relocated and that was the end of it." Leedra smiled tightly, hoping Allontis would take the hint to stop asking about her past. She was a little put out that Dexter had even mentioned it to Allontis. She wished he hadn't remembered her. It would make doing what she had to do here so much easier.

"It was just . . . a long time ago. You know? A time I'd rather not remember," she clarified, trying to soften her tone.

She looked up, unsure if Allontis was satisfied with that or not. Regardless, Cole thankfully entered the room at that very moment to break the tension, carrying a tray piled high with various goodies. He set it on a rolling table in front of Leedra.

"Oh . . . what's all this?" she said in surprise, her mouth already beginning to water in anticipation.

"Cole owns a restaurant, you know," Allontis put in.

"Yes, I heard."

"You should come and try us sometime," Cole grinned. "It's not far from Anchored. I chose our location just to be near this woman here."

Leedra smiled. She wasn't used to the banter of married couples. She smiled, unprepared for the love she saw reflected in his eyes as he stared at his wife. It left Leedra with a feeling she couldn't immediately name. She supposed it could be jealousy, but she swore she wasn't the type for that. Envy was perhaps a better word.

"I hate being holed up in this room but, bless his heart, he tries to make it interesting for me."

"We're family. That's what we do."

Leedra nodded. Of course, that's what family did. She wouldn't know anything about that, so she might as well have abstained from this entire conversation.

"That's wonderful."

She didn't know what else to say. She looked at the tray and busied herself with making a cup of tea. She offered Allontis a cup and then sat back down to work. She wanted to leave.

"So . . . tell me some gossip about the board members. Oh, before I forget: *don't* pay any attention to Lucient. I didn't think he'd actually sign up. I'm almost sorry I asked him to."

"Oh, why?"

"Don't tell me you haven't noticed the tension between him and Dexter? Dexter says Lucient's a shyster. If he doesn't seem genuinely helpful, feel free to let me know. He's sort of . . . on probation."

"I don't want to bother you with trivialities in your condition."

"Oh please. Everyone is acting like I'm a baby. I have a baby on the way but, FYI, I'm not actually a baby."

"I think Lucient is interesting. He may enjoy giving me a hard time even more than he does Dexter."

"He probably likes you."

"Oh, no. Please." Grimacing, Leedra took a sip from her cup of tea and put it down. She reached for her briefcase to find her list of discussion items to get the meeting going. While she didn't mind making small talk, she didn't want to talk about *that*.

"Dexter certainly had a lot of questions about you after the board meeting," Allontis continued, eyeing her companion.

"Really?" Leedra tried to sound nonchalant. "Like . . . what did he want to know?" She swallowed.

"Oh, things like when you came back to the area; how long we've known each other; how old you were when you left. Did you ever talk about who adopted you? That sort of thing."

"Why on earth would he want to know all that?

"You tell me."

Leedra shrugged. Her annoyance grew.

"We just . . . he and I knew each other a long time ago. Sometimes people hold on to the past. That's what I think."

"He's been through a lot, Leedra. I was thinking you could be a friend to him. You're a certified counselor."

"He's a member of our board. Isn't that a conflict of interest or something? Anyway, I don't practice."

"But you have your doctorate."

"And no one there knows that but you," Leedra huffed out.

"*I* could tell him," Allontis supplied conspiratorially. "I figure the fact that he's showing some interest in anyone outside his own family is a good sign. His curiosity is piqued. Do you know how many years it's been since that has happened?"

Leedra shook her head. She was in way deeper than she thought.

"Allontis, this is a bit much. I appreciate your faith in me,"—if that's what she could call it—"but I'm just not . . . not the one for this."

"Okay, but just . . . if he starts talking, can you please not ignore him? He needs to talk to someone."

"Okay."

Leedra didn't mean to sound like she was agreeing to anything: she wasn't. She just wanted to change the subject, but she wasn't really sure how to do it. A guilt trip was sometimes the best route, and Leedra chose her words carefully.

"I'm, um, so thankful for this job, Allontis. I will do a great job. But, uh, I just need the autonomy that this position will grant me for now, okay? For the time I'm here, I will do my best for you and the women at the shelter."

Leedra patted her hair, hating the return of the nervous fidgeting habit that'd she'd practiced so long to get rid of. Each and every symptom of her nervousness was returning in full measure in front of the one person she most needed to impress.

"All right, Leedra. I'm sorry, I just hate seeing Dexter this way. Kira is home sick today, and it's just got me thinking . . . but I'll stop bugging you."

"Kira . . . uh, his daughter is sick?" She tried to sound concerned instead of alarmed.

"Dexter's daughter. She's in Hannah's room. She's not contagious, just has a stomachache."

"Right," Leedra said, keeping a calm tone even as every single internal alarm bell started firing off in her head.

CHAPTER SIX:
HOUSE CALLS

DESPITE HER CONCERN FOR KIRA'S wellbeing, Leedra knew she had to leave. The annoyance she had felt when discussing her relationship with Dexter - even if that 'relationship' meant she'd offer a listening ear as Allontis suggested — quickly crystallized to something much more urgent: how in the world was she going to get out of there? Now that Cole had brought in their delicious-looking lunch, she knew that she really needed to make an excuse.

"You guys, I'm so sorry, but I am not feeling well. I really want to taste this food—my goodness, it looks *so* good!" she exclaimed, gesturing admiringly at the platters that Cole had set out as she stood up and reached for her briefcase. To her dismay, the entire thing burst open, scattering papers across the floor. Knowing she could not crouch because of her leg, she simply sat down on the floor to gather them, flushing with embarrassment. Cole got down on his haunches to help her. It didn't take long as she stuffed the papers haphazardly back in, not bothering with neatness, and closed the case with a final snap.

"Wow. I'm a klutz. I'm thinking about . . . uh, looking up some things on adjusting to Eastern Standard Time. I've been feeling so awkward, with this time change, I mean." She smiled, trying to keep her tone casual and airy.

"Are you sure you're okay?" Allontis asked with concern. "Why don't I make you a plate? You can warm it up tonight," Cole offered.

"Oh, uh . . . " Leedra looked at the food again, realizing that she was in fact being rude to a real chef who had his own restaurant. She supposed the extra minutes couldn't hurt.

"Of course. I'd love that." She hoped she'd sounded natural.

She said her goodbyes to Allontis and touched her shoulder, side-stepping the opportunity for an actual hug, and approached the stairs with care, lest she take them too hurriedly and land flat on her face at the bottom.

Back in the kitchen, she grabbed her coat and scarf off the hook so hurriedly that it ripped a hole in the scarf's delicate fabric. She was almost out the door when she spied Cole, busy pulling foil from an industrial sized box. "That's a really big box of foil," she said, making small talk. "Come from a restaurant supply company?"

"Nope, just Costco. Are you sure you're all right?" Cole turned, handed her a paper bag and moved closer to open the door for her.

"Oh, fine. I get a little anxiety from time to time, that's all. Well, guess I'll be seeing you all again soon."

Leedra reached out to push open the screen door to her free-dom, only for it to spring back from her fingertips as Dexter Parker mounted the top step, staring back at her with surprise.

"Leedra?"

"Hello. How are you?"

"Fine," Dexter answered, nonplussed. "What's this, home-delivered meals?"

Dexter looked from his brother to Leedra quizzically. He had been just as surprised to see her as she was to see him. He'd been trying to erase her from his mind ever since she'd told him she'd rather forget her past, which he interpreted to mean she also wanted to forget him.

"Uh, I was just leaving. Cole made lunch and I wanted to take it home—not feeling well. Allontis and I had our scheduled meeting, so now I'm headed out."

Dexter nodded. Leedra seemed fidgety to him, and the unnecessary details delivered with a slight quaver in her voice betrayed her nervousness. The question was: why?

Telling himself that he didn't care why she was acting so strangely, Dexter was swiftly yanked back to the present moment when footsteps could be heard moving quickly down the hall. His daughter ran in, her pajamas disheveled and her eyes crusty from sleep, just as the door banged shut behind Leedra. Without warning, his daughter took off after her. After a confused pause, Dexter gave chase.

"Honey—*Kira*—come back here! What's going on? Stop!"

"Lee? Lee! It's Lee!"

"Okay, okay, but... huh?"

Confused, Dexter caught Kira in his arms halfway down the garden path. The child's screams and pleas were so loud that Dexter had to hold her away from his ear while maintaining his strong grip on her lithe form as she struggled to break free.

"You had a nightmare baby, that's all."

"No, come back, please!" Kira cried in anguish. Dexter sank to his knees, holding his child as she cried. He pressed his cheek against her forehead to check for any fever that might have spiked since he'd taken her temperature that morning, but she felt normal. He looked up in puzzlement to see Leedra, the woman his child had been screaming for, slowly turning around to make her way back up the driveway. He stilled.

As she got closer, Dexter could see that Leedra's lip was trembling and her eyes were filled with tears. Frozen to the spot, he involuntarily loosened his grip on Kira, who immediately wriggled loose. Leedra's arms were open and she had dropped to her knees. Dexter and Cole, who had come outside to see what all the commotion was about, stood watching in disbelief as Kira embraced Leedra and kissed her on the cheek, as if she had known her for years.

Dexter moved closer and listened intently to the words that Leedra spoke to his girl, who up to that point had been so out of control and inconsolable but was now calm.

"I'm sorry, honey. I didn't want to be mean to you."

"Where have you been, Lee?" Kira said.

"I've just been working a lot, that's all."

"But I thought you were working for my aunt? The AEC is right up the road. It's not far," Kira admonished, wiping at the tears drying on her cheeks. "I thought something happened to you. You promised to see me again."

Dexter wanted to smile at the simplicity of the child's thinking, but he had to admit there was nothing simple in this entire situation. The distance of Leedra's workplace from this house? Questions about why she hadn't visited Kira? *How in the world did they even known each other to begin with?*

Dexter took a deep breath and looked pointedly at Kira. "Inside, now."

"Daddy, I told you there was a woman that helped me when I got snatched. This is her. Lee. You know Lee too?"

Kira leaned back slightly in Leedra's arms, looking from Leedra to her father in pure confusion.

"It looks that way," replied Dexter sternly. The truth was, he didn't know what else to say. "Look, can we all go inside, please—*now*?"

"She's coming too, right?"

"Yes. The grown-ups need to speak privately though, okay honey?"

"Well, why?"

"Kira . . . " Dexter said in a warning tone.

Leedra spoke up quickly. "Honey, look…"

Still crouched on the cold asphalt of their driveway, Leedra tried to explain, with Dexter listening intently.

"I . . . I should have told your father that I was there with you on that day. I didn't, and now he's upset because he doesn't understand any of this."

"But, why is he mad? I told him you helped me get away."

"I know . . . I just . . . he didn't know who I was."

"But you work at AEC! You're Aunt Allontis's friend."

"Inside," Dexter snapped once more.

Rather than stand and argue on the driveway, Leedra stood unsteadily and Dexter helped her, wondering why she suddenly had difficulty walking. Cole led Kira inside, though he made sure that her father and Lee were following close behind.

"What's the matter with your leg?" Dexter saw his daughter disappear inside and his attention was redirected to Leedra's obvious struggle.

"I just . . . it has been bothering me lately," she offered.

Dexter nodded. He retrieved her briefcase, the bag of food Cole had packed for her, and her purse before offering her his other arm.

His arm around her waist, she limped along, leaning half of her weight on him. With every step, Dexter grew still more confused about what had just happened.

Back inside, Kira waited obediently next to the door where she'd been asked to sit. Dexter helped Leedra up the step and led her to the nearest chair in the living room. When Dexter returned with a box of tissues for Kira's tear-stained face, he felt a flash of annoyance to see that his daughter had rejoined Leedra the moment he left. Kneeling at Leedra's side, Dexter wiped Kira's face and runny nose. He waved the box of tissues in front of Leedra's face and she quickly snatched two from it. As he continued to observe the two of them together, his jaw twitched and his mind worked diligently to put the missing pieces together.

"Well?" Dexter said, choosing to remain standing rather than to take a seat. When Cole came back into the room, he pulled Dexter aside and suggested that a less threatening stance might be better, tugging Dexter back several feet. Annoyed with his brother this time, Dexter crossed his arms and waited for someone to start an explanation.

It was Cole who gently posed a series of questions to get the ball rolling, then took a seat on the couch a respectful distance from Leedra and Kira. Dexter was reluctant to do the same, but eventually he did.

"Can you tell me this all again, from the beginning?" he said after a lengthy pause, trying to infuse his tone with a little more patience.

Leedra nodded and looked at Kira with a sad smile.

"My first meeting with Allontis was scheduled for the day Kira was taken," she began. "I was driving down this street on my way to the

Center when I saw a van pull up to the side of the road, just feet from my car. A little girl—Kira—was walking along the sidewalk, minding her own business."

"I forgot something at home for school," the child interjected.

"And I just saw these men leap out and snatch her," Leedra continued. "I didn't know what to do, but I didn't want to lose them, so I didn't think twice. I just followed them. When we got to this old building downtown, I jumped out of my car and tried to get to Kira before they took her inside. Next thing I knew, they'd thrown me in with her. I have no idea where it was: I didn't have my GPS, and I was just concentrating on keeping the van in sight—"

"You didn't have a phone?" Dexter interrupted accusingly.

"Why are you being mean to her, Daddy?"

Leedra shook her head, feeling a little ashamed. "No honey, it's just that I should have come forward sooner to tell him what happened, you know. It's not good to keep secrets."

"It's not a secret! I kept telling Daddy that you helped me. I just forgot your full name. Sometimes my dad overreacts."

"Kira . . . " Dexter growled.

"Well, you do. She was the one who saved me, and now you're acting like she's one of the bad guys. I love her."

Dexter looked at his daughter with surprise but kept quiet. With a warm smile at Kira, Leedra continued her story.

"I was two days off the Mercy Ship I'd been working on out of Africa. I had a tablet in the car but it had no signal or Wi-Fi set up yet. I'd assumed Allontis would be providing a phone as part of my new job at the Center, so I had put off getting one. They kept us for two days."

"Three days," Dexter corrected.

"Okay. I lost track. I did make a report to the police," Leedra added.

"An anonymous report."

"Yes, anonymously, because . . . well, I didn't even have all my paperwork for . . . and whatever else I needed." Leedra trailed off into silence.

"She didn't have to make a report at all, D," Cole reminded his brother gently.

"She might as well not have," Dexter snapped. He looked at his brother, annoyed, as if to ask whose side he was on.

"That's *not* true," Leedra protested. She shook her head. "I . . . I'm sorry I've caused such confusion. If even you guys don't believe me, why would the authorities believe me? No one would believe me. Anyway, I've been checking the reports and they mention a similar incident days before, also with no developments."

"Don't be mad at her, Daddy! She saved me," Kira repeated.

"Yes, your daddy's sorry he didn't believe you," Cole said firmly, eyeing Dexter meaningfully. Dexter returned his brother's look for a long moment. Finally, his features relaxed as he addressed his daughter.

"What your Uncle Cole said, sweetie, is right. I'm sorry I didn't believe you."

Kira shifted closer to Leedra, still sniffing.

"Your Daddy is right, though, in how he feels," Leedra said. "I should have come forward and made a statement. I could have talked to him and to your Aunt Allontis, actually. He was worried about you, and I should have talked to him. It was a very dangerous situation you and I were in back there, and he was scared. He loves you very much."

Dexter watched the exchange between the two. He realized that Leedra was in fact defending him, including his right to be angry, to his little girl. He was astonished at how the two had developed a bond so close in what had been just seventy-two dangerous hours. He was only moderately comforted when his daughter looked at him as if she liked him again, but with a new caution nonetheless. When it came to Leedra and his line of questioning thus far, it was clear that he wasn't winning any brownie points with Kira. He tried not to think about her current impression of him and told himself it didn't matter, because her safety was paramount right then and always.

"I'm all right," Leedra told Kira, who had begun to rub her leg gingerly. Leedra rested her hand over Kira's. "If there aren't any more questions, I'm, uh, gonna go."

"Did you see the doctor about your injury?"

"Yes, it's fine, it's fine. I just hurt myself earlier today. I, uh, banged my leg on the corner of a desk, that's all."

Dexter continued to look at her. He didn't believe her.

"They stabbed her in her leg, Daddy. With a knife. It was very deep and needed stitches. She should get a tetanus shot. Right, Daddy?"

Trying to contain his shock, Dexter forced himself back into his professional doctor persona.

"Well, let's have a look, shall we?"

CHAPTER SEVEN:
FRIENDLY REMINDERS

THE TWO-STORY COLONIAL HOUSE WHERE Dexter and Kira lived wasn't a long walk from Cole and Allontis's home. The house had belonged to the brothers' adoptive parents, but now that both Momma G and David had passed away, Dexter and Kira lived there alone. Although Leedra felt utterly silly limping through their neighborhood in the middle of the afternoon, the cooling autumn temperatures felt good on her skin and helped to clear her head slightly as she hobbled along. By now her leg was hurting something awful.

The house's noisy alarm startled Leedra when she entered and Dexter silenced it quickly by punching in a series of numbers. "Sorry," he said quickly.

Leedra nodded and walked in, expecting a similar layout to Allontis's house, renovated and imposing. Although this home had clearly been remodeled as well, it was quite different. Surprised, she glanced at Dexter and he shrugged. He likely didn't guess what she was thinking, which was that the outside of this old home did not match its interior one single bit. She limped into the kitchen and found a place to lean on the clean, cold black granite countertop, continuing to gaze around her.

"This is my adoptive mother's home. Cole and Allontis had plans to move here after they married, but then their family grew larger than expected. After my wife died, I sold the home we shared and I moved back here. This is also the house that my other brother tried to burn down a few years ago. He's adopted, too."

Leedra listened quietly as Dexter answered some of the questions that she had wanted to ask for so long. She was grateful that he did all the talking. She enjoyed listening to him. In his enthusiasm, he stood so close that his breath caressed her face, as it had while his strong arm had supported her on the walk over.

Despite the pleasure she found in listening to him, she was thoroughly annoyed about the reason they had all traipsed over to the house in the first place. She could not believe her leg had chosen that day of all days to act up.

"There are five of us adopted boys," Dexter said as he flipped on the lights, placed his keys on the counter, took off his suit coat and began to roll up his sleeves. Leedra nodded and squinted, adjusting her eyes to the bright lights. Even though it was still daylight outside, the kitchen's lights brightened everything.

Before her was a kitchen straight out of *Architectural Digest*. Like Cole's, this room was fit for a professional chef. Humongous, immaculately polished state-of-the-art appliances occupied every corner. She took in every conceivable kind of convenience, stainless steel this and space-age that, including a six-burner gas cooktop, double wall oven, French door stainless-steel refrigerator, and a door that she assumed led to a butler's pantry. Unbidden, she imagined herself cooking at the stove: a member of the family. She sniffed. Now *that* was highly unlikely, considering her present predicament.

"You really are just down the street from your brother," Leedra said, replaying Kira's earlier statement. It felt like it had taken a lifetime to get there as she limped beside him in awkward silence, but that couldn't be helped.

She was glad that just the two of them had come here. The scrutiny of both Dexter and his brother at once, even though Cole was clearly kind, had been a lot for her to handle. Also, the idea that Kira had become so very attached to her made Leedra feel genuinely sorry about having stayed away. She wasn't at all prepared to feel the emotions she was experiencing now. She couldn't believe that just three days together would cause the child to miss her so much.

"How did you, uh, get so lucky?" she said, taking a deep breath. She desperately wanted to change subjects. She looked up and around. "I mean, to be the one to inherit the house when it has a kitchen clearly built for your brother?"

She noted the way he smiled as he took her briefcase and purse to set them on the counter. "I paid for everything Cole wanted, but it's his design. After my wife died, I just wanted a change and with Allontis having a house already, they decided to stay there. I never intended to stay here this long. Anyway, he gets to use it all the time so I get free food for life."

Leedra nodded. "That's a pretty nice arrangement. I hope to go to his restaurant sometime."

He took her arm and guided her to an adjoining room. It was smaller, with few personal effects. A medical examination table sat in the center, flanked by a sink, a table and a large padlocked gray cabinet which she guessed held supplies and drugs. Dexter gestured at the equipment. "Cole has his professional-grade kitchen. . . well, I guess this is *my* in-home professional area."

Staring around a little warily, Leedra limped closer to the table. Dexter bent to pull out its metal step and Leedra shuffled herself up. Scooting further onto the table, she laid back and tried to get more comfortable.

Dexter turned on still more lights, these ones so bright that they actually hurt Leedra's eyes. The little room had no windows, and she felt her old guardedness creeping back in reaction to the tight quarters.

He opened the cabinet. Leedra lifted her head and saw how well-stocked it was, full of various supplies and clear jars brimming with all sorts of medical supplies: cotton balls, swabs, tongue depressors, gauze and a big stack of green and blue underpads. He retrieved a starchy white pillow from the top shelf and handed it to her.

She moved it under her head. It was definitely helpful. "Thank you."

"I can step out while you take off your pantyhose, or you could raise your skirt and I can cut them away."

Leedra raised her eyebrows, feeling suddenly awkward. She closed her eyes and inched her skirt up little by little. He was a doctor, she kept telling herself—but that didn't do much to stem the flood of awful memories tumbling back into her mind.

"Look at me. Look at me." He stopped and stilled her hands. "Is this too hard for you?"

She shook her head. His gentleness reminded her of the many times he had protected her so long ago. There were plenty of painful memories, certainly, but those things had never taken place when Dexter had been home from school.

"You can cut them. They have a run anyway. And I'm fine. I just haven't had a medical exam in years."

"Not even a mammogram?"

She shook her head no. She was grateful that he had stopped his ministrations, while also touched that he was sensitive enough to realize the effect this entire ordeal might be having on her.

"Okay then." Suddenly businesslike and professional once more, Dexter turned to roll up his sleeves more and washed his hands thoroughly in the small sink before picking up a pair of gloves. Then he hesitated again.

"Leedra, I can get a female doctor. I have a friend that would come over for you if I asked her. I don't have to do this. I'm just trying to make sure your leg is all right."

She blinked away her tears. "I said I'm all right. Just talk to me about something. Tell me everything you're doing, okay?" She didn't want him to think she didn't trust him. She did trust him, wholeheartedly, but this was only a small part of what she was thinking about. Sadness was overwhelming her, and it was about more than just her unwelcome childhood memories.

"I . . . didn't expect Kira to care so much."

"She's a very emotional child. You two were together in a traumatic situation."

"She's been having nightmares ever since. She wakes screaming for "Lee"—who we now know is you." He said it so coldly.

"I'm sorry. I didn't know."

"She has separation anxiety."

"What? Why?" Leedra faltered. She knew about that psychological phenomenon. She got it sometimes too, and as a child she imagined it was yet more devastating. Dexter looked at her sadly.

"Her mother's dead, Lee."

She felt like crying harder.

"I'm worthy of your trust, Dexter."

She didn't know where the words came from or why she even bothered. She felt Dexter carefully snip away the pantyhose. He pulled off her shoes and discarded the thin scraps of nylon into the trash.

"I'm worthy of your trust too, you know," he replied quietly.

"I know."

Dexter nodded. "Okay. Now, why don't you start by telling me what you're thinking about? In return, I'll tell you everything I'm doing. I already removed your shoes and cut off your nylons. Did you do this bandaging yourself?"

Leedra avoided his eyes. It was probably obvious she hadn't been to a doctor. She was a doctor herself, she reasoned, just more for the mind than the body.

"Why didn't you go to the doctor?" he said, as if reading her mind.

"I was . . . I was afraid the people at the hospital might ask me questions I couldn't answer. They might file some kind of police report and considering my line of work now, they might think I too was being abused. You know doctors and all their reporting."

She saw Dexter nodding. She felt one hand on her thigh as the other carefully peeled away the layers of gauze she had amateurishly taped to it.

"Did you put anything on the wound?" Dexter queried.

"A saline solution. It burned."

Dexter suppressed a laugh. "Well, at least you didn't say Neosporin, for a cut that looks like it's about—oh, say three inches long, and pretty deep too."

"I thought about it."

He chuckled at that, and the sound eased her tension a little.

"Did you happen to see what kind of knife they used?"

Leedra shook her head. "It was dark, I just felt it dig into my flesh and twist. They—oh, OH. Ow. Sss."

"Sorry. I am deep cleaning it now. Sit up a little more. I want to show you this. See? This here is what infection looks like. I need to put some ointment on it, and then I'm going to put this special adhesive on it and close it with better tape than you did. This . . ." He pointed, his nose wrinkled—"Whatever you did here is not working. Do you have diabetes?"

"No." Actually, she didn't know. She didn't think so.

"How can you be sure? Your wound isn't healing, and it's been over three weeks. I want you to come to the office tomorrow. What I'm doing here is just temporary."

Leedra nodded and Dexter began wrapping the leg with a bandage the color of paper grocery bags.

"I know a doctor who will let me use his office. I'll give you the address. Just come see me there and I'll fix this with the right tools. You'll also need a shot and some meds to ward off any further infection."

She looked at him, thinking to herself that she probably wouldn't go. Again, Dexter seemed to know her thoughts.

"It's safe, Leedra. You can't hide out forever."

"Does it need stitches?" she asked nervously. Dexter shook his head and she felt a surge of relief.

"I chose to work at the shelter for a reason. It has afforded me some security, being as how it's a protected location. I don't plan to hide. I just wanted time to get to know my surroundings better before I spent nights out on the town, that's all."

"Nights on the town?" Dexter raised an eyebrow at her and Leedra looked away. "We both know that's not why you decided to come home, now is it?"

CHAPTER EIGHT:
BACK DOWN MEMORY LANE

"WHAT ARE YOU TALKING ABOUT?"

Dexter moved back, shrugging wordlessly. He turned to gather a few metal pins from a jar in the cabinet and pinned the closure of the bandage in three places, pulling the material tighter on Leedra's leg. He told himself he wasn't going to mention anything about what he knew. But as he held her leg and saw to her physical wounds, the close quarters seemed to loosen his lips. Perhaps there was too little oxygen getting to his brain. He noticed some of her hard edges beginning to crumble right before his eyes. Pieces of the little girl he once knew were beginning to show.

Dexter was thoughtful as he looked at her. In his old family home, in that tiny room, his awareness of her was heightened. Though he had resolved some time ago not to trust anyone again, he figured there wasn't any reason to hold on to those old feelings. Not with her. After all, she hadn't actually pretended to be someone else. A wave of new feelings washed over him, threatening to drown out every bit of doubt and skepticism he had initially felt. He couldn't dismiss the fact that she'd been the one to save his daughter.

He took off his gloves and discarded them. He washed his hands again and picked up her shoes to help her put them on.

"Stop. Stop. I can do it. Thank you."

He stood again to his full height, deciding to address the elephant in the room at last.

"The girls. I saw the photos. They were sticking out of your date book."

Leedra was taken aback. "So you just took the liberty of leafing through my private papers? Do this to many people you're meeting for the first time?" she asked incredulously.

"I did not leaf through anything, and we're not meeting for the first time," Dexter shot back. "Not to mention, I recognized them because I have the same pictures."

He watched her as she maneuvered herself off the table and slid on her shoes. He frowned at the shoes for a moment, noting with a physician's disapproval that they were much too high for someone with a leg injury, but she put them on and made for the exit.

"I don't appreciate you looking through my things," she said over her shoulder.

"Is this really the time to hide anything, Leedra? After everything that's gone on, it's all out in the open. You can tell me anything. You must know that by now."

"Oh sure, but the problem is you don't wait for me to tell you. You snoop around. I have my *own* timetable. I'll do things when *I'm* ready, not before."

"I didn't snoop around."

"I just wish . . ."

"What?" Dexter asked, moving an empty chair at the table toward her.

"What's that for?"

"Please sit down and put up your leg," he instructed. "You should keep it elevated as much as possible."

Dexter stood and waited. Despite Leedra's obvious anger, she eventually did as he'd asked.

"See, that's what I mean," she sighed, exasperated. "Dexter, you are acting like we're still kids—like I need you to look out for me. We're not in that place any more and I don't *need* a protector. We both left, came back, and had different experiences. Things changed us. I could never have expected to run into you or to save a girl from kidnapping, let alone find out that she's your daughter. Do you even realize how surreal and bizarre this all is?" Leedra waved her hand about the space.

"I didn't change that much, and I did not leave," Dexter replied quietly. "You didn't change that much, either. You're still the caring, passionate person I knew as a boy. Truth be told, you're still running around trying to be everything to everyone, like you did back then, and it's costing you something to do that."

"People move on, Dexter."

"Sounds like you want to do more than move on. Sounds to me like you want to pretend our past never even existed."

Dexter leaned a hip against the counter and crossed his arms over each other, annoyed. He could see that there was a conflict raging within her; that she wanted to say more. It was fine with him if all she came back to Virginia for were answers. He simply wished that she wouldn't keep evading him, making him pull it all out of her piece by piece.

"There was a time when you told me all your secrets."

"Please don't."

Before she could say anything else, Dexter had gently moved aside the chair where her leg rested and was on his knees in front of her. His eyes were on her and he reached out to envelop her in a hug.

"Do you carry the photos with you, Leedra? Why?"

"Of course I carry them with me. But it . . . it doesn't matter." She pushed feebly away, but he did not release his hold.

"It does matter. You will have to let go of the guilt. You can't let it torment you."

"But it *does* torment me. I was the oldest of them and . . . Doesn't it torment you?"

"Yes, but I had to let it go or at least put it somewhere else. It can take over your life."

"Compartmentalize? Typical man."

"Don't make me sound callous," he said.

"I want to apologize."

"For making me sound callous?"

"No—I know you're not—but for earlier."

"Today?"

"No, back at the office, when you realized who I was. I told you that you reminded me of a painful time. That wasn't really true and I'm sorry for saying it. You were my only friend and protector. I loved you."

Dexter nearly drowned when her arms, once stiff and unmoving at her side, reached around his neck and clung tight. It was an effort to keep talking.

"Don't let this torment you."

"I feel responsible somehow. I still want answers."

"What if their aren't any?

"Then I will find that out and I won't be better or worse off than I was before," she insisted.

Dexter hesitated. He knew what finding answers could be like: when you found them, you could very well be worse off. After a moment, he decided to keep that insight to himself. There wasn't any need to belabor the point further right now. She was determined and he felt that determination like a hot spirit that pulsed through her entire body. He was simply worried about any fallout and wondered exactly how he could support her if the answers she sought didn't turn up. Oh, yes—he knew how that felt.

Dexter felt Leedra shift against his chest, but she didn't move out of his embrace and it felt good. He told himself to be cautious, even as his heart yelled to throw caution to the wind.

"I've thought about you all these years."

"Why did you waste your time?" Her laugh was muffled against his shirt.

He ignored her. "I wondered what you were like and prayed you'd be everything you wanted to be. You're even more beautiful than I thought you'd be."

"You're gonna make me cry again."

"Welcome home, Leedra."

When she lifted her head, he stared at her. A connection, unspoken but deep, passed between them and she sat up straighter to wipe her eyes.

"Thank you," she whispered.

Dexter moved closer, watching her lips part then close, but his chest pocket vibrated, breaking the delicate spell. Frowning, he pulled the phone from his pocket, but before checking it, he leaned over and quickly, gently, kissed Leedra's cheek. Startled into silence, she looked at him, bemused.

Rocking back on his haunches, he stood up and read the phone message.

"Cole and Ms. Kira are gonna bring over your missed lunch. They say you seem determined to get rid of it," he told her with a grin.

He was surprised by her acquiescence, seeming almost like defeat. For once, she wasn't acting like she wanted to leave right at that moment. Dexter realized that he was feeling very happy for the first time in a really long time.

CHAPTER NINE:
INCONVENIENT REVELATIONS

JUST OVER THE BORDER OF Culpeper County, about an hour away from his own home, Dexter stood uncertainly outside the old house of his biological dad, Garrison Johnson. He took a deep breath and sniffed the air, looking out over the property's three acres—mostly lush, fragrant farmland. Under normal circumstances, the approach would have been a scenic and beautiful drive, if only Dexter didn't always dread getting to the destination.

He didn't want to be there, but he hadn't been to see his father in several weeks, what with the ordeal with Kira. That had been enough of an excuse to put the old man off for a little while, but it couldn't last forever. Anyway, he had only one board meeting this week and his shifts at the hospital were almost back to normal, so he could certainly take this time out to pay his aging father a visit.

It seemed that Garrison got visibly older each time he came. That was the real reason for Dexter's hesitation. One day his father wouldn't be around anymore, yet they never seemed to be able to really talk about significant stuff from the past even when they did talk. Every time Dexter visited, they both spent hours staring into the distance, making chit chat and skirting all the important issues until it was time for awkward goodbyes, for Dexter to head back to the city and for his father to return to his post in front of the television.

Whenever Dexter came to visit, he came alone. Not with his daughter or, when she'd been alive, his wife. Ever. His father was simply off limits to the rest of his family and that was non-negotiable. Each one of the five adopted Parker brothers had had an odd, strained relationship with their "starter family," the term he and Cole had coined to describe the parental units who had launched their strange experiences in the world.

Dexter thanked God every day that the way he started didn't determine his finish. That notion turned his thoughts to Leedra. She was beautiful and his mind had rarely strayed from her in the few weeks since he'd met her again. He was excited to get to know her, but here in this particular house he wanted to shut away those parts of his heart. There were some emotions that shouldn't be mingled with the inhabitants of this raggedy old house.

Calling loudly down the hall so that his father would know he was present, Dexter entered the small rambler through the rusty and creaking front door, shifting the bulging paper grocery bag on his hip as he entered the kitchen. As was his routine, he sniffed the air. He looked over the stove, opened drawers and cabinets, searching as he always did for giveaway items: remnants of old pipes, or particular types of residue that Dexter wished he could not name. He found nothing—nothing today, anyway.

Dexter took a quick glance from the kitchen into the living room, where his father usually occupied his favorite chair in front of the television. Today, the chair was empty. Dexter looked for a space on the cluttered kitchen island to set the bag down but since he couldn't, he left it on the dining room table and went in search of his father. Down the hall, Dexter edged through another door, which would barely open due to stacks of clothes, newspapers, vacuum cleaners, an old folding tray and all manner of other clutter. His father supposedly wasn't a hoarder, but each time Dexter visited it seemed Garrison was coming closer to that label.

"Dad, you all right?"

"Yeah, yeah. I'm all right," Garrison Johnson said as he pushed the covers from his face.

"You want some help?" Dexter asked. His father shook his head.

"Lord, every Thursday seem like you come earlier and earlier. What time is it anyway?"

"It's nine o'clock, Dad. This is my normal time."

Dexter acknowledged the usual terse greeting, relieved that at least his father was talking today. He squeezed back out of the bedroom to wash his hands, find whatever soap he could to clear the sink of its dirty dishes and start to cook a decent meal.

Pushing the week's crusty dishes into the kitchen sink to soak, Dexter laughed softly to himself. Cole, his brother the chef and neatnik, would likely be horrified to see this particular kitchen. It was not only terribly dirty, with clutter everywhere, but everything in it was as old as the house. Except for the refrigerator, which Dexter had replaced a year ago, every major appliance was fifties vintage.

Once he had cleared some space to work, Dexter put away the groceries he'd brought and got to work on the bacon and eggs. Just being around Cole had made him a better cook, although Dexter knew better than to try and compete. Cole owned not one, but two, restaurants and Dexter was simply no match in the kitchen. He was thankful, however, that Cole had taught him some basics. Now, he could at least cater to Kira's picky appetite and not completely embarrass himself in front of his daughter when Uncle Cole was just a hop, skip and a jump away at the end of the street. Plus, he now had a new reason to increase his culinary aptitude.

Dexter found himself thinking often about Leedra, daydreaming about whether he could someday earn the chance to impress her—or at least try to—in the kitchen. For the most part, they had slipped into an easy groove of friendship. She had actually had dinner with him once. Granted, it wasn't exactly intimate, but it had been nice.

"Just you again?"

Dexter turned to find his dad staring at him. Lost in thought, he hadn't heard his shuffling approach. Garrison Johnson hobbled further into the kitchen, leaning heavily on his cane.

"Yes, Dad, just me." Dexter shrugged his shoulders, dismissing his dad's implication, and continued cracking eggs. What could he say? *"I'm sorry, I'd never bring my daughter around a drug addict like you in a million years? What would be the point of bringing Kira here? For her to gain some clarity about her career aspirations? I think not. No, thank you."* Any discussion would only end in a fight.

As his father slumped his old frame into a seat, Dexter put the finishing touches to the turkey bacon, one of his favorite items because it took less than four minutes to cook on each side according to the package directions. He frowned when the bacon produced no pan drippings, bracing himself for a disgruntled monologue from his father about today's paltry low-fat selections. He added the eggs, stirring them until they were cooked the way his dad liked them. He rinsed and cut fruit, though he knew he'd be the one eating most of it, and added fresh grapes and berries into the last clean bowl he could find.

He set everything before his father and took a seat across from him, only to remember the coffee and stand up again. At least the coffee wasn't an altered or low-calorie version. He fetched the two cups, added sugar and creamer to both. He placed it before his dad and sipped coffee while his father ate.

"Where's Ms. Sally?" He asked his father to break the silence. "You run her off again?"

"You know she always go out when you coming. Claim it's her only time to have any peace to herself. She ain't doing nothing but spending some of my social security check on things she don't need."

"They say retail therapy is better than a trip to the psychologist, so she's likely doing you a favor with the cheaper option," Dexter replied.

Garrison ignored his quip. "Found a woman yet? You look a little, I don't know . . . softer."

All small talk aside, Dexter was surprised that this direct observation had left his dad's lips so early. Usually they insulted one another back and forth for much longer before making any real conversation. He put down the mug he was nursing and assumed a serious expression. "Why you say that?"

"Heard you whistling down the hall. You ain't done that in ages. You barely make a peep normally, and you're certainly never in a cheery mood when you come here."

"I'm trying, Pop."

"That's just it. You don't usually try."

Dexter registered the barbed statement, but decided not to dwell on its meaning. Honestly, he hadn't realized he was whistling. He didn't think he'd done anything differently, but it was uncanny how right his father was.

"I always try with you," he said quietly after a pause.

Although the barbs always stung, Dexter knew that his father loved nothing more than to take digs at him at every turn. He knew, too, that the very fact of his being there—paying the bills his dad's meager check couldn't cover, cooking breakfast and cleaning the kitchen—clearly demonstrated how he was always trying to do right by his father. The question over his love life ignited a flicker of hope that maybe his father actually cared about his well-being and might even want to see him happy. Either way, though, Dexter wouldn't be giving the old man any details.

"I'm sorry, Pop. I wish I could talk about things like my personal life with you. I just can't."

"Yeah, yeah. You don't forgive me for breaking your precious little heart. I know all about that."

"I never said that."

"Who asked you to come here, anyway? I'm just a washed-up old man. Why you care so much about me anyhow?"

"I'm here, Pop. Isn't that enough for you? I'm here seeing about you, making sure you eat. That you got a roof over your head, that you're safe. What more do you want?"

The old man grew still, a crafty look in his eyes.

"You still mad cause I sent your little friend far away?"

Dexter stiffened. "Don't mention her. Please."

"You really did love her, didn't you?"

"I'm not talking about this with you, Pop. I'm not." Dexter didn't even know how they got on the subject. His dad just had a way.

"Then go on and get out."

Dexter stood so abruptly that some of his coffee spilled on the floor. He set it down as calmly as he could and went over to the sink to wash the dishes. His dad's voice penetrated his ears, regardless.

"Evie Carter wasn't no good for you, all right. Listen—I got something I got to tell you."

"I don't want to know. Stop mentioning her." Dexter didn't turn around, the dishes bearing the brunt of his anger in the warm, sudsy water. Why this conversation was happening now he didn't know, but he was positive that whatever his father was about to say would justify his policy of never introducing any women he had loved to his father.

His father knew Leedra as Evie Carter. Dexter was glad she had changed her name because, that way, he could keep his father from knowing she'd returned.

"I'm sorry I sent that girl away. But I know what those men did to her. I know what they did to the other girls. Finding her a missionary . . . ah, a mother, was my way of ensuring she had a chance."

"Stop. Stop. I don't want to hear this."

"I gotta tell someone, or it's going to my grave with me."

"Then take it to your grave. Let it burn a hole in your heart as far as I'm concerned." Dexter turned around sharply, water dripping from his hands, and wiped them savagely with a dishtowel. Dexter marched closer to his father, leaning into his personal space. "You take your dirty deeds to your grave. I do not care. Don't you dare unload your conscience on me. I already know more than enough about your drug use and your underage girls you picked up to do God knows what to you. Oh yes—I already know enough to last a lifetime."

Although Dexter didn't actually have all the details, he knew that his father had arranged for a missionary woman to take Evie away from Virginia. He wasn't even sure if Evie/Leedra herself knew exactly what his father had done, contacting the woman from church and making all the arrangements. Perhaps that was why his father had been talking about wanting to clear his conscience. *There was always more to the story, wasn't there?*

As a child, Dexter had testified in court about what he saw and heard in his foster home. At the time, he thought that was the end of it. If his father harbored another secret that could hurt Leedra still more, Dexter couldn't imagine a good reason to bring it all back up.

"I didn't touch no children like they did."

"Oh, you just touched the sixteen and seventeen-year-olds at the parties they had, right?" Dexter roared.

"No, no they wasn't. They knew what we was doing. It was the drugs they wanted, and then one thing led to another."

Dexter shook his head violently. He stared at his father as if he'd lost his mind, unable to fathom his calm rationalization for chasing after prepubescent girls as a grown man. Somehow, the girls being in their "late teens" made it all right. His father returned his gaze with indifference, bits of yellow half-chewed egg hanging from the corners of his mouth. Thoroughly disgusted, Dexter returned to the dishes.

The only reason Dexter's father knew anything at all about his time in foster care was because he had occasionally been permitted to visit Dexter under supervision. Even if he'd wanted to, Garrison could never have rescued his son from the foster family from hell because he himself was never pronounced safe to be around children. To this day, Garrison and this very house, was on the list of registered sex offenders and would remain on it until he died. Everyone who heard the situation for the first time thought that Dexter was the bad guy, that keeping his daughter and wife at a distance from his own father was the worst thing ever. They didn't know the truth.

"Do you know what happened to . . .?" Garrison's voice hovered near Dexter's shoulder.

"No," Dexter said, his eyes never leaving the dirty water.

"What was her name?"

"I *said* I didn't want to talk about this anymore."

"Evie Carter—was that her name? I know she made it out, but . . . well, I never did hear anything from the missionary after she took her away."

Silence.

Garrison persisted. "Just tell me now—I . . . I's trying to remember but I can't."

Silence.

"She was a pretty little thing. I threatened to report that man, but he wanted her anyway. Such a shame about what happened to the other girls, too. I tried to . . ."

Dexter felt numb. His mouth was dry, thinking about Leedra and the pain she suffered. Those men had killed those girls. Leedra was the only one to get out alive.

"I said. I do not. Want. To know." Dexter turned to face his father fully. "I don't want to know. I don't want to know about the times when you had the power to get the help you needed, the help we needed—" He tapped his chest. "And stop the abuse—and you did nothing."

"I pleaded with them not to touch you. I knew there was stuff going on in that home, but I prayed they at least wouldn't touch the boys—my boy."

"That makes you some kind of what—a saint? You gender-base your prayers, do ya?"

"What does that mean? I just tried to . . ."

"No one cares. No one cares anymore what you *tried* to do, because it didn't freaking work. Because whatever you *tried* to do was way too little, too late."

"I found that girl a nice church lady to adopt her, didn't I?" Garrison said in a wounded tone.

"Yeah, and she dragged her half way across the world to Brazil and later Africa!" As soon as the words left his mouth, Dexter regretted showing how much he knew.

Garrison paused. "How did you know where she moved to?"

"They were missionaries, Pop. Uh, back . . . back then that's where most of the missions were headed," Dexter stammered quickly. Leedra had told him more about her world travels as soon as she'd been whisked away from Virginia, how the woman—the only mother she knew—had eventually died when she'd been around eighteen and how even though Leedra had considered herself free to return to the States, she'd simply reupped for another long-term mission opportunity off the African Coast. He kept his eyes on the suds and stilled his shaking hands, feeling his father's eyes on him.

"Did you look for her?" his father asked.

Dexter was silent. He had looked. He had contacted twenty

churches in a fifty-mile radius, asking if they had a missions program. No leads. No one had been willing to give a thirteen-year-old much information about anything.

"It makes no difference now. That nasty man in that filthy godfor-saken house killed himself and that ended it. He should have served jail time—he, he should have been put under the ground for what he did," Dexter spat bitterly. "I had to testify, Dad. I had to tell them all the devastating details of what went on in that place. Our foster father was said to have taken his own life," Dexter recounted. Then and still now, he'd seen the act as only a way to escape sentencing. "Justice was *not* served, not one bit," He spat out.

Dexter squeezed a sodden dish rag viciously and began to attack every surface not already piled with trash, his efforts failing to shift the sticky film of grime that coated everything. He was trying to scrub away the hurt of his past, but that wouldn't ever go away. Finally, he threw the rag back into the water and took a deep breath, snatching up his dad's dirty breakfast plate. As his father rose and shuffled unconcernedly out of the kitchen, Dexter could already feel that he wouldn't be able to get today's particular episode out of his head. Why, he wondered, had the subject of Evie—of Leedra—come up at this particular time? It should have been long dead and buried, and he wanted no part in it. It seemed too great a coincidence that his father would bring this up so soon after Leedra returned home.

The kitchen was still far from clean, but Dexter was ready to get out of the house as fast as he could. In mutual silence, he helped his father take a shower and put on clean clothes instead of the musty robe that Garrison insisted on wearing in all seasons and weathers. He put the offending robe in a pile of equally foul-smelling garments and laundered them, wishing he could burn them instead. He cleaned, he vacuumed and he tried to be a good son.

The old man could never be fitted into Dexter's real life, despite his ever-hopeful search for a way to do so. The cruelty of Garrison's past misdeeds, compounded by his utter lack of contrition, would always separate them.

"I'm done," came his father's call from the bathroom. It occurred to Dexter suddenly how childish age had rendered the old man. He answered the call, picking his way through the junk-filled house to assist his dad with his clothes and comb his hair. He eventually got his father settled back in the living room in his favorite chair.

"Did, uh, you take your blood pressure meds already?"

"No, bring it with a Coke."

"You just had your breakfast and coffee, Dad."

"Thanks for the menu summary. Who are you, Charlie Rose? I had my breakfast. It was paltry at best, and now I want a stupid Coke. Now git."

Dexter shook his head, annoyed but not surprised by the rudeness. He trudged back to the kitchen, trying not to stomp, and snatched the blood pressure medication from the lazy Susan, already crowded with countless other orange bottles for God-only-knew-what. He double-checked the patient name on the bottle, plus the name of the medicine, then opened it and scrutinized the pill itself. Grabbing a bottle of water from the fridge, Dexter returned to set it and the pill on his father's tray table and braced himself automatically for some complaint about the absence of the requested carbonated beverage. To his surprise, none came.

"I have to make some things right. You won't like it, but I will tell you the truth. It has to come out. I'm sorry for what I did."

Dexter nodded mutely. His father paused for a beat. In that moment, Dexter realized that he didn't actually want to know the truths of the past. It would only mess with his present. He couldn't handle it. He might lose Leedra over it—and, he thought dejectedly, he didn't even have her yet.

"I'm uh, I'm going to have to go," Dexter said, before his father could continue. He was exhausted and he hadn't been there more than three hours. He could usually manage four. Garrison ignored his parting words and concentrated his attention on the TV remote.

Walking back out to his car, Dexter prayed for strength to handle the truth whenever it came—that Leedra wouldn't be hurt when it came out, and that Garrison would feel better from telling it. He wanted to believe that the old man just required some kind of peaceful absolution for his deeds and a release from the demons that plagued him. He prayed that anyone who could be hurt by the revelations soon to be spoken was no longer living. Dexter decided that ultimately, his prayers for Leedra and himself were all he could offer, and that was of little comfort.

CHAPTER TEN:
MISSING PIECES

12-year-old boy questioned about the death of two girls and possible kidnapping of two other children. The discovery of the bodies of two girls at a local house early on Saturday morning left emergency service workers and the case detective distraught, a neighbor reported. Whereabouts of the surviving girls, ages 8 and 6, remain unknown. Police and counselors were called to the home of...

WHEN A KNOCK SOUNDED ON her office door, Leedra quickly shoved the papers she'd been reading back inside their folder and called for the person to enter. Marcie, the second-in-command at Anchored, came in. Pushing the folder to the side of her desk, Leedra turned her attention to her upbeat colleague.

"Hey!" Marcie paused when she set eyes on her interim boss. Realizing the last few days' fatigue was likely evident, Leedra patted her hair in embarrassment and smiled.

"What can I do for you, Marcie?"

"Oh. Uh, this is an addendum that Senator Braxton has been working on for the Violence Against Women Act reauthorization. Attached is a note of concerns from our legal department. Lucient sent it over for your review. Sorry, I was just looking at you a little weird because you have what I call a 'deep groove' right here between your eyes." Marcie gestured. "You okay? You look a little tired."

Leedra shook her head. "I'm fine, just a migraine. I, uh, I haven't had them in years."

She rubbed at her forehead. She knew that telltale groove that Marcie had noticed. It seemed to appear whenever her migraines were just taking hold. The awful headaches had started shortly after she began gathering data and likely wouldn't stop until this whole thing was completed.

"Well, all right, but remember: that's what coming back to the city will do for you, girly. Gives us all migraines, for sure. Let's see: there's the budget-time migraine, the grants-time migraine, the reporting-and-compliance migraine . . . I guess you have all of the above, right?"

Leedra nodded. She was starting to get a will-she-just-stop-talking migraine, but thought better of saying that aloud.

"Do you want me to get you something?"

Leedra shook her throbbing head firmly. She didn't believe in drugs. Not ever. Not even for the worst pains. She had a small bag of natural remedies somewhere at home that had worked for everything from toothache to stomach cramps during her time in Africa. She'd have to remember to look for it. Fingers crossed she still had all the right items in there, because the current grade of headache was one she hadn't had in years. She waved Marcie off but smiled to convey her thanks for the concern.

Marcie left and closed the door behind her.

Leedra took a deep breath. She hadn't expected that her old wounds would be rubbed so raw by just a few weeks of deeper research into the case. Up until today, she'd resolved to do all of this stuff from the comfort and safety of her small apartment in the evenings only; last night, she had fought sleep as she wrestled with her myriad questions, tossing and turning, never gaining clarity about any of it. Eventually she fell into a restless sleep, but upon waking, she'd packed up all she'd been working on and brought it with her to work. Now her brain hurt and she needed food. She should purchase some proper groceries instead of going to Cole's restaurant, Beguile Again, every night.

Frustrated by the gap in the information that she'd been mulling over, she put her sheaf of documents into her bag and stood. She pressed the intercom to let Marcie know she was going out for a bit—to the grocery store, she said, even though honestly she'd likely end up at Beguile Again . . . again. Ready to clear her head, she locked her office door and took the elevator downstairs to her car. Perhaps she would catch a glimpse of Dexter if she did end up at the restaurant. That would be a wonderful coincidence, even though she told herself it was not a wise gamble to take.

"Daddy, look, it's Lee!"

"I see her, honey. She looks like she's deep in thought. We can . . . uh . . ." Dexter looked again but didn't wave at Leedra, who was just down the aisle in the grocery store. "Read me what's next on the list . . ."

He already knew Kira was unlikely to be deterred by his half-hearted attempt to steer her in the opposite direction. Improvising, he grabbed a box of frozen waffle sticks from the freezer, hoping the rarely-purchased treat might take her mind off the subject at hand.

Despite their new awareness and acceptance of each other, Dexter didn't want to make it seem like he was following Leedra. He just wished their getting together would happen more organically, like him asking her out on a date and her saying yes. So far that hadn't happened, and he was surprised by how much he wanted it to. Perhaps now was a perfect opportunity.

Without attention to him, per usual, Kira set off down the aisle in Leedra's direction and Dexter followed with the cart, slower but not far behind.

"Hi Lee. How are you?" Kira chirped.

"Oh, hey honey!"

Dexter watched as Lee put down a can of beans and squeezed Kira's shoulder with genuine affection before looking up to greet him.

"Hi."

"Leedra . . ." Kira started jabbering away excitedly before they could exchange further conversation, but they did manage to share a cordial smile.

"We're making some cupcakes for my class at school. Do you want to have dinner with us? Then you can help us make the cupcakes."

"Oh, ah . . . no, honey. I've just been kind of super busy and I have a little headache today."

Although Dexter was keeping his eyes down, as if poring over the nutrition information of the chocolate candy Kira had just snuck into their shopping cart, he was listening intently, his eyes unseeing. Forgetting the candy's astronomical sugar content, Dexter's ears pricked up at the word *headache*. Leedra wasn't moving, so he couldn't tell if her walking had improved. Their eyes met and he guessed she regretted how much she'd told him the other day. Now she would try to act as if everything was okay just for him.

"How are your symptoms?" Dexter inquired casually, surveying the contents of his cart.

"Uh oh, Kay Kay. Doctor alert!" Leedra joked to the child who looked back at her, her eyes concerned.

"Look at me," Dexter said.

"I'm fine," Leedra returned, although she sobered at Dexter's tone. Reluctantly, her eyes met his.

"Why are you sweating?" He moved closer.

"It's hot."

"We're in the freezer section."

"Well, you're pretty observant, aren't you? OK, OK, I have a little fever and maybe an infection. I just need to get some antibiotics . . ."

"Sure, sounds good, but you can't get those things without seeing a doctor. Over-the-counter infection meds probably won't be strong enough. What else have you been experiencing?" Reaching full medical throttle, Dexter fired more questions. "Did you go to the doctor like I told? Did they give you a prescription?"

She shook her head and swayed slightly.

Dexter moved to stand beside her immediately. His arm shot around her waist and she rested her weight against him.

"Let's go."

"Where?"

"To the hospital."

She shoved away from him, but his hand remained firmly support-ive at her back.

"Just let me walk out on my own and you pull the car around." She put her hand up as if to push him away, but Dexter saw her resolve waning the longer he and Kira stood with her. Her determination to direct and orchestrate everything was silliness.

A passerby with a small frail-looking dog in her cart regarded them oddly. Belatedly, Dexter remembered the security cameras every-where, not to mention how strange and suspicious it would look if he didn't let Leedra exit on her own. After all, he wanted to get her to the hospital, but he didn't want to make a scene, least of all one involving the police. The fact that she'd agreed to go to the hospital at all told Dexter that this was urgent, though, so he quickly sprung into action.

He crouched to talk to his daughter and his tone was stern. "Honey, stay with Leedra. Walk normally and slowly to the exit with her. Let her lean on your shoulder, and I'll get the car. Don't leave her, okay?"

"Okay Daddy. I won't leave her. I'll take care of her just like she took care of me that night."

Dexter dismissed all emotion from his immediate thoughts: The situation called for a doctor, not a caring friend from her past.

Leedra and Kira set off slowly for the exit. Taking a different route, Dexter hurried through the grocery store and exited from the back door. In a matter of moments, he had his SUV around to the loading zone. He leapt out, scanning the shoppers, afraid for an instant that Leedra had fallen before he spotted Kira's little head standing by her at the main door. His daughter was showing so much concern for Leedra that it had his heart beating triple time. Remembering that he was supposed to be observing as much as he could, Dexter hung back momentarily to watch her move toward the car. He wondered if the leg was truly her only problem.

"Listen to me," Dexter said to Kira, opening the door to usher her inside. "I'm going to call Uncle Cole to pick you up." Leedra's limp was definitely worse now, though she hid it well with her slight swaying walk. To others, perhaps, she simply looked a little drunk. She remained alert. She even smiled at a passerby who stared a little too long, but she kept moving determinedly toward the car.

"What's the matter with her, Daddy?

"She may have an infection, but she will be fine once we get her on some good, strong antibiotics. Put your seat belt on."

With everybody safely in at last, Dexter sped away from the curb for the short drive to the INOVA Hospital.

"Listen to me—"

"Please don't lecture me. You said I should just need antibiotics, right?"

Dexter glanced at the rearview mirror and at the road ahead, trying not to speed. "I won't know what you need until I run some tests."

"What kind of tests?"

"Blood work," he said shortly. If she was surprised, she didn't say anything. He rattled off some other tests she might need, including a wound culture for a bacterial infection.

"I'm concerned you have diabetes. The wound is severe, but it's also not healing. You've largely ignored what I asked you to do. So if you've developed a staph infection, it could have run deeper."

"You shouldn't ignore the doctor's orders," Kira piped up.

The hospital was close by, but the midday traffic stretched the usual ten-minute ride to twenty. Dexter pulled up to the emergency bay and was out of the car in a flash, helping Leedra inside. Kira followed close behind without prompting.

"Hey, Wally, come here." Dexter recognized a nurse he worked closely with and hailed him for a wheelchair. "This is Ms. Henderson. Put her in Room 13 and get a culture on her leg. She has an old wound there that should be healing by now, and I'm really concerned about sepsis. Do a BMP, urine culture and vitals, and I'll be there in just a second."

He addressed Leedra: "I'll be right back." He was surprised by the look of uncertainty and confusion in her eyes. Up until now she'd seemed so self-assured, even when in pain. She looked up at Walter the nurse and, with weakness and fatigue taking over, went with him willingly.

"Will you be reviewing the test results yourself?" she asked hesitantly.

"Of course. I work here," Dexter assured her. "I'm just going to hand Kira over to Cole, and then I'll be right back."

Leedra looked as if she had forgotten about the little girl who now approached her chair. "I'm sorry, honey," she whispered as Kira gently touched her hand.

"Why? You're not feeling well. It's okay. Daddy is going to make you all better. I'm going to pray for you."

"Thank you."

Dexter frowned. The entire bit seemed overly dramatic, but then again, so were most of his daughter's reactions since being kidnapped. He thought he saw tears in Leedra's eyes as he took Kira off to meet her uncle.

When he returned, they were inserting an IV and she was silent, her eyes closed.

Her eyes looked glassy when she opened them at the touch of her hand. He hoped she wasn't having some sort of adverse reaction to anything. Come to think of it, she hadn't even been given anything at this point. He completed her patient form in as much detail as he could and hung it at the foot of her bed.

"Are you allergic to anything?"

Leedra shook her head.

"I want to know what happened. Some things don't make sense; parts are missing."

"Okay, but you can't do anything if you're sick. It will wait."

"No, it won't. That night, I fell asleep . . . they drugged me and I fell asleep, so I couldn't guard the girls."

Dexter chanced a glance at Wally, who was obviously curious but didn't respond to her words of delirium.

"You're just confused. You have a fever. You will figure it out when you're feeling better."

"No, Dexter, please. Read the papers in my bag. Read them."

Dexter moved closer. Her hand gripped his and he saw how scared she was.

"Don't give me anything that makes me drowsy. Please. Okay?" Her tone was panicked.

Dexter nodded, avoiding her gaze. Half the stuff he knew she was going to get had the side effect of drowsiness.

"You need to rest."

"I can't. I can't sleep."

Dexter grew impatient as Wally made numerous botched attempts to get a line in her arm. Quietly Dexter motioned to him to call someone else up there that could do what he needed. When Wally left the room, Dexter kissed her forehead.

"This is not your fault. You had nothing to do with it."

"Someone sent me away. They helped me get away, they took Renee and I . . . I fell asleep. I feel asleep. I fell asleep on watch and I let them all down," she murmured. "I'm sorry."

CHAPTER ELEVEN:
DET. PHILIP CLAY, FBI RET.

THERE WERE ONLY A FEW things FBI Agent Philip Clay would miss about being a federal investigator. The constant noise of the office, oddly, was one of those things. At this particular moment, things was a crescendo of chaos. Phones rang constantly over the background din of computers and people talking in all kinds of different languages. Typically, the crimes in this unit ran the gamut from jumping the fence of the White House to picking tourists' pockets to illegal possession of weapons and assault, kidnapping and just down the hall, fighting national terrorism.

Clay didn't shut his door because it never made much difference to the noise level. If anything, the background noise might help him pack his belongings a little faster. He was leaving, and he supposed he shouldn't take all day to get going. Clay put down one of the boxes he'd been shuffling around the office and piled more silly knickknacks, files and mementos into it—just a bunch of junk he'd accumulated over the twenty-five years on the job.

"Hey, Boss, we almost ready? You need help loading up or are you staying till five, you know, for formality's sake? I don't think I've ever seen anyone work a full day on their last day."

His friend and Department Chief, Mark Washington, grinned as he sauntered into the office.

Clay glanced up, reaching for a stack of papers on his desk. "Listen, uh, this file here is an old case. You'll know the one. Can you see that it gets back to the archives downstairs?"

"All right. But why are you telling me? Where's your partner at?"

"He's out of town, so he says." Clay jerked his head in the direction of the exit. "Let's step out a moment. Moving all my stuff is stirring up a huge amount of dust."

The two men walked down the hall to the elevator. They rode in silence for just moments. Clay took time to process his remaining information—which was largely all completed in the days leading up to his final day. Once they were outside, Mark inquired with a quizzical glance. "Why 'so he says?'"

Clay shrugged, pushing the heavy door that led outside to the parking lot. "Because I drove by his house the other day and his car is there—house lights are on. He's up to something again. That file on my desk? I keep finding it after I know I put it back in the archives. I can just tell he keeps looking through it. Know what I mean?"

"It's odd . . . but you know you've mentioned all this before. I mean, why's he so obsessed with something from when he was . . . how old? He must have been a teenager when all that went down."

"No idea, but there's gotta be a reason."

"Officer Manning, connected to the biggest porn dealer in the Northeast? Seriously?" Mark laughed.

Clay shrugged again. He wanted to act like it was crazy too. Maybe he'd initiated the discussion just to put his own niggling feeling to rest. "Look, it ain't my problem no more. The older I get, the less I want to know. It just bothers me that I . . . ."

"That you couldn't solve that case. That you don't know what happened to the other two little girls in that place?" his friend finished.

"You remember all that?"

"Clay, how could I forget? It was all over the news."

Clay nodded. "Yeah, I guess so. You were pretty young then too, huh?" Clay continued walking through the parking lot, his eyes adjusting to the brightness of the sun.

The Chief nodded. "Finishing the academy. Look, Clay, if you couldn't solve that, you gotta know that no one could."

"The little girl though . . . I . . . it's just tragic, ya know?"

"She haunts you?"

"Yeah. Just wish I had the energy to find out why my partner is taking an interest now, of all times. Gotta be some reason. I'm just too old and out of notions to go digging."

"It's for the best. And for the record, you're not that old."

"Thanks. Old ain't dead anyway, ya know."

Mark smiled. "I know. I'm just saying, you had a good run."

"This is going downhill. I'm leaving," Clay said, chuckling. "Making me sound like an old Chevrolet or something."

"Yeah, but one that's in really good shape. A designer original."

Clay rolled his eyes. He kept walking as he turned to his colleague. "But seriously though, you gonna keep an eye on Manning?"

The Chief took a step back, his hands up, palms turned outward. "I ain't got time, Boss. I'm sorry, but I seem to recall offering you a little incentive to do that yourself by staying on and maybe working with some folks in the academy."

"Well, I contemplated it, but I think it's time for me to move on."

"You need a vacation, that's all."

"Even when I'm on vacation, my mind isn't vacationing."

"I know. You're a good man, detective."

"Whatever. You think I'm gonna die or something."

"That's morbid." The Chief staggered back and pretended to be offended.

"Maybe, but I know that's what you think about everyone who retires."

"Some do," the Chief replied thoughtfully.

"And some kick the bucket on the job," Clay defended with a snort. "Wifey's got a long honey-do list waiting for me at home. I'm doing something with the bucket, but I sure ain't kicking it yet. I'd be in trouble with the missus if I did. We're going to some church retreat next week."

The Chief was pensive and silent for a moment. He edged further toward Clay's beat-up Dodge Durango and lowered his voice confidentially. "Look, I didn't want to bring this up, but with you gone, your partner? Manning's going to make a mistake if he's not more careful. People are getting wind of his behavior. I'm not at liberty to discuss his latest lapse in sound judgment, but I know you've covered for him when you maybe you shouldn't have."

Clay sobered. He hadn't known that anyone else knew about the time he'd tried to keep his partner out of trouble. It had seemed petty, just a bit of careless foolishness, but his superior's tone suddenly made it seem more serious. It sounded as though there had been several infractions that even Clay had no knowledge of.

"Somehow I get the feeling that your leaving will be the cue for him to totally screw up." Mark continued, "Heck, probably starting as early as first thing tomorrow. First day without you."

"I thought he was doing better. He seems a little on edge, but uh, he'd been kind of obsessed with that case . . ."

"You're officially retired, Clay. As soon as you drive off this lot, try to let it go. Retirement is the time to move on from work and some of life's stresses. If Danny Manning is going to get into more trouble, it is not your fault."

"I was obsessed with the case when I shouldn't have been, too," Clay argued.

"It's more than that and you know it."

"I don't know."

"Well, then, perhaps you should thank God you don't. Our line of work sees a lot, Clay, and you're one of the best detectives, ever. Two things we don't put up with in this business are perverts and child killers. You know that."

Clay nodded. The scene he'd uncovered back then still turned his stomach. He just wasn't sure why that particular case would be of concern to his partner. Admittedly, he himself *had* become obsessed with the details of the case—the disappearance of two girls and the killing of two others—but only because he desperately wanted to know how it all happened. He might even have put off retiring if he believed that one more hour, week or even year would be enough to solve the mystery.

"Hey, try to let it go," said Mark.

"Yeah," Clay said gruffly, his mind pulled back to the present. "I'll try."

In his reflective mood, he hadn't even realized they'd reached his truck at the far end of the lot until he felt the Chief lift the box he was carrying from his arms and set it on the passenger seat.

"See ya 'round, Boss."

"Let's try that Beguile place one night. Heard the owner is a former cop."

"Yeah, that's Parker's joint. I been there. He's got real talent. Didn't stay with the DC department long though. He was smart, unlike us idiots."

The Chief chuckled and nodded, shutting the passenger door and raising a hand in farewell as he walked back to the office.

Clay smirked at the familiar moniker: Boss. He'd earned that title simply because he was about twenty years older than the Chief and just about every other investigator in the department. That was one of the reasons he'd decided it was time to call it quits. In addition to his honey-do list, the next few weeks would likely be spent making peace with unsolved cases and the aging process.

He couldn't get over Mark's revelations that perhaps his now former partner was on a road to destruction. As his truck roared to life, Clay knew he wouldn't miss this place. He certainly wouldn't miss Danny Manning. The melancholy that had been plaguing him throughout his last day had suddenly cleared, replaced only by relief that he wouldn't be around to witness the imminent fallout from whatever his partner was hiding. A boring old, church marriage retreat suddenly seemed a lot more appealing, as Clay put the car in gear and exited the gated lot for the last time.

CHAPTER TWELVE:
BACKSTORY

DEXTER WAS READING THROUGH THE information that Leedra had begged him to look over before sleep had overcome her. No wonder she was so engrossed in all of this. The volume of documents she'd gathered so far was a tangle of information – a mystery. He rubbed his forehead in frustration.

Four girls. She'd outlined each one's first appearance at the house, plus their ages, together with pictures she had cut out from the newspaper article when they were declared dead. Serena Davis, Arlene Davis, Renee Carter and Leedra Carter. Only one of them was definitely still alive. She'd also listed two boys. One was a twelve-year-old African-American male, noted only with the initials D.J. Dexter knew that was himself. The last child to have arrived at the house was indicated simply by a big question mark for his name. Age: fifteen. Race: Caucasian. An interesting piece of additional information noted that he was only present at the house in summer months.

Of those five children, Dexter purposely, for now, moved on form the unidentified white male, he knew the two Davis girls were dead; Leedra was alive; but Renee had never been discovered. Dexter thanked God for the fact that Leedra had survived as he eyed her sleeping frame. He looked back down at the papers. If the little girl had been his own sister, there would have been no way he could rest. The painful awareness hit him of how deeply troubling it must be for Leedra not to know exactly what had happened. The more he read and reviewed her attempt to fill in the blanks, the more the unanswered questions were starting to bother him, too.

He put the papers back carefully into Leedra's bag and stood up. Once again, her head started jerking and the sleep-babbling she'd been doing off and on for the last forty-eight hours started again. At least, the outbursts were fewer and farther between now, a fact for which he was thankful. Earlier that morning, her fever had broken, which meant the delirium would soon cease, hopefully.

As he'd warned, she'd developed a staph infection and needed strong antibiotics. Her vital stats were all over the place, slowing her body's natural healing. He could attribute these symptoms to the stress of her new job, or to the unfamiliar urban atmosphere after being out at sea, but mainly he suspected her growing anxiety and the mounting frustration of trying to solve something she might not be able to..

Placing a hand on Leedra's sleeping forehead, Dexter whispered something soothing and eventually her wild motions stilled. Dexter relaxed, too, when she seemed to fall back into a deeper sleep, but he continued to stand there. He'd been there half the night and the better parts of the two days since he'd brought her in. Bending down, he kissed her cheek. "I'll help you figure it out," he whispered. "I'll try my best."

He was caught off guard by his conflicting feelings. Helping her this time was bringing back his own memories of the times he'd been a boy who couldn't do anything. So what if he had been a child? Doing what adults ordered you to do, even while knowing that it was wrong, was still wrong, no matter how old you were. Feelings of helplessness still angered him and he stepped away from her bed for some much-needed air.

Outside her room, Dexter prayed that they both could handle whatever they uncovered. He prayed also that Leedra would stay in Virginia when all was said and done. If she found the information she sought . . . well, he doubted she'd come back here for anything else but that. He didn't think his heart could take it if she were to leave again.

"Come get me when Ms. Henderson wakes up, okay?" he asked a

passing nurse, who nodded. He moved down the hall to the nurse's station. He was not technically on duty, but he'd have a quick chat with the attending doctor before he headed home to take an over-due shower. He checked his phone and gave a wry smile when he saw a text that was obviously from Kira. He was astounded at how often his sneaky daughter managed to get her hands on her Uncle Cole's or Aunt Allontis's phone and text him for updates about Lee at odd hours of the day and night. He'd taught her how to text, yes, but he hadn't realized how easy it would be for her to get her hands on the phones of others with them unawares. He didn't respond but he would call her and talk to her personally. Giving away too much would only cause lots of questions and Dexter still didn't have a han-dle on how much Cole had told Allontis about this entire thing.

"So I heard on the grapevine that a woman was brought in with a stab wound the other day. You didn't feel the need to report that, Doctor?"

Dexter looked up to find Lucient Douglass blocking his view, hands on hips. He pocketed his phone and wished for an opportunity to wipe the ever-present smirk off Lucient's wide face. He ignored the barbed question with a shrug. "What are you running on about again?"

"I said, the woman who was brought in, had a stab wound to—"

"I didn't see anything suspicious," Dexter cut in shortly. He studied the overconfident man, who seemed to hang around the hospital like it was his second office, and waved his hand impatiently to indicate that Douglass was nothing more than an irritating gnat buzzing about his head.

"Lucient, why are you here?"

"I have meetings with my clientele," Lucient said vaguely. "Don't try to change the subject. You *didn't* see anything suspicious—or you didn't *want* to see it? Aren't you a doctor? As I recall, you're supposed to report anything that seems suspicious and could have been caused by—"

"Mind your own business, Lucient."

"Why? Who is it this time? Do I know her? That why it's such a big secret?"

"Who said it was anything at all for you to be concerned about?"

"Don't you realize that your secretiveness makes me even more intrigued? The nurse told me you brought someone in."

Dexter rolled his eyes. Most hospital employees liked Lucient well enough—only because they couldn't see through him as well as Dexter could, he was sure. Dexter didn't like him. Underneath the sharp suit and faux-alligator shoes was a man looking out for himself, and for greenbacks to fatten his wallet, by any means necessary. As annoying as Douglass was, there wasn't any legal way to bar him from hanging around the hospital. Dexter had to admit that he did have actual clients with whom he might have been meeting there. Still, while these clients likely had legitimate claims from real accident— everything from home injuries to workman's comp—Dexter was put off by the way Lucient conducted his business. Dexter had witnessed him using connections with the hospital staff and his current claimants to dig for more information on new prospects. His method had a cynical cleverness to it, but the practice was also sick, pathetic and completely unethical.

"Why you always seem like you hiding something Dexter? Tell me who it is. I just want to ask them some questions," Lucient wheedled.

"Why are you always in my face, Lucient? You ever heard of HIPPA laws? You need to take a refresher course. What you're trying to do is a criminal offense."

He was about to continue when the nurse approached them.

"Doctor, Ms. Henderson is asking for you."

Dexter held back from uttering an expletive.

"Henderson?" Lucient echoed delightedly.

"Lucient, you need to get out of here. This is my floor, remember, and that means whomever I want out of it has to go."

"It's not Leedra, is it? From Anchored Empowerment Center? Our new interim director! You know, I thought something was going on between you two. I saw the way you kept looking at each other. Wow. You work fast—or she does, I guess. Don't that just beat all?" Lucient laughed aloud. "Ain't that how it always happens? Well, ain't it? All the pots calling the kettles black. Always trying to keep me away from something so you can have it all to yourself, am I right? Now, what happened to her?"

"Have you heard of something called patient confidentiality? I said get out of here or I'll report you." Dexter turned fully to face Lucient head-on and took a menacing step closer to him, drawing himself up to his considerable full height. "This is a hospital. Go see your client and get out of my ward. Now."

"This is a public place. I've been wanting to get you down a long time, DP. You and your perfect family. Looks like I finally have cause to report you. How's that gonna look: you and the new interim director fraternizing? And now suddenly you're her doctor too? A bit of a conflict, wouldn't you agree?"

"The only thing I'm conflicted about right now is whether to get a restraining order barring you from this hospital or to injure my hand by knocking that smug look off your face."

"Ms. Henderson know about your wife?" Lucient continued with a mean-spirited leer. "She know that she was running from you when she lost her life? Isn't that what happened? You can squash all the speculation and stop the rumor mill right now, Dex, if you just come clean with the truth."

"Whose truth would that be?" Dexter grew angrier by the minute. He hadn't realized Douglass was so hungry for information that he'd stoop to dragging up old speculation about his wife's death.

"What happened to your wife, DP? Huh?"

"It annoys you not knowing everything, doesn't it?" Dexter retorted. "What, are you playing detective now? Why don't you just stick to being a small claims court ambulance chaser, following people around and helping them fleece their insurance like some kind of medical highwayman stalker?"

Dexter was annoyed to hear himself taking the bait. Dexter knew it was better to play dumb, but that was when there'd been no one else to be concerned about. Today, however, Lucient seemed in rare form. The old question Dexter had thought long buried obviously wasn't. He was attempting to be careful with his words because he didn't want Leedra in the middle of what was a three-year battle that apparently refused to end. He took a deep breath, searching for more ammunition to get them away from the subject of Leedra.

"If you have to hang out looking for some poor soul limping toward the exit to get your claimants, then I'd say you run a crappy practice."

"You shut up."

"You wouldn't have to listen to me if you'd just get out of my face. I *work* here."

Lucient's face soured. "Look at you. Always getting the beautiful women. I been looking at her. I see how beautiful she is. You two kept making eyes at our meetings. Then she let you chase her around the conference room table—"

Before he could stop himself, Dexter's fist had balled up and connected with Lucient's face. The man staggered backwards, his dramatic howling causing several nurses to rush toward him and assess his "injury"—a split lip. Considering his profession, this would no doubt be described later as much more serious than it actually was. Dexter turned to walk away, knowing with regret that he was exiting the situation about three minutes too late.

CHAPTER THIRTEEN:
CORDIAL CONVERSATIONS

"HOW DO YOU FEEL?"
"I'm all right." Happy to be anywhere except the hospital, Leedra watched cars flash past the window as she sat beside Dexter in his SUV.

"Where's your apartment?"

"Turn here," she said, pointing.

The luxury SUV made its way through downtown Alexandria, along Washington Street toward her garden apartment. Ever since she'd returned from the Mercy Ship, she'd lived not too far from the Anchored Empowerment Center, in a set of newly renovated residences. As Dexter drove through her neighborhood, she thought about how much the area had grown and changed. With the addition of the metro station and some other significant renovations, she now found some places unrecognizably nice, especially all the housing for the influx of people. Leedra was thankful just to blend in, here in this growing city.

"Is the Krispy Kreme still down Route One?" she asked.

"It is. You remember that place?"

"You can't forget a staple of nostalgic Americana." She grinned and looked out of the window again. The many renovated shopping areas and new buildings seemed to battle with the old, more homely-feeling town. She liked change as much as the next person, but there was something charming about the older parts of the city. She'd been so happy to see trees when she first moved back here that she'd angled all the furniture in her tiny apartment toward the window, with its view of the scrubby shared garden.

"You can park over here, next to my car. Did I ever thank you for fetching it from the grocery store parking lot, by the way?"

Dexter backed his car into one of few vacant spots. Leedra knew Dexter likely had helped her avoid one more day in the confines of the hospital. She was thankful, but guessed he might be more attentive now than before simply because he felt responsible for her most recent ordeal. She reflected abashedly that it was actually her own fault, having failed to heed his advice about the wound.

He rushed around to help her out of the SUV and grabbed her hospital-standard-issue dirty linen bag from the back seat and helped her to the second floor. She hopped up every stair with an effort, thanking God with every hop that she hadn't leased a place on the fourth floor.

"You're lucky you didn't tell me you lived up two flights before we left the hospital," Dexter chided in a playfully warning tone.

He unlocked the door for her and she found herself waiting for him to make a comment about the numerous moving boxes scattered around, or her minimal furniture.

"If you think this is sparse, don't look in my fridge!" she said in a rush before he could form his own assessment. "It's hard shopping for one. I haven't quite got the hang of it yet. On the ship, someone made our meals and you just ate what was put out. The locals brought us plenty of food, fruits and vegetables. I personally find all the choices at your local Wegman's completely overwhelming."

"That particular chain can have that effect regardless of where you're from or what you're used to," Dexter smiled. "They take the visual display to another level. How about some water?"

She nodded. She was fairly certain she had that at least, in her bare fridge. He headed into the kitchen.

When he came back, he propped her leg with a cheap folding chair and pillow before seating himself in a small armchair, the only other seat in the small living room. Tired from the trek upstairs, Leedra smiled.

"Are you hungry?" Dexter asked.

She didn't want to admit she was starving. The part of her that wanted him to leave battled with the part that wanted him to stay.

"Let's see what I can find, shall we?"

She listened to him rummaging around in her little fridge. She could see his face from her seat on the sofa and laughed at his exaggerated frown as he opened her fridge wide. He sniffed each item he plucked out and made faces before throwing several things dramatically into the trash. Eventually he was able to salvage an unexpired egg carton and a sealed pack of American cheese. He held them up, yelling "Eureka" in mock triumph.

"Oh look—there's ham in here, too! Odd choice, isn't it?"

"I gave up a lot of my favorite deli meats while I was out at sea," Leedra explained. "When I got back, I wanted every kind of processed meat I could find. I still haven't been to Five Guys, but I keep hearing about how great they are."

"Oh, that's debatable," Dexter harrumphed proudly. "Cole's burgers and steak fries are way better. We'll have to go."

"I've actually been getting dinner from there most nights. I wonder if he knows it's me ordering the eggplant parmesan to go almost three times a week?"

"You should try the veggie lasagna."

"How is Kira?" Leedra sipped her water, finally feeling her strength return after the hobbled journey up the stairs.

"She's a little put off about a certain cupcake incident, but I'll make it up to her."

"Oh? What happened?"

Dexter smiled sadly. "We made them together the night you went into the hospital, but we forgot a couple key ingredients and they . . . didn't turn out so well. She was so tired when I got home late that we didn't have time to try again."

"I'm sorry. It's my fault."

"It's not your fault. She was very worried about you. She waited up late for a status update when I got home."

Leedra looked at him.

"Um, you don't have to do this, you know."

Leedra tried to stand but the couch felt like a sinkhole. Dexter moved in front of her, took her arms and pulled her up.

"Thank you," she said once she was upright.

He stared at her for a couple of beats.

"Look, uh, what did you tell Marcie—or did you . . . Did you tell Lonnie I was in the hospital?"

Dexter shook his head, surprised.

"Well, how did you explain my not showing up for work today?"

"I told Marcie that you weren't feeling well."

"She's gonna tell Lonnie." "I asked her to keep it confidential for a few days and that you'd explain to Allontis yourself—that you would keep on top of any work, but that you may need to work from home for a few days."

Leedra nodded thoughtfully. "Thanks for the cover, but my list of different explanations is growing longer than Lucille Ball's list of answers to Ricky Ricardo."

"She's very understanding, Leedra. I'm sure Cole has told her some version of everything, anyway."

Leedra nodded, still unsure. A pause.

"I looked at some of your notes," Dexter said.

"You did? Why?"

He raised his eyebrows.

Leedra blushed. "Look, I know that I was a little delirious when I went into the hospital, but what I said about your helping me . . . I . . . I was just stressed out. You don't really have to help me."

"What if I want to?"

The question, delivered quietly yet not missing a beat, seemed so loaded that Leedra looked at him, trying to assess whether he was serious. After begging him to help her, the whole idea suddenly seemed like a big mistake. Perhaps this was a journey they shouldn't embark on.

"Did you have a reason for getting up? Otherwise, you need to stay off your feet—just another day or so."

Leedra nodded. "I have to use the restroom."

She limped to the restroom, Dexter leading the way to clear the obstacle course of boxes from her path. Leedra looked at him gratefully and thanked him before closing the door. The confines of the restroom gave her a short reprieve, but her head still swam with the fact that he was right there in her condo, cooking her a meal. She looked at herself in the mirror, embarrassed by how awful her appearance was. After washing her face and brushing her teeth, she quickly applied some moisturizer and painted her lips with a sheer gloss. It wasn't much, but at least she felt a tad fresher.

She re-entered the kitchen and was surprised to see that he'd already set the table. On her plate was a delicious-looking omelet. She looked at him and then back at the food.

"Sit down here, so your leg can be up . . . like this." He deftly placed her leg back on the folding chair he had brought from the living room.

Her kitchen was small, but with him there it seemed extra tiny.

"I was gonna say that . . . while I appreciate your being here for me, taking care of me and doing this, I think that perhaps . . . we shouldn't get involved in another project, too. The work at the center may be enough for both of us."

"I'm resigning from the board. Lucient said something unflattering so I . . . punched him."

"You *what?*" Leedra sat up in consternation. "Dexter, you *can't* resign. I—Allontis—asked you to be there."

"Lucient and I don't get along. He's a shyster and I want out."

"Please don't resign. I've enjoyed having you there."

"Why not? You and I can talk freely if I'm not on it and Lucient can stop all his speculation about us."

"He speculates about us?" Great. Just what she had wanted to avoid.

"Pay no attention to that. He just has it in for me. He's always making inferences and false accusations. Then he runs away."

Leedra was quiet as Dexter blessed the food. She took a bite of her omelet and smiled.

"This is really good."

Dexter exhaled audibly. "Thanks."

They ate briefly in companionable silence.

"I'll talk to Allontis about Lucient. Perhaps he should be the one to leave the board," Leedra said.

Dexter rolled his eyes. "He'll make a legal stink over wrongful dismissal from a volunteer thing. That's his life's work: casting accusations around in search of money."

"That's a strong assertion."

"It's the truth."

They continued to eat. Leedra hadn't had an omelet this good in a long time, if ever. Somehow, the cooking made her even more intrigued about the man sitting across from her.

"What made you decide to become a doctor?

Dexter glanced at her and set his fork down. "Thought it would provide some variety. In the ER, I get to see the whole gamut, from children to adults, the critically ill to the hypochondriacs, not to mention women threatening to pop out a baby right on my ER floor. But the patients that don't do what I tell them the first time—now they're the ones who cause me the most grief."

Even though he smiled as he said it, Leedra felt a pang of shame that she had not listened to him and taken better care of herself. "I'm sorry," she offered.

"It's all right. We're only the fifth most likely establishment to be sued in the area, and we have a lot of difficult patients." He winked at her. "Anyway. It gave me an excuse to take care of you."

"Just like when we were children," she added softly.

Dexter stood up abruptly. Leedra noted the pain on his face and remembered the article she'd been reading about his testimony.

"Not quite. As a boy, I was helpless—just a kid—and you and all the other girls suffered as a result."

"That's not true, Dexter."

She didn't blame him. Not in the least. She was sorry she'd ever made him feel that way. Her harsh words to him when she'd first arrived had only been an effort to make him leave her alone. She hadn't meant it. She stood unsteadily to join him.

"You made life there easier. You helped put them away. No other children were placed in their care. Wasn't that the best result? No one else suffered like we did."

"But *you* suffered. The greatest kind of suffering."

Leedra nodded. He had moved closer and cupped her face tenderly in his hands. She touched his hand.

"Do you—do you really remember Renee? I've never heard you mention her by name."

"I looked at your notes," Dexter replied. "I can't say I really think of her a lot. She was quiet, almost like she wasn't there at all."

Leedra nodded. Of course, he'd looked at her notes. She'd begged him to look at them during the height of her delirium. How embarrassing.

The moment he withdrew his hand from her face, she missed it. She took his other hand and held it tight.

"I think she had a speech impediment . . . they made fun of her."

Leedra looked back at her omelet. She'd managed to eat most of it and it had been delicious, but that was the whole problem. It was impossible for her to eat much of anything with all this weighing so heavily on her.

"If you're sure you will help me, I . . . I have something to show you," she whispered.

"Show me."

CHAPTER FOURTEEN:
DANNY BOY

DANNY ENTERED THE DARKENED ROOM with both arms outstretched, just as he always did when he had to visit this particular part of town. Two men approached, one from each side, and frisked his pockets for weapons and recording devices. When he turned around, the man behind the desk turned on the lamp and leaned forward into the pool of weak yellow light.

"Tell me again. I'm not sure I understand why exactly it was so hard for you to get one girl, keep her for a few days, bring her to the holding spot and then give her to me for our little outfit? Seems pretty simple to me."

Danny did not answer but continued to stand at attention, meekly returning the gaze of the man in front of him. He started to approach the desk but felt a heavy hand on his shoulder, preventing him from moving any closer. He relaxed his body, ceasing all movement, and the hand was withdrawn. He had learned to show no resistance when he encountered potential trouble.

He hated coming there. He was only present now because he wasn't in good standing. Usually he did what he was asked, and if he did it right he could avoid these little trips downtown. His eyes itched, as the haze of cigar smoke and the fumes from an incense stick on a corner table formed a cloud that hung in the center of the room. Danny choked back the acid in his throat and decided not to complain about how stifling the room was becoming. He blinked rapidly.

He hated smoking.

He was also getting tired of rehashing the same old story about the botched job that had, after all, taken place more than a month ago anyway. There was no way to change the outcome, except maybe to try again in the very near future. That was his plan.

"You could be real rich right now. Man, *I* could be richer right now. But now I gotta clean up your mess."

"They told me some woman got in the way. What did you want me to do?" Danny protested.

A sigh. "You're always outsourcing, Danny."

"I have a high-profile job. It's best for me to lay low."

"Well, as a result of your 'laying low,' you botched another job. I'm starting to regret making you mid-Atlantic regional manager. Now I got transportation, food costs and housing fees all adding up because I ain't got a full shipment to send off. Your dad was better than this, son. He died a legend. Got me all the girls I wanted and the photos too. Shame he had to go out like he did."

"Don't mention him. He wasn't my dad. He was my aunt's husband, which I keep tellin' you over and over again." Danny's jaw clenched.

"Well, that's the problem then, ain't it. You keep telling me stuff I don't care nothing about," the man roared suddenly. Danny flinched. His voice returned to normal as fast as it had raised. "I need you to make this right. I want you to work a different area. You still connected in the right spot?"

"I'm . . . on desk duty right now," Danny stammered, knowing that being on desk duty was quite different from being out in the field, with free reign and unlimited access to the people he needed.

"Oh man, Danny, now what can I do with that? You get all the information on the kids just by patrolling the streets. Their parents don't miss 'em, we take 'em off their hands—practically a public service. Now Frank here has got to double up on his detail in Juvenile Detention just so I can get a good assortment to pick through. Shame, Danny. Shame."

The man took a deep drag on his cigarette. He was silent as the mouthful of smoke filtered through the air.

"Geesh, this is just like back when you was sixteen. You used to get those good pictures, but you messed that up too. You been around here a long time, Danny, but you're slacking. Maybe you getting too old for this? What are you now, almost forty?"

"I said I'll get some more."

"Do that. Your partner's retired, so you ought to be able to have a little more freedom—once you get off of desk duty, that is. Ha."

"H-how did you know about Cl—about my partner?"

"What are you talkin' about? 'Ey you guys," he said as he looked around, "Danny here don't know I'm Santy Claus. I see you when you're sleeping and I know when you're awake." A low, sinister chuckle. "Now get outta here. You make me sick."

The man laughed mirthlessly and puffed more smoke into the heavy air between them. Mixed with the incense, it gave Danny a headache.

Knowing there really wasn't anything he could say in his own favor, Danny turned and left the warehouse: an abandoned old pile just across the Virginia border. If he could just catch a break, he wouldn't have to keep coming back to this place.

His stupid uncle wasn't a legend at all. He had been a drug addict and all Danny remembered him doing was hosting addict parties, mostly for men that came over to get high and look at the little girls he paraded around them. Danny had been so sick of everyone back then. He just wanted quiet. But he'd been constantly surrounded by other kids, mostly annoying little girls, bugging him, never giving him a moment's peace, not for a single solitary week in the awful summers he had to spend there with his dufus aunt and her disgusting husband. He had gotten distracted back then . . . but now he had a quiet house all to himself. Zero distraction. Since his uncle and his aunt were dead, though, someone had to keep supplying that area's particular chain with young children, girls especially, and the pictures they were paying a pretty penny. Danny transitioned into that role without issue. So, he wasn't flying the planes he'd always thought he'd fly for the country. He didn't need the military at all with their stupid rules and medical requirements. He'd been able to find a more lucrative gig.

No one even knew that he was the hero of the story back then. He'd saved them all, Danny told himself. No matter what anyone said, no matter how tragic it seemed—*he* had saved them, rescuing them from being further tainted. Tainted goods did not sell.

He was a good person, despite the talk about him at the office. Everyone was just against him. He would get it right this time. Old Philip Clay wasn't going to be an issue any longer, retired to wither away and die. Danny would never retire. While desk duty wasn't ideal, it and his partner's absence would give him the freedom to do whatever he wanted, his own way. No one was looking over his shoulder anymore—at least they wouldn't be once he got back into their good graces—so he'd only have to walk the straight and narrow for a little bit longer. With duty in the office, administrative junk work, he surmised he'd be able to gain more access to the archives and he could find out the rest of the names of everyone in the foster home. Just two is all he needed, because everyone else was dead. Two people eluded him and he had to take care of them because he had vowed never to leave a job half done.

CHAPTER FIFTEEN:
RETREAT! RETREAT!

LEEDRA WATCHED THE BOARD MEMBERS as they completed a team- building exercise. Looking around the facility, she hated having to reschedule the board retreat not once, but twice to accommodate everyone's conflicting schedule and her own absence that had set her back a few days. But no one seemed to mind, and Leedra was eternally grateful to Marcie for doing such a great cover job. She made a mental note to thank her later.

She would have to tell Allontis what a good idea it had been for everyone to get to know each other on this retreat—away from the office and the confines of the cramped board room, learning more about board service, each other and how to identify and work toward shared goals for the Center.

Now into the second day of the two-day retreat, Leedra found that out here at a beautiful conference center in Loudoun County, even the loudest initial resisters like Mr. Douglass seemed more open. Even after last week's conversation, Leedra hadn't ended up asking anyone to leave the board. Dexter hadn't said anything more about the incident. He and Lucient had evidently either decided to let bygones be bygones or were just biding their time, Lucient perhaps hoping for a second even worse offense to top off his list of grievances. Leedra was hopeful they would continue to set aside their differences and work amicably together. At least they'd managed to steer clear of each other for the better part of the two days.

At this particular moment, things were calm, probably because Dexter was outside on a hospital phone conference while Lucient was attentive to and even interested in what the leader was writing on a flip chart. To Leedra's annoyance, he still found time to look toward the back of the room and make eyes at her from time to time as she observed the session. She reasoned that she could handle a flirtatious glance or two simply by ignoring them. She hoped that he got the hint to keep his distance.

Dexter and distance, however, was another matter entirely. She wished they could both turn off their respective urges to discuss their secret project, but during every break and lull, they seemed to gravitate toward each other. Despite the seriousness of their topics of conversation, there was an intimate bond forming as they tried to put the pieces of her nightmare back together. Deep down, she knew that the call and the subsequent conversations may only be encouraging something beyond a rekindling of their friendship, when she knew there shouldn't have been.

She had gotten caught in the moment. He made her feel safe, but she had tried to caution him that once she had her answers, things might not be the same between them.

It was nice not to be forced to work on such an emotionally taxing issue alone, but that's all this was: work. It was a partnership toward a goal that would be—should be—severed when all was said and done.

As the group of folks closest to her chatted amongst themselves, Leedra straightened up to find them all gathered before her expectantly.

"Oh, is that—uh, we're breaking for lunch, right?" she said with confusion. "Okay everyone. I'm sorry, one second . . ."

Leedra took out her schedule, scanned it quickly and announced, "Okay people, we will dine in the cafeteria. Just have your ticket numbers out and name badges showing, and they will stamp your card. Please note—" Leedra flipped through the notes she'd hastily written earlier. "Checkout is at two o'clock this afternoon. Please pack up and bring all your belongings to this room after lunch. We will be leaving straight after the last session."

Formalities complete, she moved to secure her papers, picked up her things and tailed the group as they headed for the cafeteria. She was hoping Dexter would join her, when Lucient slowed to walk beside her instead.

"This is a nice facility, Ms. Henderson."

"Yes, it comes highly recommended by some business associates of Allontis," she replied, trying to remain cordial.

"I admit that I didn't initially see the need for this retreat, but it's been interesting. The facilitator is really quite good."

"I'm glad you've found it useful."

Lucient glanced at her. "You know, sometimes I see you and the great doctor in deep conversation. Is there anything I can help with, perhaps?"

"No, he's just, uh, helping me with an issue about some records I'm looking for." Leedra hugged her portfolio tighter as she walked.

"Oh, well, I can see how you two would have a shared connection, what with both growing up in foster care."

Leedra wasn't sure where this was going, but she wanted to move past it. "Not a connection exactly, but of course he's one of five adopted siblings. As Allontis's brother-in-law, as well as the medication manager at the center, he and I do work quite closely together."

Her hesitant intonation made the statement come out sounding more like a question. She didn't want to admit anything to Lucient, but her tremulous tone alone spoke volumes. He touched her arm as he replied softly, "I can understand how his relation to your boss would give each of you some . . . inside benefits."

Leedra took a step away from Lucient. He made no attempt to be subtle about his eyes wandering all the way down her body, finally moving back up to meet her gaze before he continued. "I could be of assistance to you too, if you'd give me a chance. I may be able to, ah, investigate some things for you as well. In my line of work, we're always investigating child support evaders, insurance fraud, medical malpractice—that sort of thing. I know a lot of detectives who are reasonable. I've recommended them to the women here and to Marcie."

"I'll keep that in mind. Obviously, your contribution to the Anchored board is to provide access to those resources to our residents," Leedra returned crisply.

"Can I get you some food?" Lucient said, changing the subject.

"No, thank you." She moved closer to the table and put her bag down firmly. "I'll just, uh, hold this spot for the group and wait for some others to return before I get my own meal. Thank you. I'm not terribly hungry."

"Leedra, look, I know that Dexter is quite charismatic. I care about you. You're doing a great job and I . . . I just want you to be careful. Some people aren't always as they seem."

Alarm bells went off in Leedra's head, but not due to Lucient's implications about Dexter. This caution was exactly what both Allontis and Dexter had told her about Lucient himself. She couldn't be swayed as far as Dexter Parker was concerned—certainly not by some creep who looked at her suggestively whenever they were in the same room together.

Still, she was now preoccupied by Dexter's character. Was Lucient Douglass the type to just make things up about him? Was it all false, she couldn't help but wonder, or was there some truth lurking in the suggestions? She pushed the lingering doubts from her mind. She didn't want anyone to bother Dexter or say any negative things about him, to her or to anyone else.

Her desire to tell Lucient to get away from her reared up so strong she had to bite her tongue to keep from making a harsher retort. No wonder Dexter had slugged him. She could only imagine what Lucient must have said to provoke Dexter's anger.

"You've gotta eat. You should keep your strength up. We wouldn't want you to end up back in the hospital, now would we?"

Leedra recoiled. "What? How did you know about that?"

Lucient smiled, an oily grin. "Oh, I'm at the hospital a lot. I'm always there seeing my clients, you know. Dexter just mentioned that you had taken ill. Now, you sure I can't get you anything?"

"I'm certain." She was now angry. She sat down to drive home her signal that she wanted to be left alone. To say his revelations rattled her a little was an understatement. Why would Dexter have told him anything about her? That annoyed her. She went from feeling protective of him to doubting his motives in the span of thirty seconds.

She watched as Lucient sauntered off to join the food line. Perturbed that he could rattle her so easily, she returned to her own thoughts. Lucient wanted a rise out of her, that much was clear, and she noted with some frustration that he had gotten one.

As those who had been served first returned to the large table, everyone seemed to be opening up. They were chattier than when she'd first met them.

"Great location! I like this place," Nurse Dupont remarked as she sat down, hanging her purse on the back of her chair.

"I'll be sure to thank Allontis for you. A friend of hers arranged everything for us," replied Leedra modestly.

Ella joined the group, nodding hello and saying a quiet grace before digging in. The two football wives and the banker chose seats not far away, the three of them chatting amicably as they dove into their food. To Leedra's dismay, Lucient returned to his vacant seat next to her as soon as he had his salad and coffee in hand. Leedra kicked herself for not having blocked the chair with her purse. At her elbow, she heard Lucient clear his throat.

"So, uh, I'm really starting to understand more about the plight of the women we're here to serve. I thank those of you who were brave enough to share stories earlier today," he began grandly.

"I'm glad you feel the time was beneficial, Lucient," Leedra responded firmly, keen to nip any grandstanding in the bud. "It's imperative that we all get a sense of what we're up against and who we are fighting for." She saw Dexter enter the cafeteria and had to keep from shooting her hand up to alert him to where they were sitting. He spotted their group quickly by himself, so she could pretend she hadn't even noticed him making his way toward them.

"Perhaps we should offer some personal safety classes to the women," Lucient continued.

Leedra nodded. "We have them annually."

"Right. Of course," Lucient said. "But maybe we should have them more often, for any new women who come."

"That's a good idea."

"Greetings, everyone."

"Doctor Dexter!" Most of the women greeted him in unison.

Leedra gave a cordial smile before looking down at her phone, try-ing not to hold his gaze for too long.

"Missed most of the day there, Doctor. This is a long ways to come if you're not going to participate," jibed Lucient. "I was on call this weekend. Sorry," Dexter said.

"Right," Lucient replied, rolling his eyes.

Leedra watched the two. Dexter remained calm. "I'm gonna get myself some food now," she announced. "Uh, how's the salad? It looks good."

"It is. Try adding the dates—delicious!" Ella chimed in.

"Okay. Be right back."

Dexter joined Leedra in the food line and gave her arm a subtle squeeze. Thankfully, the buffet was laid out at food stations separated by partitions, so the others couldn't see.

"How are you?"

"Fine. Look, did you tell Lucient about my being in the hospital?"

"What? No! I . . . he overheard your name at the hospital because he's always there, looking for his next victim. Leedra, he's a terrible lawyer. I told you what happened." Looking surprised and somewhat hurt, Dexter moved on to the coffee station.

Leedra surveyed the salad bar's various greens, raisins, sunflower seeds, dates and banana chips before selecting some fruit. She was aware of a man whom she didn't recognize standing beside her and she saw him look quickly at her before getting his salad. She looked away. Her hand shook briefly, and as she put her spoon down, the metal clattered noisily, splashing fruit juice onto the fiberglass sneeze guards.

"Are you all right?" In an instant, Dexter was at her side.

"Yes," she hissed. "I'm fine. I'm fine."

"Look at me," Dexter demanded.

"Stop it—just leave before me, OK?" She saw he was skeptical. She didn't want them to be seen exiting together. "I said I'm fine."

"Miss—excuse me, Miss?"

The man from the salad bar was standing feet from her.

"I'm sorry, um yes?" she replied.

Dexter remained beside her and she saw the man become aware of this powerful presence at her side. She was a little embarrassed, but a part of her found the social buffer comforting. To the strange man, it likely made the whole scenario that much more suspect.

"Can we help you?" Dexter was the first to speak.

"I just—uh, your friend looks familiar, that's all. What is your name?"

"I'm Dexter—who are you?" Dexter said curtly.

"Forgive me. I'm Philip Clay. I'm a detective—uh, retired. Sorry, hard to turn off my ask-questions-first mode," the man said with an apologetic smile. "My wife says I gotta relax, be a little more civilian-type. I'm here on a church retreat. This is a pretty place."

"Yeah, it's nice. This is my co-worker, Lee."

"Hello. How are you?" Leedra said, relieved to hear mention of a wife, and feel Dexter's hand grab her arm and squeeze.

"We gotta get back. We're at a conference and they only allow a certain amount of time for eating, you know?" Dexter said.

"Yeah, I know. I don't miss those days of work and their conferences and meetings and such!"

"Take care now," Dexter said in parting.

"Yeah, uh, y'all do the same..."

Leedra let Dexter usher her away from the food stations. She gripped her tray firmly, even as her palms sweated and perspiration dampened her armpits. She was thankful that the group had dispersed, all most likely fetching their luggage and checking out before the second half of the session commenced. Dexter took a seat at their table and patted the one next to him. She was grateful that none of the other board members were still present.

She sat down next to him and he touched her leg under the table. Wordlessly, she grabbed his hand and squeezed it briefly. She bowed her head and listened absently as Dexter uttered a blessing over their food.

When he finished, she calmly looked at the appetizing salad she'd put together, but her mind raced, reviewing what had just happened. Together, she and Dexter had filled in more of the chart she'd started to list everyone involved in their past, including the man they'd just met and who she would not have recognized without his full disclosure. What were the chances? Her mind couldn't participate in this.

"He's the first officer that was on the scene at our foster home, right?" Dexter asked.

Leedra stared at him, unseeing and shook her head. She couldn't forget his name, even though she'd never really knew what he would look like. She'd read his name a thousand times in the newspaper article and now that he'd said exactly who he was, it set her nerves on edge.

She looked at her watch. It would be another four hours before they could discuss what just happened behind closed doors. She looked at Dexter, her food forgotten. Though she was in a state of uneasiness, he retuned her gaze with one of silent reassurance and calm. Even though the day was almost over, her nightmare continued.

CHAPTER SIXTEEN:
COLDS CAN RUN HOT

PHILIP CLAY HAD TO MAKE himself stay away from the federal government building for a week after returning from his vacation. Early that morning, however, he found himself abandoning a fresh list of honey-do's just to come back here once more—just to sit on the side of the street in a random parking space that was adjacent to the old familiar building. Just a civilian and no longer a part of the group inside, he had a good good view of it from afar. A place he was supposed to have left for good weeks ago.

Seeing that woman at the conference center had haunted him so much over the last day of the marriage retreat that his wife commented with some irritation about how preoccupied he seemed. She'd even suggested he go and talk to the Chief about whatever work-hangover stuff was bugging him this time. The woman he'd seen at the salad bar had reminded him so strongly of the age-progression photo he'd pored over for the last twenty-five years. The thing was, he was sure he shouldn't have needed to make a trip to his old office to get the picture he was thinking of, because he could have sworn he kept that photo in his wallet. Tattered and creased after years of carrying it around, he had held onto it just in case. He never entirely gave up hope. The thought of the young woman he had seen at the retreat both scared him and reinvigorated his old investigative skills. And the man with her—Dexter. Was there any chance he knew the truth about her, too?

Clay searched his wallet once more. Not finding the photo, he shoved the wallet back into his back pocket in frustration.

His best efforts at database searches back in the day had yielded only sparse results, which he'd collected in a file that currently should reside in the archives on the lower level. There was only one way to get it—even though he'd have to be escorted in and around the building and he may not be able to get his hands on it all, because he no longer held any authority whatsoever. He did have favors to call in and he'd use them to find the information he sought. Deciding to lay his niggling question about that woman to rest once and for all so he could chalk it up as a coincidence and move on, Clay exited his truck and made his way inside, hoping that when he left, he would have the answers he sought.

"I think we should talk to him."

"Why would we do that? What good would it do?"

Leedra had been standing in Dexter Parker's home for all of five minutes and she was already itching to get on to her regularly scheduled meeting with her boss. She no longer limped and she was glad. Favoring her leg had been a nuisance and she was finally feeling back to normal. Somewhat impatiently, she tried to see the reasoning behind arranging a meeting with the detective who'd worked the case those many years ago.

"I know this business of our chance meeting at the retreat seems like fate, like a sign almost, but I don't want to contact him."

"Okay, but I was thinking—why don't I talk to him for you? Do you want some hot tea, by the way?"

She nodded. "Thank you," she said quietly. It was difficult to stay on the defensive when his tone was so conversational and caring, and when he was looking so good in regular clothes. He was obviously off work today. He was barefoot, too, and that alone disarmed her. She found herself wondering whether he had to custom-order his extra-long jeans, and his soft baby blue cotton shirt had her wishing he'd hugged her in greeting as he usually did. Now he was offering to meet the retired detective for her, demonstrating that he genuinely cared for her by taking on the necessary awkward footwork on her behalf.

Still, Leedra hesitated. "I don't want anyone to know."

"But honey, we have reached a road block and we need to seek outside help from somewhere. He seemed like a good cop. We might be able to trust him."

"Don't they all *seem* trustworthy?" Leedra returned, pacing the kitchen. Their schedules had been so busy since the retreat that this was the first private meeting they'd had to try and process all the new information. Taking a seat, she sipped the hot tea Dexter set before her. It had a deliciously calming effect, but not enough to balance out her concern about Dexter's idea.

"I could get Cole to see if this guy is aboveboard. Would that make you feel better?"

"Not really."

"Leedra, please?"

Leedra looked out of the window, feeling torn. He wanted to help her, and just recently, she'd begged him to. But they were moving at a pace that seemed like a windstorm, and she was nervous.

"He's bound to have answers," Dexter persisted.

"And what if he doesn't?"

"Then we're no better or worse off than we were before."

"Oh, but that's where you're wrong. We'd be worse off: one more person we're not sure we can trust would be involved," Leedra pleaded. She stood up and was caught off guard when Dexter pulled her into his arms.

"Listen to me. I know that was a painful time, but remember that the people who hurt you are dead. If we want answers we have to dig a little deeper, and we may have to involve at least one or two more people."

"Who else besides Clay?" Leedra hadn't planned to accept the idea. Though she was hard-pressed to admit it, she was beginning to see his reasoning.

"Look at me."

"No."

"If you don't look at me, I'm going to kiss you."

Startled by his sudden change of tack as much as by his boldness, she blinked up at him.

"The detective is retired and I was thinking that even though he might not have the answers we need, he probably knows who does. We can see if any other children were placed in that home before us. In your notes, you wrote about 'a guy'—you don't remember his name? We might figure out who he is or how he plays into all this. We might even see if our foster parents had any biological children."

"That other guy, maybe he was their son," she said with a start, then shook her head in frustration. "I don't remember his name. He didn't have the same name but he gave me the creeps."

"That guy only came for the summers, right? He arrived later, didn't he?"

Leedra nodded.

"So, anyway, I thought I'd ask Cole to look into it using some of his old police-buddy contacts. If Cole figures that this Clay guy is aboveboard, I'm going to meet with him, alone. I'll tell you what he says."

Leedra lowered her head to his chest and listened to the lull of his heartbeat. She was afraid of what he'd find, and she didn't want anything to happen to him. She didn't have a family and she didn't have anything to lose. He had everything: a daughter to raise and people who loved him.

"Okay, but promise me you'll be careful," she whispered, hugging him tight. Even though she wasn't certain there was danger, she thought about everything she had already lost. She didn't know who or what to be afraid of, which left her feeling afraid of everything.

"I will," Dexter said. "Now, please take some of this tea to Allontis. She's just down the hall in the library. The doctor gave her permission to move around, just not too far."

"What?" Leedra stiffened. She felt suddenly embarrassed that his sister-in-law, her boss, was there, at his house. She backed away from him, trying desperately to get her guard and professional demeanor back up. It always took time to feel normal again whenever she and Dexter had been so close together.

"Don't worry, okay?" Dexter said.

"Impossible," she returned glumly, but managed a rueful smile. She knew he was talking about the situation they'd discussed. He was a guy: he probably hadn't given a single thought to what his sister-in-law might have to say about the two of them. She needed to remember that to Allontis, she was, first and foremost, an employee.

Before she could leave the room, Dexter pulled her close again in a strong embrace. He lifted her chin and held it gently between his fingers for a brief moment before placing a soft kiss on her lips.

Leedra carried the two cups of steaming tea down the hall, gazing at pictures of family members she had yet to meet. The corridor almost seemed to tell her a story as she moved along it. The hair and the clothing styles significantly improved as she neared the end. Every single person was smiling or laughing, showing pearly white teeth. They all looked so very happy.

She wanted to linger to study the photographs, to clear her mind of the unexpected emotion Dexter's heart-stirring kiss had elicited, but she'd almost reached the library. Light spilled into the dim hall from the room ahead and she turned the corner to find Allontis sitting on the small settee, waiting for her. Leedra pasted on a smile that she hoped conveyed an all-is-well impression, even though she felt butterflies rise in her stomach.

"Well, hello there. Look at you!" Allontis exclaimed. "You've certainly been quite busy, haven't you?"

CHAPTER SEVENTEEN:
THE TALK

"W-WHAT? I DIDN'T—" LEEDRA STOPPED herself mid-
stream, supposing she should ensure they were definitely
talking about the same thing before she jumped to guilty conclusions.
Last she checked, her boss didn't have x-ray vision, nor was she tele-
pathic. She set the tea tray down on a round side table and handed
a cup to Allontis before correcting herself and starting again. "Sorry,
busy? What are you referring to?"

"All these reports—four to be exact—plus a grant application draft."

Without another word, Leedra simply put her arms around the
other woman's shoulders and squeezed.

"Wow," Allontis smiled. "Your hugs are improving. Dexter must be
rubbing off on you."

"You could say that." Willing her nervousness to take a hike, Leedra
sat down in the leather loveseat opposite her friend, taking in the
beautiful airy room.

"Isn't it lovely?" Allontis smiled.

"Almost as beautiful as the kitchen," Leedra agreed, quietly observing the parlor-like decorations of the cozy room. While it was smaller
than the kitchen and with less of the latest gadgetry, the library's
flawless design made it perhaps more stunning still. Built-in slate gray
shelving lined every wall, and the tasteful antique seating area featured accents of lavender, velvet pillows and a black lumbar roll. In
the corner sat a small decorative secretary desk. The coffee table sup-

ported a pretty stack of leather-bound books beside Allontis's laptop, and the thousands more books on the surrounding shelves had small chalkboard labels indicating every conceivable subject: from cooking and travel to history, design and the classics. There was even a kid's section in a cozy corner, complete with a jaunty purple lampshade and two beanbag chairs. A copper and wrought-iron chandelier hung above it all, casting a bright yet soft light perfect for reading.

"It's exquisite," Leedra breathed, awestruck.

Allontis laughed. "Girl, I am so glad for the change of scenery I cannot tell you."

"It must be difficult." Leedra focused her attention on her boss and tried to keep her eyes from roving over their wonderful surroundings. She pulled her briefcase onto her lap, ready to start the meeting.

"Can we just talk for a little bit?" Allontis asked. "I enjoy hearing about all the wonderful work you're doing for the center, but I was really curious about how *you* are doing—you know, personally?"

"Oh, I'm fine." Leedra put down the briefcase but kept her hand on the buckskin handle. She didn't really want to talk about how she was doing, but this was her boss asking, so she likely had little choice.

"Leedra, you don't feel you can talk to me. I'm sorry to realize that. Everyone is keeping stuff from me these days and I'm getting a little sick and tired of it." Allontis rolled her eyes. "I know I've said this before but it bears repeating: I'm your boss, but I'm your friend too."

"I know, Allontis. I'm sorry. I . . ."

"Why didn't you tell me about the kidnapping?"

"I just . . . I didn't want to bother you." She bit her lip.

"Didn't you know how relieved we'd all be? I can't tell you how grateful I am to you, forever indebted. Your purpose here is so huge. You have to believe that."

"I don't think so, I mean, it's not really. I just. . ."

"I love my niece. Can't you see you were an angel sent to protect her? Don't shake your head at me, Leedra, and please don't cry. Please don't cry. I'm so happy you were there."

"I know, but I shouldn't have kept it from you this long. I'm so sorry."

"Guess what, though? Every single one of you, even that little rascal Kira herself, is guilty of keeping this from me, now aren't they?"

Leedra looked away.

Allontis continued. "Cole said that Dexter was hard on you at first, but you have to understand, he was only worried about his daughter. Then when he got to know you, he was likely to be concerned about you, too. Even more so when you felt that you couldn't trust him."

"I do trust him. He is a great person." Yes, that was the ideal way to describe him: Leedra congratulated herself on sounding so detached.

"So when you knew each other as kids, you were good friends?"

"Yes, we were in the same foster home. He was a wonderful person then, like a big brother. He was kind to me and he looked out for me. I wasn't sure how much to involve him in this latest stuff."

"You mean in finding out what happened to your sister?"

"Yes. I really don't know much, just that the two other little girls died. I was sent away, and the fourth of us—Renee—was never found. I only recently accepted the information that she was my sister. Children would just show up at the foster home and no one ever even told us if we were related."

"Do *you* think she made it out alive?" Allontis's eyes were piercing.

"I, uh, I don't know. A part of me doesn't want to find out, but another part of me becomes ill over how desperately I want to."

Leedra paused, unsure how much Allontis knew and how much more to share about the various incidents, as her friend wordlessly passed her a box of tissues from the table. "Thank you." Leedra dabbed at her eyes.

"I need to ask you something."

"Okay." Leedra took a deep breath. She reached for her briefcase again, trying to signal a change of subject.

"What will you do once you find what you're looking for?" Allontis persisted.

The question hung in the air. Leedra had pondered the answer often, especially since Dexter had been helping her.

"What do you mean?"

"I think you know what I mean."

Leedra was thoughtful, but decided after a moment to be straightforward. "I will wrap up my life here and then I'll be going back to mission work," she lied. She didn't want to admit that when she'd arrived. It was ultimately because she was tired of life at sea. But she decided right then it was best to pretend she wasn't sticking around so no one could be didsappointed if she didn't.". While all of this wasn't completely true, it was for the best.

"And Dexter?"

"What about Dexter? He has work here and a life. I'm not sure what you mean."

"So you wouldn't say there is something going on between you?"

Leedra looked at her boss helplessly. "Would *you*?"

"Leedra, I'm cooped up in my room all day, every day and even I can tell that the man is falling for you."

"No, no, that's not true! We're just working closely together. That's all, Allontis. That . . . *has* to be all."

"Says who? Has he kissed you?"

Leedra blushed crimson. "Well, we've hugged and . . ." Obviously, a move to the library from the confines of her bedroom had liberated Allontis's thoughts as well. Leedra was completely caught off-guard by this line of questioning.

"You think the man has no feelings for you whatsoever?" Allontis continued.

"I think . . . well, it doesn't matter what I think or even what I do, it matters what I say. And I say that a relationship of that kind isn't part of this at all."

"There's nothing wrong with falling in love, Leedra. Regardless of your past, will you just give your future a try?"

"I'm sorry you think there is more to this than there is, Allontis." *Deny, deny, deny.*

"So you're saying that you won't stick around, not even if you fall in love? You're here only for answers about your family and when you have those you'll move on?"

Leedra didn't respond. She simply looked at her boss, unseeing. When her vision focused, she saw an emotion on Allontis's face that at first she couldn't identify. *Pain.*

"My time here was always temporary, Allontis. You drew up the contract yourself," she started out, her voice catching at the emotion wanting to burst forth. "You'll have your baby and you'll be able to get back to work, back to normal." She was getting annoyed at this personal interrogation and her face and neck grew heated. "If Dexter has, I don't know . . ." Leedra lifted her hand in a dismissive wave. "Something else on his mind, then that's unfortunate."

Allontis nodded and Leedra tried not be affected by the defeat she saw in her eyes.

"I'm asking you to promise me that if you feel something, Leedra, if you feel that pulling in your heart, that you won't ignore it, okay? It is the greatest feeling. I was like you once. I thought I'd make it on my own, single. I was in the process of adopting a child independently when Cole came into my life."

"That's very nice, but I don't want those things. I'm happy for you, but I don't want those things." She felt like a parrot.

"You think you don't, but I already know you can see something wonderful in Dexter and in Kira. I used to get so angry when Momma G—that's Dexter and Cole's adoptive mother, who lived in this house—when she would talk about the family I was gonna have one day. I used to think she was doing it just out of pity."

"Please stop. I don't make promises any more," she said leaning forward, terribly tired of this conversation to the point where she felt indignance creep in as she spoke. "You know why? Because I swore to those little girls in foster care that everything was going to be all right, and now here I am, with two of them dead and one of them as good as."

"I know it pains you, but that's not your fault, Leedra."

"Stop it. I can't take it. I may say something I'll regret."

It hurt her to be so cutting and cold to her boss. She might even be fired for how disrespectful she was acting, and she hated herself for it. Yes, Dexter offered comfort, but it was just for a little while until she got through this pain and discovered the truth. She'd maintain that until she found what she needed or her contract at the Anchored

Empowerment Center ended, whichever came first. Perhaps she needed to do a better job of keeping her distance from him. From that day forward, she would do just that.

Leedra didn't believe in happy endings. She believed in the ultimate ending: death.

She pulled her briefcase up onto her lap and hoped the move signaled to Allontis that she was done talking about this. She waited a beat until eventually Allontis wiggled her fingers over her laptop to rouse it from sleep and finally they got down to work.

CHAPTER EIGHTEEN:
CLANDESTINE ENCOUNTER

DEXTER ENTERED HIS BROTHER'S RESTAURANT, Beguile Again. Despite trying to focus on the task at hand, he was still annoyed that Leedra had left so hastily after her meeting with Allontis, cutting out any chance of getting her alone for a meal together. For the last few days, Leedra had been unavailable every time he called. The heart-to-heart chat he'd asked Allontis to have with her didn't seem to have worked. In fact, it had apparently done exactly the opposite of what he'd hoped and scared Leedra away from him. Not the desired result.

It had been his sister-in-law's idea to ask Leedra straight-out if she felt anything for him, and it was evident in the way Leedra had behaved since, that either she didn't reciprocate his feelings, or she did but had decided the risk they carried was too great. Dexter wasn't sure what the women had talked about, but the dismal look on Allontis's face when she emerged from the library spoke volumes. It hadn't worked in his favor. Allontis cautioned delicately that immediate results were unlikely.

Dexter headed for the restaurant's back office. He was undeniably nervous about the meeting he'd set up with Philip Clay, but according to Cole's report, the man seemed honest and his integrity was intact.

Stepping into the small room, Dexter nodded to his brother, the only other person present, save for a handful of kitchen prep staff working in the back. He shook hands with the man, reintroducing himself, although they had met before at the conference center. He took a seat across from Clay.

"I thought I'd just cut to the chase," Clay began.

"I'd appreciate that," Dexter replied coolly.

Clay nodded and laid out four photos from a thick folder, placing them in a neat line across the wooden tabletop.

"These are pictures of every adult the Department talked with in relation to the night in question." Dexter sat forward, surprised how forthcoming Clay was being without preamble. They didn't know each other, but Dexter supposed before he left, Clay would also want some answers to his own questions. If that was going to be the case, Dexter knew one of them had to go first.

"Number one I call the Ringleader. Donald Suthers was your foster parent. Supposed fatal drug overdose, but we don't know for sure. Lots of drugs found throughout the home, stuff we didn't even know about or have names for back then, opioids, oxycodone before it was a big deal, morphine, over-the-counter content like aspirin, even analgesic substances we didn't know could be an additive. All of it was boiled, crushed into powder and mixed with new stuff to form deadly combinations."

Dexter nodded grimly.

"Suther's wife," Clay continued, pointing to the next snapshot. "Jean, found dead at the scene and then three children. There were three other men we know to have been in the house. They were all suspects who might have been able to tell us something about what happened, and their DNA was found in the house that night. Two of the three men are dead and the other is just aging somewhere, but still lives in the area. Number one, this guy, hit by a car ten years later. This man, number two: deceased."

"Number three here, is Garrison Johnson. No arrest, no priors, just a local client we observed frequenting the home for his monthly supply. He kept a low profile—functioning addict, so they say, which just means he had a nine-to-five that he managed to get to every day. They say he had a kid and a wife who passed around that time, too, but I never did find out anything about them. Sometimes I want to believe he was just in the wrong place at the wrong time." Clay shrugged. "I didn't always believe his claims during questioning that he knew nothing about what happened, though. Truth be told, even as a junior detective, I always felt like he was lying about something. Anyway, didn't have any reason to hold him, so we had to let him go . . ."

Even though Dexter had sat back in the chair, looking at the photographs of the three men and his former foster father from so long ago, it brought back all the painful memories. His eyes lingered on the shot of a very young Garrison Johnson.

Right then, Dexter could tell the truth about what he knew about Garrison Johnson or he could continue to pretend he knew nothing. He didn't have to own up to knowing him because his last name was different. He cleared his throat loudly as it began to clog with emotion. He was unaware his father had been questioned that night. By the time the investigation was full-on, Dexter was being processed in the foster care system. He had a new home and a new set parents. He was given a new last name to protect him because Momma G and David were involved in his life and they had saved him. He had been questioned and his account had been videotaped, but as a minor no one would have to know who he really was. Dexter wondered if his father might have been the one to omit more about him in the questioning, or had it really been Momma G and David? Dexter could see a plausible reason to hold this information back from the Detective, but it wouldn't help Leedra and regardless of whatever new scrutiny he had to suffer, he would always do everything to help her first.

"You doing all right? You look like you seen a ghost."

Dexter was gazing past Clay's head to the door. He nodded. "I was adopted. Garrison Johnson is my biological father."

CHAPTER NINETEEN:
TRUTHS APPEARING

DEXTER MAINTAINED HIS COOL EVEN as his blood pressured spiked. The information from Detective Clay about his father had him flooring the gas pedal in his SUV before Cole could talk him out of it. The vehicle couldn't move him fast enough. He felt a blinding rage from which there was no escape, rolling around in his gut and rotting him to his core. He might commit a crime when he got where he was going. No matter what Dexter did, his father's choices had cost him so much and were about to cost him yet one more precious thing: Leedra.

Dusk was falling when he got to his father's house. The old man was passed out on the couch, the television blaring and the room dark except for its faint light. Rushing down the hall, Dexter shoved open the door to his father's room, pushing it so hard that the force dented and crushed the boxes behind it. The old wood of the door began to splinter with the force.

He'd orchestrated his life so carefully. He'd met a great set of parents, Momma G and David, who had worked hard to help change the trajectory of his future. He hadn't even tried to erase his past. He'd just considered it all his cross to bear and he'd shouldered it as best he could, taking care of his father year after year, seeing to his needs, his personal care, his meals, his doctor appointments, his medication, and working lights and plumbing and a roof over his head. Why, God? Why?

His heart hurt with grief. The walls were closing in and Dexter felt like he couldn't breathe.

"What you doing in here at this time of day?"

Dexter glanced over his shoulder as his father shuffled blearily in, but he didn't stop tearing into each moldy moth-eaten box in turn. He dumped the contents roughly onto his father's bed as he searched for the evidence that he was sure was there. He hoped and prayed that there was something there to be uncovered, but all he was finding was the magazines and print outs you could get on free sites: modern stuff, disgusting stuff nonetheless, but hopefully not images you could go to jail for and certainly not images that indicated they were from twenty-five years ago. Dexter's nose ran and he swiped at it. He was sweating. Boxes were stacked so high that they blocked the window and likely the air vents too. He felt claustrophobic and ill.

"Tell me what you wanted to tell me, Dad. Out with it. I'm ready to listen. Tell me the truth. Now! Tell me!" he yelled. He stopped long enough to look at his father over his shoulder. When the man had nothing to say, Dexter continued digging.

His father moved closer, tugging feebly at Dexter only to be pushed back. "Get off me. Get off!" Dexter warned and gave a final shove. The old man fell dramatically onto the bed. The little energy he'd summoned was spent.

"Stop looking through my stuff."

"No. It's here, isn't it? I'm going to listen to your pathetic excuses just one more time. I'm listening this time, so you tell me. You think you gonna die or something? Well, you're still here now and people want answers. I want answers."

His father sighed, rubbing his forehead. "I had a job and a life and I was trying to get my son—you—back. It wouldn't have looked very good if they knew I had any dealings with those people, now would it?"

"You *are* 'those people,' Garrison," Dexter clarified coldly.

"No, no. Now, I wasn't like 'em. I had a drug problem, y'see," the older man clarified in a wheedling tone. "But I wasn't no killer. Don't you see I would never have been able to get you back if they found out? At least I had supervised—"

"I know, I know. Stupid supervised visitation to see me . . . A lot of good it did! Eventually, you stopped coming around altogether, anyway."

"You're right, it wasn't no good. I couldn't take you nowhere, not to a ball game or out for ice cream . . ."

"You've told me all this before. Skip ahead, will ya? Were you there that night? Did you lie to the police? Did you lie? You said you didn't know what happened, that you left early that night . . . and . . . and . . ." Dexter began to stutter. The fact that his father might have had the missing piece all along and been sitting on it caused him to shake with anger.

He wrenched open a smaller box and his hands stilled in disgusted shock. The pictures he saw, the images instantly and permanently ingrained into his brain, made him sick—but this was what he'd been searching for. Quickly, he grabbed the box and ran for the back door, as his father yelled after him.

There was a rusted metal wheelbarrow outside the house. He snatched some old newspapers from a teetering stack, balled them up and threw them into the barrow. He took some matches from his pocket and tossed in handfuls of the hateful pictures as the fire snapped to life.

His hand paused when a handful of photos stuck together caught his eye, illuminated by the flickering firelight. He dropped the box on the ground and crouched low to get a better look at them, holding the faded images toward the light. One depicted a group of children, him and five others, including the one boy they couldn't identify. Another was of Leedra and . . . was that Renee? He assumed so. They were fully clothed and they were laughing, Leedra's arm around her little sister, both of them smiling. Little Renee had two missing front teeth.

Tears ran down Dexter's face. He wiped them hastily. In a rush, he realized what burning the pictures could mean for the case. Burning the evidence. He stumbled back into the kitchen and filled a glass with water. He drank it, filled it up again and went back outside. He doused the fire but left the box where it lay: a sad heap in the dirt.

"How could you, Dad? Now you'll probably go to jail, finally. Do you realize that? I can't help you any more. I tried. Do you know where the body is?"

Silence.

"I said, do you know where her body is?

"She was already dead when I got her. I thought she was alive. I was trying to get them out—out of there, but the other two had been strangled and I was too . . ."

"Too high to help, right? And they called you a functioning addict. Not when it counts, you don't. Not when it really, really counts. That's why you couldn't do anything. You were high."

"Forgive me, son? Everybody left me—your mother left me. She had a miscarriage and it turned me into an addict. I loved her. I loved you."

Dexter had had enough. His heart hurt still more at the reminder of his mother and what she had gone through before she died. His father might have even driven her down—Dexter would never know. He stormed through the house, desperately trying to control the impulse to shove everything out of his way as he stumbled through the hulking mess of junk blocking every door. He checked his pocket, ensuring that he still had the two pictures. Tears clouded his vision as he headed out to his car.

He loved Leedra. He didn't think he'd ever love anyone again, but he'd managed to find love for her. And being connected to this mess could have devastating effects on their fragile new relationship. He thought of the two little girls in the picture, hugging each other close and laughing. Few moments like this had existed in their lives, Dexter was sure of that. The girl on the right was Leedra and the other, Renee, was dead. Only his father knew where she was.

Sitting behind the wheel, Dexter's energy drained from him as the realization set in that his time coming there had been completely wasted. He'd tried to help his old man, only for everything to blow up in his face. He would also now have to tell the detective that he'd burned some of the photos, in anger and without thinking, but there were more in that house. Conflicted, he considered burning the photos in his hand, but he wanted Leedra to have something that showed her and her sister in a happier time, rather than just an image from the back of an old milk carton.

He thought despondently about what the legal system would do with an old man brought up on charges of . . . he wasn't even sure what. Garrison Johnson was frail and ill, and he likely couldn't stand any kind of trial.

As he put the SUV into reverse, he looked back at the old sagging home one last time. He would never come back there. He wanted nothing more to do with the man in that house. He thanked God for saving Leedra, even if the truth would ultimately drive her out of his life forever. She was safe—that was the main thing—and as soon as the case was reopened, she'd have the closure she sought. If his father had helped her escape back when she was a child, fine, but even that knowledge was of very little consolation.

CHAPTER TWENTY:
KID CONVERSATIONS

LEEDRA WOULD HAVE TO SEE Dexter eventually, most likely in just another few minutes. She kept looking at the clock on the microwave as the hours snailed by.

This unexpected encounter was unavoidable. When she'd arrived at the house earlier, Allontis was sweating and in pain and Cole was in a state of panic. Without thinking twice, Leedra told them to get to the hospital and that she'd watch the kids until Dexter made it home. So now there she was, waiting.

The children were well-behaved enough. Kira and her cousin Hannah, whom she'd just met, played a game while three-year-old Jacoby watched. Jacoby was still a little fuzzy from his nap, but seemed content with the honey-oat cereal he was now shoving into his mouth. Leedra's back-up plan of ripe bananas and sliced apples lay on the kitchen table, in case the crunchy cereal either lost its appeal or got finished. Cole had hastily explained where she could find the things she might need before he'd dashed out the door. He hadn't started dinner but she supposed it would soon be time for the kids' main meal. She doubled-checked everything so she had a plan rather than face the prospect of a hungry screaming baby on her hands later.

While the girls seemed fine, she needed something to do besides standing by the kitchen counter. "Are you girls hungry?"

"Do you know how to cook?" Hannah spoke up. She'd stopped playing her game with Kira and was looking at Leedra skeptically.

"Uh, of course I can cook, just not as good as Uncle Cole. I can make you . . . something."

Leedra raised her eyebrows, reading the reactions that skittered across the children's faces about her declarations of cooking prowess. If only she hadn't been in such a perfect kitchen at that moment. Even the slightest bit of disorder could have given Leedra moderate hope, but after all, Cole ran a restaurant. It occurred to her that the concept of cooking in this family might be something altogether different, and now that she'd offered, she was getting quite concerned about the outcome.

Resolving to do something, even if it was ultimately nothing more than a grilled cheese sandwich and a bowl of microwaved soup, she opened the fridge—and stood in awe.

It was packed. There were several packages tied up in butcher's paper, likely holding freshly killed meat. Three kinds of cheese, each looking like it came from the local dairy farm, were nestled on a shelf. In the fridge door sat brown eggs neatly contained in a carved wooden block with the inscription, "farm fresh." No cardboard containers in this house. She closed the fridge. *Well. That was intimidating.*

"Uncle Cole's fridge is intense, isn't it?" Kira piped up.

Leeda nodded. "That's the understatement of the year."

She could do this. She checked the cupboard and pulled down a few items. In a matter of moments, they'd have a meal. No promises on the outcome except that it would be edible. Thank goodness there were no pets for the children to slip their food to if they didn't like it.

Washing her hands, she worked diligently on a simple pasta dish and listened to the children's laughter and antics in the background. Every now and then, she checked on them over her shoulder, seeing little Jacoby beginning to fight sleep. The whole scene had her reminiscing about her own little sister.

On autopilot, Leedra browned the meat in the pan and dumped it onto two paper towels to blot off the excess fat. She strained the cooked pasta in the colander and ladled generous helpings into a large white oval dish, together with a little white sauce, sautéed veggies and the browned meat. She topped her creation with shredded cheese and put the brim-full ceramic dish into the oven.

Leedra was still thinking about how she had tried to protect her sister and the other girls all those years ago. She'd been the oldest and she felt responsible for them, even at such a young age. Despite all the notes and research, she was frustrated because she saw absolutely no progress on her quest to find answers. Even coincidentally running into the cop at the retreat had seemed like a fluke, but if it hadn't been for that, she'd likely have chickened out entirely and stopped trying to find out anything at all. Dexter was right: they needed to talk to him and she needed to tell him the truth about her identity. *But they'd need more evidence than just her identity to open the case,* her mind interjected. They'd need new information. Dexter had never told her the outcome of the meeting he had had with the detective, and part of her didn't want to know. *He can't talk to you, if you avoid his calls.*

"Something's burning!"

"Oh!" Ripped from her reverie, Leedra looked down at the stove in front of her. Burning the house down would not be a good move. She grabbed a set of potholders, turned off the burner and removed the empty pot that was now completely burnt. Despite not actually having burned any food, the girls still looked at her like she was pathetic. She smiled back at them. Disaster averted.

"All is well," she said with relief. She placed the pan in the sink and ran cold water over it, making a mental note to replace it. A sizzling sound filled the air. She turned to check the oven, hoping the good smells from there would help to change the girls' minds about her abilities in the kitchen. The cheese was melting nicely and it was almost ready. All she had to do was to avoid burning that too.

"Do you want us to set the table?"

"Yes, please. Let me know if I can get anything down for you."

Kira nodded. She ran around the kitchen island and pulled open one of the drawers. "The dishes are here," she said, pulling open one of the built-in drawers. She lifted plates while Hannah grabbed forks and napkins from another drawer.

"Remember there are only three of us, honey. I'll just have a little something."

"Daddy should be coming any minute. He went to see his father today. Uncle Cole says Daddy is always sad after seeing his daddy."

"Oh, well, why?"

"He's dying."

Although sadness shadowed her heart, Leedra held back from posing any of the myriad questions that came to her at once. "Right, um, okay. Would you girls like some garlic bread?"

"Do you think that Uncle Dexter will let you see him before he dies?" Hannah asked Kira, reaching to place the forks on each of the napkins.

Kira shrugged. "I don't think so."

"He must have done something pretty bad," Hannah said. "Even I still get to see my daddy. He's in jail, but Cole takes me to see him a couple of times a year."

Leedra turned around and pretended to busy herself, separating the rolls as she listened.

"Daddy says no children can be around his daddy."

Alarm bells went off in Leedra's head. Her hands shook a little as she placed the rolls on the foil in the toaster oven. She bent to pull the heavy dish from the oven and put it quickly on a trivet in the middle of the table, warning the girls about how hot it was.

Her pride in the look of her dish took an immediate back seat to the discussion about Dexter's father. *Who was he? What was he like, and what had he done that could possibly mean he could never see his own grandchild? Why hadn't Dexter ever mentioned him?*

The toaster oven dinged and Leedra turned to retrieve the bread and set it too, on the table. The girls made encouraging noises about Leedra's creation, even paying a few real compliments before they all sat down at the table. The girls were the first to grab her hand on each side and bow their heads.

"Hold Jacoby's hand, sweetie," Leedra reminded Hannah, who was sitting nearest to the toddler currently chewing his cubed apples to mush. She hoped she'd cut them small enough. The exasperated look Hannah gave her was hilarious, but Leedra smiled encouragingly instead of laughing out loud.

"Do you know where he puts his hands? Anyway, he doesn't like it," Hannah protested. She touched Jacoby's chubby arm gingerly at the wrist in lieu of holding his sticky hand, even though he didn't understand and kept wiggling away.

"Malonnie says he's a typical man, whatever that means," Kira added.

Leedra did laugh at that, looking back and forth between the two girls. She thought they must be the funniest pair on the planet. Of no real relation, they seemed almost sisterly, just like her and Renee.

"Is Malonnie what you call Allontis, Hannah?"

"Yes, it means Mama and Lonnie together," Kira interjected.

Hannah nodded proudly. "Yes. I came up with it. She's not my real mother, but I still feel like she is."

"That's a wonderful combination of the two."

There was silence as they all bowed their heads and Hannah began the prayer.

"Dear Lord, please let Malonnie be okay. I love her so much and I thank you for blessing us with her. Let our new baby be okay and help Uncle Dexter get along better with his father and find a wife also. Amen."

Caught off-guard by the last part of the prayer but determined not to say anything, Leedra sat a little straighter when she heard the jangle of keys at the front door. She was hoping it would be Cole and Allontis here to rescue her, but when the door swung open, it was Dexter's eyes that met hers.

CHAPTER TWENTY-ONE:
FIGMENTS

WHEN DEXTER ENTERED HIS BROTHER'S house, the scene that met his eyes seemed like a lovely dream in contrast to the nightmarish day he'd had so far. He turned to close the door, rubbing his eyes to make sure the tableau really did feature all the people he loved most, almost nervous that it would all just evaporate as a figment of his imagination. It was all so perfect, he nearly went back outside to check the numbers on the door. He felt like the father on "Leave It to Beaver." While "Honey, I'm home" ached to leap from his lips, he had to remind himself that that wasn't his reality: not yet, and maybe not ever. At that moment, Dexter just wanted to make time stand still.

"Hi Daddy, you okay? We've been trying to reach you. Where have you been?"

"Hey, Uncle D."

"Hi, ladies."

"Daddy, Aunt Allontis is in the hospital and . . ."

Kira trailed off when Hannah shot her a look.

"I heard, sweetie," Dexter replied. "She's doing good, but they're going to keep her overnight for observation. Just some early labor pains. That means baby wants out of there, but he has to bake a little longer, 'kay?"

He caught Hannah's eye, who looked sad. The oldest of the three children present, she was also the most sensitive. Dexter crouched to her level and she hugged his neck tight. He'd known she'd be worried, even though she was the more worldly street kid of the two girls. She'd had a rough start with a drug-abusing mother up until three years ago, when Cole—who turned out to be her biological brother—and Allontis had saved her from the nightmare. Hannah was masterful at keeping her emotions in check and seemed much older than nine. For all her smart retorts and comedic antics, she was pure softness underneath, surprisingly like Cole, and just like another woman Dexter knew, too. He chanced a glance at Leedra. Not to be left out, Kira joined in the hug and Dexter embraced them both, giving each little girl a kiss before straightening up.

"Time to get ready for bed," he said, stretching. The girls groaned in unison. Dexter looked at Jacoby. The energetic three-year-old, slumped in his high chair, was already knocked out.

The girls put away their game and he was surprised that neither made much of a fuss. He thanked God for their compliance.

"Daddy, Lee made a pasta bake. Do you want to try it?"

"If Lee made it, then of course I do. She's never made me anything before—and I'm her *doctor*."

The girls giggled.

"It's uh, nothing—just a little something I threw together," Leedra said, flushing.

"Let's try it," he said over his shoulder as he went to wash his hands. He grabbed the last clean plate and heaped on a good portion, then picked stringy cheese from his fingers and tasted it. "Gooey, huh? We'll have to get Uncle Cole a gooey-meter for his kitchen. What's in it?" He lifted the warm plate to his nose in approval.

"Sausage, pasta sauce, cheese, broccoli . . . it's ooey-gooey good," Kira said.

"Yes, ooey-gooey! I really liked it," Hannah added dramatically.

Dexter sat at the table and blessed his food quietly.

"Umm-hmm. I like how you two are so vested in the conversation here. That does not mean getting ready for bed got moved off my request list, by the way. Go put your pajamas on, and at least pretend to mind your own business."

Eager to get back to the room where giggles and hushed conversation would ensue, the girls shoved their remaining food into their mouth before running off to Hannah's bedroom, where they found an extra pair of pajamas for Kira.

"How are you?" Dexter asked Leedra when they left.

"I'm good," she smiled.

"I'm gonna put this one down and then I'll eat." He indicated the sleeping toddler and took a quick forkful before he stood, chewing thoughtfully. "This *is* good."

"Well, don't act so surprised. I *can* cook."

"Um hmm." Dexter set the fork down with a grin and moved to pick up his nephew from the high chair. He flipped up the tray and deftly unbuckled the lap belt. When he went to grab Jacoby up, Leedra touched his arm hesitantly.

"Can . . . Can I hold him?"

"Of course. He's like a bag of bricks, but he's pretty cute for a linebacker. Sit down, I'll put him on your lap."

"He's beautiful," she breathed once the child was in her lap. She wriggled until she had a comfortable position and the child moved his head around in his sleep until he found the perfect spot smack dab on the rise of her bosom.

Dexter sat back down across from her, his eyes riveted to the peaceful scene of woman and child, until she caught him looking. He quickly looked back at his food.

"He has eyelashes for days and he smells like warm milk and apples."

"Apples? Really?"

"I gave him apples while we ate. I didn't know if he ate table food yet," Leedra said apologetically.

"You're kidding? It was a wonder he didn't throw the apples at you until you gave him some of your food. I guess he gave you a pass because you're new. Do you ever think about having children, Leedra?"

"No . . . No."

Dexter's fork clattered to his plate as tears filled her eyes.

"Where's his bedroom?" she asked.

Dexter stood up with her and he was silent as he led her down the hall. She followed slowly behind, the baby on her hip.

When they entered Jacoby's room, Dexter flicked on a football-shaped lamp near the bed and reached into the crib to pull back a plush blanket by its soft glow. The room was painted a gentle, neutral yellow, with accents of green and blue. A menagerie of stuffed animals was bunched on the dresser and piled on the floor below. A floating shelf held wooden letters that spelled out Jacoby's name above a sweet rocking chair, changing table and toy chest.

"What's the matter, Leedra?"

She shrugged, revealing nothing. "Here." She handed over the boy and Dexter laid him tenderly in the crib. He made short work of removing shoes and pants and replacing them with darling little PJs while the babe slept on. After a beat, Leedra spoke again.

"You all make family life look so perfect. I've never seen anything like it. Perfect girls, perfect toddler—I mean, you have everything and it looks so great. Watching you all is like being at a sumptuous buffet . . . but having a ton of dietary restrictions."

"Aren't your restrictions self-imposed?" Dexter said softly.

"It doesn't matter."

"It matters to me. Maybe you won't *let* yourself have these things—but you can, you know?" Dexter moved closer to her. "What would you do if I told you that I loved you and I want you to stay in my life?"

Her response came without hesitation. "Run away."

Dexter nodded. If only he had been kidding. How he wished her response weren't true.

"Why haven't you remarried?" she asked him somewhat defensively, wiping carefully at her eyes. "You're eligible, plus you work with all those nurses at the hospital. What's the problem?"

Dexter shrugged. "I realized I'm in love with someone who thinks they don't need it—or can't let themselves have it."

"Well, you better leave her alone. She's obviously crazy," Leedra laughed.

"I'm in love with you, Leedra"

She shook her head.

"Yes, I am."

"Well I can't give you anything in return."

"You can't, or you won't?"

"This is your fault." Leedra turned on her heel and abruptly left the room.

Stung, Dexter took a quick look at the sleeping child and replaced the little lamp with a night light before exiting. He left the door cracked and followed Leedra back to the kitchen, where she was cleaning with tight-lipped determination.

"Would you grab some foil to wrap this up?" was her only acknowledgement when he entered. Dexter watched her.

"Stop. Look at me."

"No, you stop. You know I'm not . . . I'm not here for that."

"What if 'that' is here for you?"

"Please, Dexter. Please." She tried to turn away, but in a moment, his arms were around her.

"You make things so difficult." His lips gently but firmly met hers. When at last she returned the kiss, finally letting go, it was everything he'd wanted and more. His tongue slipped past her teeth and he felt her gasp, but she didn't pull away. Her hands clasped his neck and she stood up on the tips of her toes. Dexter hugged her closer and pinned her against the sink. He wanted her in every way, right then.

When they finally pulled apart, she laid her head on his chest and her arms wrapped around his waist. "I want to love you, but there's a barrier between us," she said softly. "It's greater than my past, although that alone has messed me up and kept me from truly living. Really, until you tell me the truth about everything, I don't know if I can love you at all. Perhaps you're just one more person with something to hide."

She broke their embrace and turned to grab her coat.

"Wait—please?" Dexter's arms felt bereft with her no longer in them. He felt a surge of desperation. Moving to the door, he pulled his coat from its hook, reached into the pocket and pulled out the two salvaged photographs. Silently, he handed them to her. He saw her bottom lip tremble at the sight of her sister in the picture he gave her, and he held her hand until she eventually pulled it away. Dexter took a deep breath.

"I will tell you everything there is to know."

He had planned to tell her the truth all along; he just wished he'd had more time. Today's kiss would be all he'd have to remember her by when she left, because after she heard what he had to tell her, Dexter was sure there was no way she would choose to stay. Without further ado, Dexter delved head-first into the story of his father, starting as far back as he could remember and finishing with what he'd learned just that day. For the first time in his life, Dexter held nothing back.

CHAPTER TWENTY-TWO:
PARTING WAYS

THE NEXT FEW DAYS WERE a whirlwind of activity. Dexter found himself back at the police station with the one picture Leedra had left behind when she'd gone home the other night. He hadn't been able to contact her since, and he was getting more and more worried that his story, almost a confession, had pushed her away just as he'd feared it would. He hoped desperately that she was okay. He wasn't sure the extra information even made a difference at this point, but he had a sudden and urgent need to come clean to the police about everything he knew. Now there he was, spilling everything to the detective on duty.

"Do you believe your father has anything else to hide, Mr. Parker?"

Emotionally exhausted, Dexter shrugged. "I didn't know about the extent of his addiction till a few days ago. He told me that the girl was dead when he tried to take her to the hospital—that she was already gone."

"Are you sure he didn't confess to killing her?"

"No. I don't believe my father actually killed anyone, but I just found out about all of this."

Dexter wanted to stop associating his father with murder. He just couldn't believe that. He wasn't sure of anything right now, but that seemed impossible even as his heart and mind argued. "I didn't even know he was there that night until this week. Look, I also burned some of the photos. I didn't want anyone to see the girls . . . like that.

I started burning them in a blind rage, but then I stopped when I found that one there."

"So your fingerprints are on some of the pictures–on some of the evidence?"

"Y-yes . . . but . . ." Dexter looked at the man in front of him, who returned the look without emotion.

"That's not good, Mr. Parker."

"What about the statute of limitations?"

"Unfortunately, Mr. Parker, this is a murder case. The statute of limitations doesn't apply here. Your father will be charged with possession of child pornography. If more comes out, his situation will only become worse."

A knock sounded on the door. In walked a second detective, followed closely by Leedra.

Dexter did a double take. She looked at him briefly but did not say anything, only clutched her purse closer to her in a death grip.

He felt as though he were watching a movie. She was his only focus. He longed to reach out and hold her hand, but her eyes told him that would be a bad idea.

"Ah, Ms. Henderson." The detective who had been listening to Dexter's tale stood up and moved to shake her hand. "I hadn't expected to hear from you so soon."

"I don't know why not," Leedra responded curtly. "You already made it clear to me that the longer things take, the more time is wasted. Twenty-five years is long enough."

Dexter couldn't keep quiet any longer. "Leedra! What are you doing here?"

"What are *you* doing here?" she snapped, addressing him directly for the first time.

He saw the pain in her eyes before she had time to hide it. She turned away from him and spoke directly to the detective.

"I want to reopen the investigation. My real name is Evie Carter. I went missing as a child twenty-five years ago and I want to find my sister, Renee. I'll help you put those responsible away."

Dexter's mouth opened in surprise.

"Wait, what does that mean? Why does she have to come out of hiding to open the case?"

"Mr. Parker, you bringing this evidence about your father today, coupled with the fact that Ms. Henderson—ah, Carter—is still alive and willing to help us review the case, constitutes sufficient grounds for us to go back over all the evidence."

"Honey . . ." Dexter reached out to touch her arm and it hurt when she shrugged away. "I'm sorry." He shoved his hands in his pockets. "Can we just talk for a minute?"

"I'm done with that."

Dexter nodded. In that office, at that particular moment, he realized that any attempt to connect with her would be fruitless. "Just, uh . . . Leedra, just think about what you're doing. This could destroy you. We can hire a private detective. There are other ways to keep your autonomy."

"Don't you tell me that. This has already destroyed me. Scratching around for little pieces of my own puzzle here and there isn't working. I want full-on answers. I want all the resources the department is willing to provide. I appreciate the help you've given me, but now it's time to move on."

Dexter watched as the two detectives escorted her out of the room, away from him. This wasn't how he'd envisioned things going, but he wasn't mad at her at all. He knew Leedra resented him because of what his father had done. Nonetheless, Dexter felt as if Leedra could have done more to uncover the truth before resorting to this. Having the whole thing swept under the rug, not knowing, had surely been better than the pain both of them were experiencing now.

He had long had a suspicion that his father would end up costing him everything. He was happy that Leedra was finally going to do what she felt she had to, but he knew that in doing so she had been saying goodbye to him. She'd walked out on him after he told her about his father's past transgressions, as he always feared she would.

As she'd left, her eyes had told him that they would no longer be working on things together—on anything. He wanted to believe she'd be fine on her own, although he was worried that getting to the truth would only expose her to more trouble and grief. He hoped for her sake that she could find the truth and that eventually she would be all right, able to move on with her life.

CHAPTER TWENTY-THREE:
REPETITIONS

Recent information could reopen a twenty-five-year-old cold case. Detectives remain tight-lipped about details of this week's developments, but acknowledge having new evidence on the mysterious disappearance of eight-year-old Evie Carter, who went missing over twenty years ago . . .

A LOT COULD HAPPEN IN TWO weeks. That was Leedra's first thought as her eyes scanned the morning paper's headlines at her desk. She frowned and set the periodical aside. It was just the usual parade of convoluted speculation, innuendo and drama that her eyes skimmed until they glazed over. The articles only created more open questions and guesswork. Nobody really seemed to know any more than she did, which was not comforting.

At her recent meeting with the detectives, she'd felt like she'd been on trial. They had been welcoming and encouraging at first, but now that they knew she'd been Kira Parker's rescuer, they hadn't even said "thank you" or "good job." Just more questions that usually came across as accusatory. *Why did you do that? Do you realize that what you did could implicate you in the crime? Do you know the men? Why can't you give us a better description of them?*

And on and on. If she'd only known they were planning to interrogate her instead of asking about the reason she'd come forward—to find her sister—then she wouldn't have agreed to the interview in the first place. She considered ruefully that the questions they were firing at her were normally reserved for common criminals.

According to the detectives, she may have to make an official statement in the coming weeks, going back over reports to recreate the
horrible night. In the process, she would have to come forward and
tell the world she was alive. She dreaded that, and more than anything, she dreaded doing it all alone. She tried not to cry, but it was
no use. Nowadays, she cried every single day that Dexter didn't come
through her door or call her. Much as she hated to admit it, she
missed him.

When her desk phone rang, Leedra stared at it, wondering if she
had caused Dexter to get in touch by sheer force of hope. She picked
it up, knowing that while a call from Dexter would be a wonderful
thing, it was highly improbable. Any caller at this point, though, was a
welcome distraction from her present state of sadness.

"Hello, this is Leedra."

"Hello, Leedra. It's been a long time, Leedra."

Leedra's back straightened. She looked at the phone's LCD display, but the caller's number was unlisted. "Hi—uh, wh-what do you
mean? Who's calling?"

"You were always so polite. Look, I can't talk long, but you need
to think about things pretty carefully before you do anything rash. It
won't be good for you to come out, not after all this time. Evie should
remain unknown. It's better that way. It's been so long, why bring it
all back up now?"

"How do you know Evie?"

"I know *you*, Evie."

"Wh-what are you talking about?"

"Don't lie to me, sweetie. I don't like liars. Remember Renee?
Sweet little Renee, always saying she didn't do it. We all know she did
it. You were always covering for her, cleaning up her messes, weren't
you?"

"No . . . look, who is this, please?"

"Just an old friend. I've been waiting for you. It's been a long time.
I look forward to seeing you soon."

"Hello . . . hello?"

Leedra waited a beat longer, but when she heard a soft click on the other end, she replaced the receiver in the cradle with trembling hands. She took several deep breaths as fear began to close her throat. She picked up the card of her assigned contact detective and dialed his number.

"Hello, Detective Roy? I need to tell you about a phone call I just received at work."

She told him everything she could recall. It didn't seem like much, but he asked a lot of questions about it and she answered them all. When he had gathered all the information he needed, he asked her to come down to the station.

Leedra hung up and was standing to grab her keys when the phone rang again. She picked it up, hoping the short tips the detective had just given her would be more useful this time. "Hello?"

"Ms. Henderson? Can you comment on the case of the missing Evie Carter? Sources say you and Ms. Carter are the same person. Is this true? Why are they investigating the case? What new evidence do they have? Were you the one to bring this evidence to their attention?"

"No comment," Leedra whispered hastily and slammed down the phone. She stared at it a moment, stunned, wondering why reporters were always so busy peppering people with their questions that they never paused to allow time for responses.

She picked up the phone once again, took a deep breath and pushed the button to call Marcie's line. A busy signal. Odd. She left her office to stick her head around Marcie's door. As she walked down the hallway, her ears were bombarded by ringing phones and beeping sounds that indicated several callers. When she reached the other, smaller office where Marcie and the intake counselor shared space, she found the two women with their heads down, both glued to their phones, their voices repeating "no comment" over and over again like stuck records.

Leedra was horrified. She approached Marcie's desk. "Just hang up," Leedra mouthed, when she saw that the caller was giving Marcie no opportunities to respond.

Marcie did as she was told, but the phone rang again as soon as she placed it in the cradle.

"Just . . . don't answer for a little bit. I'll figure out what to do. I want to speak with both of you in my office—now, please."

Once they entered Allontis's office, Leedra shut the door behind them and asked the pair to sit down. They looked exhausted, although it was barely lunchtime. Marcie looked ready to beat someone up through the phone line, if she could figure out how, and the intake counselor, a younger woman who hadn't been at the center more than two years, looked as if she were simply doing her best to cope.

Leedra took a deep breath. Now was the time, she knew, to come clean to her staff once and for all. With a nervous heart, she began the complicated, surprising story of who she really was. It was imperative that she shared this now because the women sitting opposite her had a duty to protect the lives of the Center's women, as well as the rest of its staff.

"I want to empower you both to answer all these calls effectively," she finished at last. "I'll craft one for you, if I can just have some time alone. There will be people calling about me for the next few days, because as I've told you, I've been a missing person for a while now."

Throughout her spiel, the expressions facing her ran the gamut from intrigue to disbelief and then to disgust about the abuse she had suffered, and finally to awareness. Her colleagues now knew what they had to do and how they could help her.

"As long as you don't waver in maintaining that you don't know anything about it, I hope they'll eventually go away," Leedra assured them. "Just in case, I'm going to find out how we can change our main numbers. If you can dig out our old press policy, we can update that too and circulate it to all our staff and contractors. We'll need to see what we can share with the women to help protect them from all this, not to mention the confidential information we hold."

Leedra sighed with relief. She was glad she could finally be honest with them. Both women worked hard and they'd been her first contacts when she was completely new to the office. As they stood to leave, Leedra touched Marcie's arm.

"Marcie, I just wanted to thank you especially and tell you how much I appreciate you. I also need to tell you that, um, I'm going to resign from this position. I'll have to tell the press about this before long, and I don't want any negative publicity for the Center. The police will likely want to make my identity public within the next few days."

"You can't leave!" Marcie gasped. "Allontis will be devastated."

Leedra shook her head. The truth was that *she* was devastated, but personal detachment was paramount in this now very public case. Work gave her purpose. She'd likely have to lay low for a while until the case was resolved, if it ever was. The alternative involved going back out to sea aboard the Mercy Ship, where the press only came around every few years for a news magazine story for *Sixty Minutes* or *Sunday Morning*. Out at sea was where the real peace was, a million miles from the fishbowl of Washington, D.C. What had she been thinking, coming back to this city? She should have stayed out at sea in the first place. If nothing else, her heart would never have discovered Dexter Parker. Leedra forced her attention back to Marcie.

"She'll be more devastated if there's any compromise of security at her precious center. This is strictly between you and me until I know for sure that she can handle it, though, what with the pregnancy scare and all," Leedra said firmly.

Marcie looked at her. "Why are you crying? Going public will get you one step closer to finding your sister, won't it?"

"I just feel in my heart that she's gone."

"Oh? But you don't know that for sure, Leedra. And am I right in thinking you'll miss Dexter more than anything?"

Leedra shook her head hastily, wondering if her feelings had been that obvious all along. "I'll just miss this place. It's great here. You're all good people, doing great work. I would have liked to see what else I could do here to keep growing the Center and to go after more money for you."

"That sounds well and good, but Dexter has called me a couple of times—just to see how you're doing, he said. He told me to tell you that you can call him any time."

"I have a lot to get past," Leedra said simply. She patted Marcie's arm, who took the hint that her supervisor was done conversing: about Dexter and about everything else. Impulsively, Leedra gave her a hug before closing the door behind her.

Leedra sat down heavily and started up the computer. When the "new e-mail" icon popped up in the top corner of the screen, she clicked open her e-mail inbox to see what was there.

The e-mail was from one of the detectives and the subject line read, *"Do you recognize this picture?"* She tried to blow up the image, peering at the computer screen to try and make out the details of the pixelated black-and-white thumbnail. She downloaded the image next, which only marginally improved the quality.

Throat tight, she rose from her desk chair, grabbed her keys and purse and called through to Marcie that she was going to her scheduled meeting with the detectives working her case. That picture meant there was even more to discuss, and her recollections were suddenly coming back to her full throttle.

CHAPTER TWENTY-FOUR:
COMPLICATIONS WITHOUT EXPLANATIONS

"HE'S IN JAIL?"

Dexter looked at Cole and nodded as he finished up his phone conversation with the detective working the case about his father. He and the detective had been in contact regularly—every other day, it seemed—and while all the news he'd received so far had been bad news, Dexter was thankful for it nonetheless. At least it was information; at least it was something.

Cole sat across the table from him. As they had in many other late-night conversations, they sipped coffee and discussed everything, from how long Dexter planned to take leave from work to how long he'd keep Kira out of school. He'd taken her out recently, when the press had started hounding him even outside her school. Rubbing salt in the wound, Kira asked Dexter every day if they could invite Leedra over, if they should take her lunch, and if they could call her. She wanted to know why Lee was seemingly being punished for things that she, Kira, did not understand, and why Dexter would not supply the necessary answers.

The fact was, he didn't have the answers. He missed Leedra as much as his daughter did. Together at bedtime, they prayed for her each and every night: that she would get through the coming months. Dexter's own time off from work didn't help matters either. Everyone was going stir-crazy. Late each night after Kira was all tucked in, it seemed all Dexter did was stay up watching the local news, scouring the familiar story that was reported for any fresh details.

Eventually Dexter spoke, breaking the lengthy silence. "I don't know what they will do if Garrison becomes ill."

"Do you want them to call you if something happens?"

Dexter shrugged, "I guess I do." Honestly, at this point, he'd sacrifice his father and never speak to him again if he thought that would bring Leedra back into his life. Both then and now, he was realizing, it was his father's secrets that had kept him and Leedra apart.

Dexter squeezed his coffee mug in his hands, pressing the cup until the burn stung his palm. "It doesn't matter what happens. I put my information on all of his documentation. That's how they even know I exist, because I put *my* name down there. If I hadn't done that, Dexter Johnson could hide, pretend he doesn't exist. I put down Dexter Parker and my real number. I should have lied."

"You don't mean that, D. Honesty is always best."

Dexter shrugged again. There was no worse feeling than defeat. He was the next of kin; It wasn't a question of *if* they would call him, but *when.*

His phone, on silent, vibrated and rattled against the table. Dexter looked at the screen and, not recognizing the number, pressed the button and put it to his ear.

He listened for all of ten seconds, and when the call ended, he stood so abruptly that the half-filled coffee mug sloshed to the floor and the ceramic cup smashed into pieces.

"Hey, hey, Dexter—what's the matter?" Cole stood up to stand in front of him while Dexter's mind raced a mile a minute. "Dexter, who called you? Stop! Tell me what they said!"

Dexter was at the door. He didn't think to grab his coat and ripped the door open so fast that it banged against the wall.

"Wait, wait! Did they say something about Leedra? Was that Leedra? Dexter, talk to me so I know what's going on."

Dexter looked at his phone as if it were a foreign object, gripping it so tightly it felt like part of his hand. His brain and fingers worked together just long enough to dial her cell phone.

"No, I gotta go see if Leedra's at her apartment. She might be in danger."

"Fine, I'll go with you—you're not going without me. Just please tell me what they said?" Cole implored, as he grabbed a towel, wetted it and quickly sopped up what he could of the coffee and the broken ceramic. Holding everything, he put the wet towel in the sink before he reached behind the open door to grab both his and Dexter's coats and his keys from the island counter.

Dexter stared at his brother, unseeing. "They said: 'stop your girlfriend or I'll kill her.'"

On the drive to Leedra's apartment, Dexter's nervousness increased with every mile, worsening still further when they didn't find her at her home. Even when they saw that her car wasn't in her unit's assigned parking space, he and Cole continued up the steps to her second-floor apartment and knocked, waiting a moment for any signs of life. As they feared, there were none.

Cole drove them to the Anchored Empowerment Center's office building, one of several in a large complex. Dexter spotted her car immediately.

He watched Cole punch in a series of numbers and then use a set of keys to access the office that only he, Allontis, Marcie and now Leedra had. They went through two security checks and then took the elevator to the fifth floor.

Dexter and Cole stood in the office hall. Dexter called Leedra's name, but there was no answer. They entered her office. In the dimness, they saw light filtering from around the bathroom door. Dexter caught Cole's eye and pointed silently to a blanket covering the sofa and a pillow that looked like it came from Leedra's home.

There was a small noise and the bathroom door swung open. Leedra emerged, and when she saw the two of them standing in the office, she froze.

"What are you doing here?" she squeaked in fright.

"Leedra, what are *you* doing here? It's ten o'clock at night!" exclaimed Cole.

"I work here," she said, as if that answered it all. She graced Cole with a fake smile. Dexter blew out a pent-up and doubtful breath. He looked around the office, which was pretty large, and noticed an open suitcase on the floor. A few clothes spilled out of it. Other telltale signs that she was moonlighting there long-term were evident: the old takeout Styrofoam trays that littered the space, the coffee maker she must have brought from home, and—the most obvious of all—the slippers she wore.

The office was eerily quiet. When Dexter crouched low in front of the sofa to look at her, the haunting look on her face somehow made him angry.

"Don't look at me like that," she snapped.

He looked at her intently, more closely. Her hair was disheveled from sleep, her face was devoid of make up, and the skin under her eyes was dark and puffy with exhaustion.

The longer he looked, the sadder he felt.

"I'm all right . . . th-thanks for checking on me, both of you. Thank you."

Dexter stood to take a seat beside her. Cole stepped out of the room and Dexter seized the chance to pull her into his arms. "Tell me what you need. We don't have to talk about anything other than what you need."

"They threaten me. They call me all the time. I can't escape them. I can't go out there. I'm afraid. I'm just tired, all the time," she said, reluctant to be held. "The feds don't seem to be helping. I call them when I get threats, but they do nothing. I don't know what to do. They can't trace the person making the threats. I can't sleep. I *need* sleep. I can't do this. I'm not any further along despite telling them everything I know *and* telling them the truth about my identity. I don't have anywhere else to go." Leedra's eyes filled.

"You need to take time off to process this."

"They call the office. They call my cell phone. They call the main office number. They won't leave me alone. They want a story. They want everything. I don't know who to trust. No one can keep these people away from me. They're calling me. They . . ."

Dexter nodded.

"Are they calling you?" she asked.

"Yes, but not very often," he replied.

She nodded. "Reporters call me all the time too. This is the only place that has twenty-four security on the lower level, so I just stay here. Someone from the paper, someone else from some daily news magazine . . . I . . . I can't take it."

"Why didn't you call me or tell me?"

"I thought you wouldn't want to hear from me."

"Why?"

"Because . . . because your father is in jail."

"He was in possession of the pictures—it's the punishment he must face. He's ill. He won't last long there," Dexter said hurriedly.

"But he didn't kill Renee."

Dexter looked at her. "How do you know?"

Leedra stood, moved to her desk and pulled a photo from a thick file.

"They gave me this picture. This is your father, right?"

Dexter moved over as she sat back down next to him, the picture in her hand. He looked at the picture, then back at her, as if the picture told them nothing.

"It's *Christmas* in this photo," she said meaningfully.

Dexter shrugged.

"The man, there," she pointed. "He came from the church the day after Christmas. Two years in a row. In the Santa suit. You truly don't recognize him? That's Garrison—your father."

CHAPTER TWENTY-FIVE:
PRESSING INQUIRIES

CHIEF MARK WASHINGTON HUNG UP the phone and stared at the cowering junior detective in front of him.

"You want to tell me why we're not further along on Ms. Henderson's case, Danny?"

"I dunno why you're asking me," Danny spluttered. "I'm not working on that case—Roy is. I don't take the information. I just enter what they've written from the report. I just file the paperwork."

"That's just it, Danny. According to Stevenson, you were seen in Archival several times. You don't have any old cases, so what have you been doing down there?

"I . . . uh . . . look for things people send me to retrieve . . ."

"Is that right, Danny?"

"Uh . . . Yes, sir. I—"

"Oh, save it, Danny. You don't file the proper paperwork, and if you're going to plagiarize old police reports, then at least correct your damn spelling."

Danny's neck heated as the Chief of Police threw the papers at him. He watched them all scatter to the floor. The Chief continued darkly.

"We have a problem. I'm conducting an investigation on your reporting procedures. If I recover more than just a few, ah, *padded* pieces of your prose, then we're going to have a *real* problem. Turn in everything you are working on. You go get it now and bring it to my office."

"Look, Chief, I just . . . I'm just going slow because the woman—well, according to the reports Stevenson wrote—the woman, this Leedra Henderson, is really Evie Carter, sir. She was with Kira Parker, that little girl. She's the one who mysteriously brought the girl back."

Danny noticed that he had the Chief's attention at last and continued rapidly. "You know, there's been talk of an international porn ring in the area. Kidnapping girls, you know, Chief, and laying low for a period of time before selling the children on to a larger criminal organization. What if this Henderson-Carter woman is one of the front people for those sickos? She's nice. What if she gets close to the children and then she makes off with them? They trust her, but—"

The Chief cut him off. "You think the child's own father wouldn't be able to see through an act like that?"

Danny's color rose. "If he were in love with her, he wouldn't be able to see through it. She could be *working* him for a time, to-to . . . Anyway, when I go to the archives, I'm just reviewing some of the cold human trafficking cases—see if I can get a pattern going, ya know, Chief? That's all."

"That doesn't explain your need to fudge information on unrelated cases, or why pieces of information are missing."

"That I don't know nothing about, Chief. I mean, why would I have a need to steal information? I'm not working on any cold cases. Man, . . . I mean, Chief—Clay was *obsessed* with that one cold case—remember? *That* wasn't me. I mean, you saw that yourself. I just . . . I use some of the old wording sometimes to help me with the details I put in, for, uh, similar cases. I seen others do it all the time, to beef up the description box. I just . . . I just should read though everything twice before submitting it. I'm sorry."

"You are on administrative leave until further notice." The Chief's tone was cold.

Danny halted his monologue and nodded. He looked at the Chief and moved meekly to pick up the papers that had been thrown in his face. When he stood up, stacking the sheets into some order, he had regained some of his composure.

"Just think about what I'm saying, all right?"

In control once more, Danny moved to the door and left his boss's office. Standing out in the corridor, he paused and listened for just a moment as the Chief picked up the phone.

"Clay? Yeah, it's Chief. I spoke with management, and I got a green light for you to consult on the special project, so I need ya to get in here."

After straining to catch what the Chief was saying, Danny smirked. So, his stupid partner was on his way back. Figured. Danny walked quickly back to his desk to do what the Chief requested. Give him all the information about recent cases he'd been working on. He would do that all right. He wasn't working on the Henderson case, but he hoped that he'd planted enough doubt to cause the Chief and others to look at her with renewed scrutiny.

Once that woman was in the public eye, he could get rid of her and get back to his "side job." He was doing real well here so far: biding his time, slowing down the progress of the other detectives. He was a master at this, he reflected proudly. He wished Clay were there. He'd been so useful for Danny's purposes—so trusting. One time, when Clay went to the doctor to see if he had early-onset Alzheimer's, his partner Danny was the only person he had told. Danny smiled to himself at the way his mind worked.

If the Chief was going to consult Philip Clay about this intricate case, then that was the next seed of doubt Danny had to plant. Doubt didn't require much to take hold. It was like a match—a tiny insignificant sliver which, when struck against an abrasive surface, could burst to flame and raze large building. A little match, just like a seed of carefully planted doubt, could destroy everything in its wake. All Danny had to do was plant it and once planted, it would spread like wildfire.

Danny began the appropriate paperwork for his leave. He didn't like the stares he received as he moved through the halls of the office. He'd worked really hard to control his paranoia and this situation was causing it to surge. Surely no one could know that he was being placed on leave this soon after the Chief had told him. He had to be more careful. Silliness. Leave was a welcome break. He moved a little more assuredly and lifted his chin, realizing how this time away would allow him to nip everything in the bud. Finally, he could clean up the mess his aunt and uncle had made some twenty-five years ago.

Dexter was still thinking about Leedra's revelation as he drove them down Interstate 95. His brain kept plaguing him about the stupid picture. *Your father played Santa Claus and you didn't even recognize him.* Dexter drove in the silence. He was driving Cole's car. Cole had taken Leedra's car back to the garage of a friend to throw off any reporters and certainly the person who had started calling. The local news station grew fuzzier the further away they got from the city, even though he would have preferred that they not listen to anything at all. With Cole's help, he and Leedra had come up with a plan to do their own press conference: to take control without waiting for a bunch of federal investigators to do nothing. First off, he was going to take Leedra away for a few days' rest, to escape the terrible pressure of the media's scrutiny and also to stop sleeping in an office not meant for an extended stay. After they got their bearings and solidified the plan, they'd face the world and they'd make progress—together—this time.

Cole had made some calls and told them what to do. Dexter found that he was able to exist in another mode: protector. He could do that. If she was willing to come with him, merely to permit him to help her, he could do anything for her.

The photo didn't mean Garrison wasn't the same person the police had arrested: an awful man. As many years ago as that was, Dexter reminded himself, it was still the fact. Everything was simply catching up with Garrison. Undoubtedly, he had just played the part of "upstanding citizen" long enough to make a few rounds handing out toys donated by well-meaning church-goers and getting that photo op. How long had that taken him?—a couple of hours? Surely, his father could stay sober for a couple of hours—he'd had to work, after all. Hadn't that Philip Clay guy even said that his father was a functioning addict? So, he had to have been free from the influence of drugs at least eight hours a day, long enough to go to work, plus this hour's extension around the holidays to take gifts to a bunch of indigent kids.

Maybe it was his only way to see you. Dexter batted the idea away. *He would have had to care to do that,* he concluded. He never believed his father cared that much. His heart wouldn't allow it. Regardless, it was too late. Or so that's what Dexter kept telling himself.

He could only hope this Santa picture meant something good. He imagined that such a hope was likely the sole reason Leedra had agreed to come with him and that she seemed willing to allow him to help her. Or her exhaustion over the issues that plagued her was winning out. He looked over at her as he drove along the dark highway.

He reached over, and with his eyes still on the road he put a caring and gentle hand on her leg. A hand squeezed his in return. He was surprised that she still wasn't asleep, despite the pillow propped against her window and the blanket over her knees. He hoped that would change when they reached their destination.

After just a moment, her hand loosed on his and he put it back on the steering wheel. "I'm gonna take care of you," he whispered, hoping to himself that he was able to do what he promised.

The house they were approaching, which he hardly ever visited, was just a little over an hour away in Severn, Maryland. It looked like most homes, but it was quiet, in a pleasant rural area with no other houses for at least three miles in either direction. It was also like Fort Knox, with an alarm, motion-sensor cameras and lights and a six-foot wrought iron fence around the entire property. A safe haven.

"What is this place?" she asked drowsily. As they pulled up to the garage, lights immediately flickered on and lighted all the walkways and the driveway. He opened the garage using the key fob that he kept on his keyring. "It's the Parkers' home-away-from-home." Dexter drove the car in and closed the garage door behind them. He led her inside, deactivating the alarm when its shrill beeping sounded, and set down her suitcase just inside.

"Do you want to go take a shower and get to bed? We can talk in the morning. You can get some rest first."

"Can we have a little tea? Is there any here?"

"Sure."

Dexter set down the keys in a bowl by the door and led her through the foyer and living room. She took a seat on the couch facing the kitchen. Dexter noticed that she was rubbing her arms and wrapped herself back up in the blanket she'd brought with her.

"What sent you looking for me?" she asked, half to herself.

"I was worried about you." He hunted through the many musty cupboards in search of tea. Having not visited the place for quite some time, he had difficulty remembering where everything was, but eventually found a box of tea, which he was relieved to find, had not yet expired.

He set the kettle on the stove and exited the kitchen. The fireplace was just opposite the sofa, with a raised brick hearth, and he got to work balling up pieces of newspaper and setting them under the logs in the cavity. Memories caught up to him of the horrific pictures that he'd burned just a few weeks ago at his father's house. His throat felt dry when he thought about the images, and he'd only seen a few. He cleared his throat to address Leedra, who was dozing on the soft couch.

"I uh, I got a disturbing phone call, Leedra, and it scared me." He wouldn't lie or hide the truth any more, even if he thought he was doing her a favor. That sort of thing had already destroyed what little they had.

"They threatened to hurt me, didn't they?"

"Yes, but they won't hurt you. We'll fight this together."

"Someone doesn't want the truth to get out, Dexter. What we're doing is forcing it out. It can't be your father, though, now that he's in jail. Doesn't that give you some hope? He's too old and not very agile. Do you ever think perhaps he was framed, too?"

Dexter nodded thoughtfully. He brushed the dust and ash off his hands and went to sit down next to her.

He stared into the fire. The flames were already taking hold of the wood, illuminating the otherwise dark room. The only other natural light source was a skylight, through which they could see the full moon. The fire was chasing the empty-house chill away. His arms around Leedra, he held her close, reveling silently in the smell of her hair, the warmth emanating from her and the softness of her body pressed against his.

"Thank you for sharing the pictures and trying to believe the best in an impossible situation," he said softly. "While it answers some things, it doesn't absolve my father of his wrongdoings. It does not make him innocent or take away his numerous bouts with addiction. And everything he has done took me away from you, then and now. He must know all that happened; he *must* know. It's like he flip-flops. He gives part of the story—and other parts I guess he insists on taking to his grave—but why?"

"I don't know." She shook her head.

Dexter could feel Leedra drift off in his arms. Her body gradually sagged against him, pressing him deeper into the couch. He reached over the side of the sofa to a wicker basket that held extra blankets and pulled one over her to cover her legs and feet. He stood, careful not to rouse her, and went to turn off the tea. When he returned, he lifted her gently to return to his spot and kicked off his shoes as he shifted to cradle her more comfortably in his arms. She turned on her side and also kicked off her shoes, bringing her feet up onto the sofa. "Tomorrow will be better," Dexter whispered, the crackling snap of the fire the only other sound in the air.

"It won't look any better, except for the fact that you'll be here with me," she returned. Her mumbled words were slurred, but he understood them perfectly and he smiled. He hugged her closer and her hands held his tight until they loosened once more: she'd finally fallen asleep.

He prayed for safety and rest to prepare for whatever awaited them—and for the strength to win against it.

CHAPTER TWENTY-SIX:
PEACEFUL AWAKENINGS

WHEN LEEDRA WOKE, THE SUN from the skylight made her feel warm and safe, like she was in a cozy cocoon. The quietness was welcome: not a beep, not a car horn and no blaring of sirens had roused her throughout the night. This morning, she simply drifted awake easily, without the immediate dread of the day's discoveries, and for once, unprovoked by harsh sounds or harsher nightmares. She felt arms around her and stared at the ceiling, blinking away the sleep from her eyes. She would bask just a little longer, long enough to get her bearings and enjoy the space around her. She felt calm and serene. However fleeting this feeling might be, she would take it. She also knew that the calm feeling had less to do with the house's peace and quiet than with the safety her companion provided simply by being present. For once, she felt safe—protected.

She wished she could prolong this sense of quiet security. If they could just stay there forever, she would. Sadly, reality entered her mind as she woke fully. She recalled the late night drive, the cover of night surrounding Cole's loaner, luxury car as they drove, and how her inability to stay awake now that someone else was at the helm had helped her rest for the first time in weeks.

Some time in the middle of the night, her limbs and Dexter's had become entangled; perhaps having tried to get comfortable in her sleep. She now pinned Dexter to the sofa. She turned slightly to admire him as he slept, his even breathing causing his chest to rise and fall rhythmically. There was stubble on his chin and she noticed a little gray hair beginning to come in—just one or two.

Gently, she touched the rough hairs on his chin with her thumb. How she'd give anything to be with him and to fast forward things by just a few months, to the part where they'd gotten past their trust issues and had reached the end of this unsolved mystery that kept her constantly on edge. Her mind toyed with the idea of what that would look like: a shared moment of intimacy between them. Something in her replied that she wasn't ready, that it would mean different things for both of them. For the first time in a very long time, she remembered desire and how it would get you into all sorts of trouble, if you weren't careful. In other relationships, she'd never felt the love she truly desired. They'd provided empty, temporary gratification, but once the desire was fulfilled, it was gone by the next morning. That was obviously why she'd run away from it until now. Even the current situation seemed like setting herself up for everything to backfire. It was scary to want anyone that much.

She did love him. She wanted to tell him. Not even her past, nor his for that matter, could make her stop loving him. Tears came to her eyes. She just wanted to love and be a part of something so badly. Without further consideration, she kissed his slumbering lips, tentatively at first. Before she knew what was happening, his eyes opened to look at her half-lidded, with a drowsy reciprocation of her desire. His hands, first slow and tentative, quickly turned strong, hard and pulled her closer to him. Her own hands traced up his chest and everything inside of her came alive with hope. His strong arms pulled her up, encircling her as their kiss deepened, hands splayed on her back, pressing her still closer. She wanted so much more.

His tongue sought hers. When his hand dipped lower, caressing her bottom, it snapped her back to reality and she froze. Her eyes blinked rapidly; her body was still responding, trying to do more, even as everything else in her fought to flee.

"Dexter, stop. I'm sorry. I'm sorry. I . . . gotta stop. Excuse me." Mortified, she martialed her spaghetti legs into working order only to fall somewhat ungracefully off the sofa onto the plush carpet in a heap.

She managed to scramble up and find her footing, willing everything to coordinate properly. Not entirely sure where she was going, she ran up a set of stairs and dived into the first bathroom she saw.

With the door closed, Leedra closed the toilet seat lid and sat down heavily on it, taking deep breaths. The desire felt like it would not abate. She closed her eyes, willing it away. After a few minutes, there was a knock on the door. She stood to open it but Dexter wasn't waiting there when she looked out. She looked down to see he'd left her suitcase outside for her. She smiled, somewhat relieved and dragged it back into the bathroom.

She decided on a shower: if nothing else, that might help her hit the reset button and wash out the lust-crazed woman she'd just become from her brain.

Thirty minutes later, she felt immeasurably better. Desire was likely still lurking, but she got dressed, selecting a long blue-and-white-flowered dress that she'd often lounged in when secretly living at her office. "Sounds like a CNN documentary," she said out loud to herself in the mirror. She laughed at her reflection. She hadn't done that in a while: smile, make a joke at herself, laugh even and feel like everything just might be okay. Well, everything except the investigation, anonymous threats on her life, sleeping at work, not to mention the confusing I-love-him-I-love-him-not feelings for the man downstairs.

She searched her toiletry bag for a comb to tame her hair into some style befitting a woman who *hadn't* just been frolicking on the leather couch downstairs. She brushed her teeth and looked at herself in the mirror a final time before exiting.

As she approached the stairs, something heavenly greeted her nostrils. Going down, she saw Dexter standing at the stove. He must have found sausages somewhere, which he was now prodding around in a sauté pan on the stove as he stirred a second pan of what looked like porridge, only white.

"Do you like grits?"

"What's that?"

She shrugged when he looked at her as if she was crazy.

"My world traveller doesn't know what grits are?"

"It's like cream of wheat, right? Just a different texture?" Leedra laughed at the look on his face. She moved toward the coffee maker and he handed her an empty cup. The machine was one of those fancy pod ones. Thankfully, there was a similar model at the office, so she knew how to use it just about. She retrieved the box of pods next to it and was bemused, even a little annoyed, at the vast array of options.

"Try the caramel—you'll like it," Dexter suggested.

"Thank you," she said, relieved.

"Cream of wheat is disgusting, by the way," Dexter added. "Grits are made from corn. Most people I know put butter in them, but if you think it's like cream of wheat, I guess you've probably been around people that put sugar in them. That's just blasphemous."

Leedra grinned. "I'll try it. It all smells so good. Do you want some coffee too?"

Dexter held up his cup to indicate that he already had some. Leedra nodded and sat at the table, waiting. He finished cooking, plated the food and brought both plates to the table.

"I'll go to the store later. Sorry there are no scrambled eggs. We can have some tomorrow."

"Oh, it's okay. I can live without eggs."

Dexter held her hand and said the grace. "My dad, David," he clarified to note his adoptive father who he often spoke more fondly and certainly more freely of, "used to, uh, mix his eggs and grits together with the sausage. Then, we all started doing it, only because he did it. Now, it's pretty much a Parker habit."

Leedra listened while digging into her food. She cut her sausage into smaller pieces and pushed them into the grits, wondering if that was how his father did it, and scooped it up to take in the taste of both. "Oh, I like it. It's good," she said, covering her mouth to speak.

She ate, thinking. The simple breakfast plate was just enough and it hit the spot. She took a piece of toast, tore it and used it as a vehicle for the last of her sausage.

"Dexter, about this morning . . ." Leedra set down her fork and looked at him.

"Don't mention it." He avoided her eyes.

"I want to," she insisted. "I felt embarrassed and foolish. I believe that ultimately we will have those things between us—in time, but first I need to be free of my past."

"We're working toward that—I know. I'm very patient, Leedra."

"That's an understatement." She smiled. Finally, he met her gaze.

"Just know that whatever we would do, it's not wrong or inappropriate. I'm here for you, as long as it takes."

Leedra nodded. She noted Dexter's unusually serious, even somber mood. He didn't eat his food, just looked at her intensely.

"I have a good friend, Cashell, and she is coming up here to meet with us today. She's basically a glorified publicist, an Olivia Pope character."

"Who's Olivia Pope?"

"She's a fictional character on TV, based on a real person. She cleans up public relations nightmares for the wealthy."

Leedra nodded. "Sounds interesting."

"Cashell has helped our family out in the past. Some stuff that Cole went through with his father back in the day, and some more recently when my wife died. She's worked for some pretty high-profile people and she makes the process easier, especially when you're unsure of what to do. Her clients tend to be people who aren't sure who to trust—like us right now."

"How did she help you after your wife died?" Leedra asked.

"She assisted with crafting information to send to the press and wrote us an official statement. Working with her, I learned that if we can control what we put out, there's less room for error—and less extra time for other people to put out false information. Plus, they will start calling her office for information, which may reduce the calls to you or me personally."

Leedra sat up straight. A part of her wanted to tell him that she trusted him completely, and she hoped that the fact she was there with him alone spoke volumes, but dread after dread besieged her, making her feel as if she were delusional for trusting anyone at all.

She prayed she could handle yet another load of truth that was about to come out.

"Okay, she sounds like a valuable ally, Dexter, but when your wife died, why would you have had to *craft* a message at all?"

CHAPTER TWENTY-SEVEN:
AN HONEST REVELATION

"I WANT TO TELL YOU JUST one last thing. It's pretty much the only thing left about me that you don't know, okay?"

Dexter wasn't sure he could stand reliving the pain of what had happened all those years ago, but with Leedra looking so confused and with so much else at stake, he knew he had to try. The only reason he'd kept his secrets to himself for so long was that, after three years, he was just starting to feel normal again. He was finally putting it all behind him. Loving or trusting anyone again was a major step for him. He drew a deep breath and began.

"So, first my wife cheated on me. I knew about it and we were trying to work it out. I forgave her. I believed in our marriage and I wanted to try to work it out. Then, we found out she was pregnant . . . with his child."

"Oh, Dexter, honey. I'm sorry."

Dexter winced. The only part he knew for certain was the part he'd just told: that his wife had left him. As for his wife's motives and final thoughts, all he could do was guess. He'd never know for certain.

"So, uh, she drove off one night after we had an argument," he continued. "I did not chase her, whatever those news reports might've said. I stayed home to look after our daughter, and then I took Kira to Cole and Allontis's house for the rest of that night. The police came in the morning and told me she ran her car into a tree."

Dexter sniffed. He wasn't crying over his wife—she hadn't cared about him or their marriage. No, he simply wished she was still alive for his daughter's sake, to be with her during the tough times and to witness how much she grew each and every day. That was the part that pained him.

"I knew where her lover lived. The accident was a mile from his house. Cashell, Cole and myself are the only ones who know she cheated on me or that she was probably driving to see him. I don't even think Cole told Allontis. To everyone else, it looked like any other accident, except to this one cop—for whatever reason, he didn't believe that I had nothing to do with my wife's hasty exit. To him, her death seemed suspicious, and he thought perhaps that I'd somehow pushed her over the edge. This particular cop seemed bent on making me look guilty and it escalated. I held back the fact that she was pregnant and when they found out later, it made it seem like my motives were certainly even more dishonest. I didn't want anyone to know how much I hated her for what she'd done, and I didn't want anyone's pity over what had happened." Dexter cleared his throat. "I still maintain that it was an accident, too, to protect my daughter and honor her mother. Do you think that's wrong?"

"What?" She reared back as if she were repulsed. "Dexter, no, of course not. Dexter, that is a wonderful, noble thing. Every parent should keep more adult subjects away from their children. It's sad that they have to know any tragedies at all."

Dexter watched Leedra as she paced the kitchen, her bare feet silent against the tiled floor. It was obvious something else was heavy on her mind.

"What are you thinking?" He scooted his chair back from the table and stood. Just to do something with his hands and move on from relaying the past, he picked up both their plates and put them in the sink.

"I'm thinking about how angry I am. I'm angry at *her*, for what she did to you. How could she? When your friend Cashell gets here, perhaps she will agree with me that it's better for you not to come to this press conference after all. I don't want to make you rehash this pain all over again ... I'm sorry. Oh Dexter, I'm sorry for not thinking this through more. This will hurt you so much more than I realized. I never meant to hurt you."

To Dexter's surprise, as soon as he turned from the sink relieved at her response, Leedra rushed into his arms of her own volition this time. He felt her hands on his face and he closed his eyes. When he opened them again, he kissed her palms. "I'm sorry I kept this from you for so long. You've told me everything and I'm—" Her fingers silenced his lips and Dexter just stared at her.

"Thank you for trusting me with this. I trust you completely, and I believe you'd never do anything to hurt anyone. You're honoring the best parts of your wife by not tarnishing her memory for your child. I don't think many people could do that, especially when they were being persecuted for withholding information. Especially when she is to blame for everything: her unfaithfulness and even her death. That's so sad."

Dexter took a deep, cleansing breath. Sage as she was with her thinking, Leedra's reaction both amazed and vindicated him. No one had reacted to his story the way she had when they first heard it. Not Cole, certainly not Cashell. Almost everyone else had insisted that when Kira was old enough, she must be told the truth about her mother. Dexter had always wondered what good that would do. The truth would solve nothing; it didn't change his wife's calamitous mistake. It might have absolved him of any wrongdoing sooner, certainly, but nothing would be different.

"Maybe I wasn't paying attention to the signs. I just thought we had hit a rough patch and that we could work through it, even go to counseling. Naïve, I suppose, but mostly just stubborn—unwilling to give up on us . . ."

"You didn't give up. You forgave her, even after discovering she was carrying someone else's child. Even after death, you forgave her. You allowed her to be remembered as a wonderful mother who died in an unfortunate accident that you had nothing to do with. Whichever way you think of it, she was someone special to you at one time, even if she was not wise enough to remain faithful to you. I don't know how anyone could do that you—I can only imagine how hurtful that is. One indiscretion shouldn't wipe away all your memories of the good times, though. I've seen how people are. They lock onto one bad deed and forget decades of good that came before."

Dexter nodded. "I do try to focus on the good times when Kira and I talk about her." Dexter couldn't believe how strongly telling his secret to Leedra increased his love for her. He wanted her in his life forever. She accepted what he said without question or suspicion when others, Lucient Douglass for example, would not. Lucient and others like him would rather concoct implications that Dexter was somehow responsible for his wife's death, or insinuate that he had something to hide. He had been desperate to hide the truth, but also to face scrutiny about his wife's fidelity and whatever that said about him and their married life. To others, it was weak to want to honor a dead, cheating woman's memory for his daughter. No one seemed to understand that or why he would care about his wife so much considering what she'd done. It wasn't about her at all.

"I want to make something clear to you, Leedra. I'm not in love with a dead woman, okay?"

Leedra nodded.

"Look at me. I'm telling you this to clear the air, to clear everything between us. I love you. I'm in love with you."

"I know that . . . I believe that . . . and I—I love you, too. I always have." Her lips sought his, this time of their own emboldened volition, and he returned everything she gave without hesitation.

"Cole, honey?"

"Hmm?"

"Did you know that I have resorted to gossip, social media and interrogating eight- and nine-year-olds to get information about my own family?" Allontis exclaimed. "The kids still have this rock-solid loyalty to you and your brother—and now to a woman that I hired, too? Leedra just got here and the children already think she's wonderful. I feel duped."

Cole stood at the dresser in their bedroom and dried his limbs with a towel after his shower. It had been an unusually busy night for the restaurant. He turned to look at his wife of almost four years. Even though he smiled and rolled his eyes, he would proceed with caution. He knew that she and Leedra had become very close, so he knew Allontis was likely kidding about being offended at how the girls adored the new woman in their lives. Kira was taken with Leedra because of the scary experience they had shared, of course. Cole's little sister Hannah, who tended to be a bit more judgmental and discriminating about new people, was warming up to Leedra pretty fast as well.

Allontis knew that Leedra had saved Kira from kidnapping, a fact that had further endeared her to the entire family. Cole liked Leedra well enough too. Recently, though, he'd been distracted by wondering just how much he should tell Allontis about Leedra's past connection to Dexter. He considered all the added emotional baggage that Leedra Henderson might bring to his home, not to mention his brother's. Ultimately, the only thing Cole was truly only concerned about was the impact all this might have on Dexter and Kira. Cole and his family would be fine. They had to get through this pregnancy, and that meant keeping a certain detachment from all the family's other issues to minimize his wife's stress level. Besides, their own family drama had occurred some time ago and everyone had emerged unscathed. He wasn't going to go borrowing trouble from other people's lives. He would be there for his brother, but his priority had to be his nuclear family: Allontis, Jacoby, Hannah and their new little one.

He pulled on an undershirt and tightened the drawstring on his sweat pants before climbing into bed next to Allontis. He closed the laptop, took it gently from her fingers and placed it on her nightstand. She made a face.

He scooted closer to her. "You know why I don't tell you all that's going on, don't you? You internalize your family's problems and you start stressing. Now I'm going to tell you just a few things, but before I start, I need you to know that everything is going to be all right."

"Please tell me. I want to do something. I promise I'll read some romance novels or something to calm down after you tell me," Allontis wheedled.

"I'm not sure those are any better. They can be full of tragedy too," Cole smirked.

Allontis laughed. "Yes, but they are about *other people's* problems so there's some detachment, and they always work out in the end anyway."

Cole shrugged. Sounded good. "Okay, here we go. I'm worried about Dexter because his father is going to be investigated for possession of child porn."

"Oh no. We had a feeling it was something like that . . . so that's why the girls never get to see him, huh?"

"Yes. Also, it turns out he knows something about what happened to the girls in Leedra's foster home all those years ago. You know she was there with Dex, right?"

Allontis's face darkened. "I knew they grew up together but—oh no, he didn't . . . You don't think Dexter's father had something to do with that filthy stuff, did he?"

Cole sighed. "In my heart, I really don't believe that he did anything to the girls, but it looks as if he knows more than he has told anyone, and we're not sure why he's keeping it."

"Have your old friends down at the station been helping?"

"I put a call in to a couple of buddies. I no longer have as many contacts as I used to, and this is a federal case, way bigger than my time in DC as nothing more than a beat cop. There is this one guy I had checked out, though, Philip Clay. Apparently, he was at the conference center during the board's retreat. Turns out he was at some church's annual married couples weekend thing—well anyway, he spooked Leedra, kept staring at her as if he knew her. Crazy coincidence: turns out he's the very guy who was on her case all those years ago. Dexter and Leedra have been working together to reopen the case, and they found out this Clay person was one of the first responders. He just retired."

"Oh wow. And Cole? I'm pretty sure Dexter loves Leedra."

"I know. Since he was a child. Kind of like us."

"You didn't love me when we were young! I was a nuisance."

"Yeah, the finest nuisance I'd ever seen with those beautiful light eyes," Cole smiled lovingly.

Allontis chuckled and sighed. "I don't look so good now, huh? Pregnant, laid up here in this bed? It's driving me nuts."

"I realize pregnant women often feel a little lackluster, but let me tell you, you're the most beautiful woman in the world. I love you. In just another few months, all of this sitting around will produce a perfect little me . . . or you, of course."

She laughed. "Thank you for acknowledging my contribution. I'm sorry for being so down. I just . . . I want Dexter to find love again. Do you think things will work out between them?"

"Yes, I do, but . . ." Cole grabbed Allontis's hips, pulling her down further into the bed. He adjusted her pillow. Flat on her back, her belly protruded more and he stared. His hands covered her bump as he marveled at his newest child's growth just within the last month. When he spread his hands across her belly, his thumbs were getting further and further apart. He couldn't believe how much his life had changed in the last few years. He was a husband, a big brother and a father now, and the woman lying beside him had given him all of it. He could tell his wife wanted to say something, but not while he was praying for them: a ritual he did every night. He asked that God would continue to bless them, protect the formation of the child as well as Allontis's own life. This pregnancy had been a little bit tougher than with their first, Jacoby, but he believed everything would be okay. He uttered his prayer aloud and ended.

"Amen," Allontis said.

Cole kissed her belly and laid his ear against it, just enjoying listening to whatever sounds issued from inside her. He lifted his head slowly and looked at her. He shifted positions so that he lay on his side and kissed Allontis with all the passion and love he had. She meant everything to him.

He thought of his brother having had all this at one time, or so it had seemed, and then losing it all. That sort of total loss would devastate Cole—he was sure of it. In his brother's shoes, he wasn't sure he'd take a second go-around with such an awful tragedy always hanging over his head. He'd likely say "no thanks" to anyone else if, God forbid, something happened to Allontis. It was the very reason he'd run away years ago, to avoid entanglements and attachments that only ended in loss.

Giving himself a little shake, he kicked the negative thoughts away. His eyes moved back to the woman beside him.

"Baby, it's still a tough road ahead. Lots of things left to be uncovered. Leedra wants to find the answers that weigh on her heart, and you can't blame her. I'm certain Dexter will help her and wants to be there for her all he can. I just pray the two of them can handle what they find out, if and when they are able to do so, and that the obstacles aren't so impossibly hard to overcome that it tests them and they decide to part ways. That is what worries me most."

Cole was done talking. His reasoning astonished even his own ears. He was a deep thinker, he always had been, but he never talked with anyone so much as he had just opened up to his wife. He was sure that was why she was now looking at him so curiously. He could see her mind thinking, figuring, absorbing. His lips sought her again.

"You're so wonderful," she smiled. "You make fatherhood and husbandry look sexy."

Cole laughed. "Isn't husbandry care of animals and farming?"

"Yes but the archaic meaning is the care of household," Allontis said proudly.

Cole was thoughtful, smiling. "Really?"

"Got a lot of time on my hands here. That was Dictionary.com's word of the day."

They laughed together and kissed, showing their passion for one other.

"Now, where are those novels? Want to read to me until I go to sleep?" Smiling mischievously, he reached a hand under her pillow and retrieved her e-reader. He knew all of her secrets. She would likely be up another hour reading, as she almost always was when he came home after a late night closing down his busy restaurant. She was usually up to greet him when he arrived. Often, he would go to sleep with her bedside light still on, trying not to let her sleep patterns affect his own.

"I just downloaded a few more today. I'll read you something." She laughed, snatching her device from his hand.

Cole laughed and pulled her closer as he waited for sleep to claim him. Her soft reading lulled him into a peaceful dream state. Saying a final silent prayer that the same rest and happiness would come to his brother and Leedra, he added a plea to God that whatever was going to come to light wouldn't take too much longer.

CHAPTER TWENTY-EIGHT:
BACK TO REALITY

TWO WONDERFUL DAYS HAD PASSED in the Maryland cabin, hidden away and secluded from the world—but in Virginia, just a bridge away, Leedra's real life remained in turmoil. It was time to stop hiding.

She stared at the bedside table, adorned with a vase of fresh flowers courtesy of Dexter. He'd been to the store again that morning after making a delicious dinner the night before: eggs to go with her second taste of grits. Afterwards, she'd slept like never before in her life, mostly in his arms. Safe. Loved. Cared for. Her heart beat faster just thinking about their time together, but right then, she made herself sit up, take a shower and get dressed. They would return to Virginia today and meet with Dexter's publicist, Cashell. The days ahead promised to be an interesting time.

Leedra showered, got dressed and headed downstairs, but stopped at the last step, listening intently to the voices below. A woman's stern voice was telling Dexter that he should think twice about . . . whatever it was they were talking about, which Leedra had not picked up.

"This could be terrible, Dexter, and you know it—" the voice persisted.

"Hello?" Leedra moved the rest of the way down the steps and the voices stopped altogether. Two faces turned to look at her, each with clearly different thoughts.

"Hey, come here a sec," Dexter said. "Did you sleep well?"

She nodded, suddenly shy. She knew that somehow their relationship had changed in just the short amount of time spent at the Maryland house, and she liked the newness it had. They held nothing back from each other now, which was wonderful, but it would take some getting used to if he was always going to display his feelings for her so openly—especially if he was going to do it in front of others.

Dexter moved closer to her. He hugged her and kissed her fully on the lips in greeting.

"You ready to talk to Cashell?"

She nodded, though his words might as well have been in Greek, because Leedra could not stop looking at the other woman in the room. Cashell Bruer looked like she belonged on the runway, certainly not sitting behind some desk at the local Public Information Office. She was a black woman with striking straight hair touched with subtle red highlights, lots of makeup that accentuated her large eyes, and a blue designer suit that seemed to hug her in all the right places. In short, the woman before her looked like she'd stepped out of an Essence magazine photo shoot. Leedra stopped herself from looking down at her own lackluster duds and her bare feet, which made her feel small and dowdy next to the woman in six-inch heels.

"Ms. Henderson. Cashell Bruer—nice to meet you."

"Hello, how are you?"

"I'm well, thank you."

Dexter led Leedra over to the sofa, and Cashell reclaimed her seat across from them.

"I suppose you might have overheard me telling Dexter that this won't be an easy exercise, considering his past interactions with the police, coupled with the determination of the press to get the drop on every story, even if their fill-in-the-blanks strategy churns out falsities and innuendo. The Parker family has experienced a lot of tragedy and I just—well, Leedra, I think it's best that you do a lot of this release of information—on your own. I will be there to advise you and I'll write you a detailed list of responses to possible questioning."

"I agree," Leedra said, realizing this woman meant business. Leedra scooted forward to the edge of the sofa. Despite Cashell's intimidatingly glamorous image, she had already started liking the woman more and more. Cashell clearly wanted to protect Dexter; Leedra simply hadn't known until now that the two of them wanted the exact same things. Perhaps a bit of jealousy had kicked in before, what with Leedra having been upstairs while Dexter was downstairs alone with this striking woman. The man was obviously clueless about how women, just like men, sized each other up when a member of the opposite sex was involved. Her newfound love for Dexter had her feeling both jealous and possessive for the first time. Ever.

"I was just telling Cashell that I disagree with her strategy," said Dexter. "I will be there."

"Yes, okay. There in the next room." Cashell clarified.

"Is there a kind of private room where he could watch it on television?" Leedra asked hopefully.

"Leedra—" Dexter said in warning.

"No, it's okay. Listen, there's nothing wrong with your being there. Just not beside me, okay? Not anywhere the cameras can link us." Leedra looked away. Dexter was looking at her as if she'd lost her mind.

"I believe there is a room, but you can always meet him somewhere," put in Cashell.

"I'll be there," Dexter repeated firmly.

"All right, fine. I'll be in touch with some talking points." Cashell said. "I'll e-mail them over to you both as soon as I get back, and if I'm missing any details, call and let me know. The press conference will be tomorrow at noon. I really need you to read and review the bullet points before then. We'll only have limited time to discuss them tomorrow. I'll also send you a statement and I'll touch base with the Bureau Chief, too."

"How long will it last?" Leedra asked.

"Hopefully, not more than an hour. It will take a while to get started—that's usually the most nerve-racking part. The complications of getting everyone in and assembled are just silliness really. It's like everyone feels they have to get in a row and strike some sort of pose they feel favors their best side. Taking a senior class picture requires less effort, but just remember to pack a bit of patience while all the men are striving for their prime spot in front of the cameras." Cashell smiled and stood. "I'll see you both there, early. I'll e-mail any last-minute changes."

Leedra returned her smile, thanking her, and shook her hand briefly in parting. Dexter squeezed Leedra's hand and moved to see Cashell out the door.

When he returned, she stood. "So, this is it?" she said.

"Uh—what is it?" he returned.

She looked around, taking in how spacious and inviting the place was. "Can we . . . can we come back here for a few days when this is all over and bring Kira?" she asked in a rush.

"Of course, that would be wonderful."

"I miss her. Thank you for waking me to talk to her earlier. I know she misses you so much."

Dexter nodded. "I needed this time with you. She knows I love her and that I'll always be there for her. Anyway, her Uncle Cole's cooking is a fair tradeoff. He makes her whatever she wants whenever I have to be away."

"Cole is not her daddy, though—make no mistake," Leedra assured him.

"And make no mistake that if I were with anyone else but you, she wouldn't take it nearly as well. She's glad I'm spending time with you. Now, about that meeting just now? You and Ms. Bruer seemed to come together like long-lost teammates—good going for having just met less than an hour ago. The pair of you ganging up to tell me what to do? Now, that part I'm not so sure about. I'm not leaving you with anyone tomorrow, under any circumstances. You wait for me. We stay together and only separate for the hour of the conference."

Leedra nodded. His firm protection of her comforted and delighted her.

"I love you," he said.

"I love you, too." They packed up the few items they had and prepared to leave for home, hoping this time around, the mystery would finally be solved.

CHAPTER TWENTY-NINE:
STAKEOUT

DANNY MANNING LURKED AROUND THE county building, scoping it out. As he looked around, he noticed that not much had changed since the last time he'd been there—years ago, whenever the last press conference was held that involved his department.

He moved aside the mop and bucket he'd been pushing and pulled his cap low on his head.

Building maintenance staff were already assembling chairs in the main room where the conference would be held. Other than that, the hallway and room were largely empty.

He walked through the day's events. He wasn't going to be a part of today—at least he wouldn't have any parts in front of the camera. Danny was a behind-the-scenes kind of person. Right then, he was checking things out, playing it out in his mind so he could be ready for one person in particular and avoid certain other people at all costs, less he blow his carefully crafted plans.

Ready to ditch the prop of his bucket and mop, the metal wheels on the bottom of the dirty water bucket squeaked as he pushed it back toward the maintenance closet. He tugged on his jeans and cap when he saw that Bruer woman enter the building. A draft of cold air blasted him in the face and he looked down to avoid contact with her. He looked at her, her designer suit, her straight hair, all public persona and all fake. He might have found her pretty, if he was into women like her, but he wasn't. He'd never like someone that defended criminals, spinning words to make them look better in the heat of the media's truthful light. No doubt she'd worked for the good doctor. He remembered her from just a few years ago. Always on television, always lying and spinning copy to fit the story she wanted you to believe.

After her, a group of men, wheeled in microphones, a podium and more chairs and two six-foot-long tables. They took them to the conference room. The woman turned to sit on the bench and when a uniformed officer approached her, coming briskly down the hall, Danny ducked into the supply room just feet away. He set the mop and bucket aside and listened intently as the woman introduced herself as Cashell Bruer.

"Ms. Bruer?" Chief Washington said as he approached.

"Chief Washington. Good to see you again."

"Same here."

"Is Detective Clay here, already?"

"Yes, my clients agreed to see him before the announcement to the press. He's meeting with them now in the staging room." "Yes, well, it doesn't seem like there is much time, but I hope before we're ready, they'll have enough time to give Clay the ability to piece together a few more details about the case."

Danny kept listening, but it seemed like their voices diminished. He noted that perhaps they had moved away, either down the hall or into the conference room across the hall.

He smirked. Clay was on duty, huh? Danny gritted his teeth in annoyance. Clay, conveniently called back to resume his stupid role, playing detective, not even three months out of retirement. Danny wondered how much they were paying him for his "consolatory advice" on a case he hadn't solved when he had twenty years to figure it out. There was no way he'd get any further with it given an extra hour, no matter who he was meeting with.

Danny wanted to laugh. "Hilarious," he whispered aloud in the maintenance closet. Clay would feel so stupid to know the truth. He wished he could see the look on his face when all was said and done. But one couldn't see much of anything, if they were dead.

Danny ensured the closet looked as he'd found it before flipping the light switch and closing the door behind him. Patience was the only thing he needed right then. If he could keep his cool and bide his time just a little longer, he'd be able to do what he wanted.

Moving down the hall, he found the door marked "Stairs" and took them back to the garage.

CHAPTER THIRTY:
PRESSING DETAILS

PHILIP CLAY LOOKED AROUND THE gray room with its large metal conference table and bare, stucco walls. It was a holding cell until show time. Leedra and Dexter took their seats at the table, just to Clay's right.

Clay had had plenty of time to get over the fact that Evie Carter/ Leedra Henderson were one in the same, as well as alive and well. He'd successfully unearthed the wrinkled picture he'd been searching for on that day he went to the office. He was still not sure how it had got put back there—but after talking with the chief, he had a good idea. Now was not the time to think that through. The woman he'd been looking for and wondering about all these years was sitting inches from him and for some reason, perhaps to confirm she was real, his hand reached out to touch hers. When Dexter, the man who had been with her at the conference center's cafeteria eyed him disapprovingly and leaned forward, Clay took his hand back quickly.

"I just want you to know that I work for the truth," he began hastily. "Whatever it costs, I'm here. And in my career, I have always been seeking the truth."

Leedra nodded. "Thank you. That's, uh, good to know. It was Dexter, who ultimately encouraged me to speak with you. In a million years, I never expected to run into anyone from that time. I'm just glad to know you're here for justice."

Relieved, Clay got down to business. He opened his folder—the one he had carried around and that had remained on his desk for the last twenty-five years. Wear and tear on the folder and the contents were evident in the frayed corners and the numerous coffee, grease and other unidentifiable food stains that soiled the front and back of the once cream-colored jacket. Finally, he had the chance to review everything with Leedra and Dexter themselves, asking a number of clarifying questions. With so many years having passed, there was no guarantee of any new information coming up at all. He still hoped that rather than being called back there just to play lead investigator and appease the press in their questions that he would eventually find the whole truth this time. His throat felt dry and he cleared it nervously. He tried to keep from staring at Leedra, but his eyes could not look away.

Clay was finally able to remember Dexter Parker, but only through the reports he'd read over the last few days. He had read the deposition given back when Dexter was just twelve years old. Due to the stringent protections around the boy, owing to his young age at the time and the things he might have seen, Clay really hadn't had any direct interaction with him during the first and subsequent investigations. Dexter had been going through the process of being permanently adopted at the time. Though he hadn't seen Dexter, other than photos of him as a youth, he had read the twenty-page transcript of the boy's account more than a hundred times.

Back in the present, Clay began a new line of questioning directed toward Dexter.

"You, uh, were gone to basketball camp for the week?"

Dexter nodded. "My adoptive parents paid for me to go. They'd hoped that I'd be with them once I returned, so they obtained a scholarship for the program."

Clay nodded before continuing. "Best thing that ever happened to you, I guess."

Dexter nodded. "They were, yes."

Clay could see and feel Dexter's annoyance at the questioning, so he moved on to Leedra. "So, uh, we know that Mr. Johnson said he helped you, Ev-Ms. Henderson, escape, but we aren't sure what happened after that. He says that he carried you to the basement and locked you in a small room to keep you safe."

"Yes, that's what I remember, but then I fell asleep. I got told later that they gave me drugs and I assumed that they drugged all the girls," she replied.

"He says that he gave you the key. To get out of the basement?"

"There was a key around my neck but I—I woke up in a hospital. I didn't know what the key was for. In the hospital, they just told me that my foster sisters were dead. After that Mr. Johnson found a woman from the church's missionary group. She took me to Brazil and then later to Africa."

Clay nodded. He'd had all these facts but he was now finally able to piece them together in some sort of timeline—something none of the police had hitherto managed to do. "Mr. Johnson says that he was not into child porn. He stated that he had relations with minors but that they were always about sixteen and seventeen—they weren't, like, children."

"When someone is a minor, they are a child." Dexter, who had been largely silent, spoke up, looking at Clay dead on.

"You're right—of, of course. I'm very sorry, Mr. Parker."

Flustered, Clay watched as Leedra swiftly took Dexter's hand. He held it, but otherwise remained closed off.

"I believe Garrison," Leedra said quietly.

"Why do you believe him, Ms. Henderson?" Clay asked. "We have evidence that he lied back then. He could still be lying."

"As I told Dexter, there is no longer any reason for him to lie. Mr. Johnson is already in jail, his health is failing . . . and I don't think anything will likely save him. He was in possession of the pictures, okay, yes, but I don't recall him being at a single photo shoot—that's what they called them. I don't remember him being present, so I don't believe he took any of the photos or was even a buyer. No, my foster father and his buddies did all of that. Alone. That's what I believe."

"She thinks because he played Santa Claus a couple of times, he couldn't possibly be guilty of anything," Dexter interjected.

"Mr. Johnson played Santa Claus?" Clay asked.

"Over the course of two Christmases—that I *can* remember. I told the detective this, and he gave me a picture he'd found in Mr. Johnson's things."

Clay nodded again. He searched through the papers of the folder and found the photo. He looked quizzically at Dexter.

"You didn't know at the time that the man who visited the house playing Santa was your father, Mr. Parker?"

"The boys rarely got presents. Only the girls," Dexter rejoined.

Leedra chimed in. "That would explain why the boys couldn't come. They used the presents as a bribe to make us take the pictures, to make it . . . fun." She looked as though she were about to be sick.

"How did they get you to do the pictures otherwise?"

"We were children. We couldn't not participate. They beat us, but in very strategic places—bruises wouldn't look good in the pictures. They gave us makeup and stuff that night, like it was a special occasion or something."

"But this particular photo shoot was around Christmas?"

"When you're a child and someone tells you Santa is coming? It could be in the middle of July and you'd still do whatever you could for the opportunity. We had photo shoots year-round. The picture is obviously from a past Christmas, but the abuse was all the time."

"This is my first time seeing this photo. So, this is Mr. Johnson?" Clay asked, pointing.

Leedra nodded. "Yes, I can tell by his eyes. They are kind."

Clay paused. "Wasn't Mr. Johnson ordered to stay away from children?"

"He wasn't yet accused of being a sex offender at that time," Leedra offered. "That's another reason his possession of the pictures seems difficult to believe. He was 'only' guilty of neglecting Dexter, of allowing school truancy—as well as all his involvement with the drugs, of course. That ultimately led Child Protective Services to his house, and it goes down hill from there. Any sex offender wouldn't have been able to have any contact with children whatsoever."

"Perhaps coming dressed as Santa was Mr. Johnson's only way to see you, Mr. Parker," suggested Clay thoughtfully. "You know, the church could have been implicated in the crime if they hired Mr. Johnson to play Santa, or even permitted him to volunteer, with the knowledge that he wasn't supposed to be around children."

"Exactly," Leedra spoke up. "Why take the risk, just to help someone play with his child? That's a good reason, sure, but not enough to risk the entire congregation and the church in such a scandal. I just don't believe he is a sex offender—and anyway, the church was probably helping him with costs or something to do with his drug problem. That's plausible."

Clay let the theory go, even as Leedra kept looking at Dexter, imploring him to see her reasoning. The information they all sought, he reminded himself, wasn't about Mr. Johnson's guilt or innocence but about Renee Carter and what might have happened to her.

"Just a couple more things. Mr. Johnson says that someone gave him the boxes of pictures by accident and that for some reason he couldn't return them."

"He what?" Dexter snapped.

Clay was patient. "That's what your father says: that the boxes were not his. It sounds like he was accidentally allowed in when the photo shoot was in session. Perhaps there were other girls there? He tells us he was supposed to receive a hefty supply of drugs in return for keeping quiet about whatever he saw that night."

This entire thing was just making him sad. Someone had to pay for all the pain suffered by so many people, Clay reflected, and frustratingly he still had no clue who. He wasn't even close.

"If my father says they switched the boxes on him, he could be telling the truth because he could not very well go back to them and say, 'Sorry but, uh, you guys gave me pornography instead of drugs—your bad,' now could he? He had to keep it even if it wasn't his," Dexter said clearly annoyed.

"Wait—that must be it!" Clay exclaimed. He stood up and pulled out his phone.

"What must be it?" Dexter asked, nonplussed.

"Your father wanted the drugs, of course, and he had driven away that night thinking he'd gotten them. After he left, maybe he became suspicious. Perhaps he discovered that he didn't have what he was supposed to have, or maybe he saw something that he shouldn't have while he was there. Anyway, for some reason or other he came back later and everyone was dead. In this other photo you gave the police, everyone is dead except you, Leedra, and one other boy—is that right?"

"I guess. None of us knew that other boy," Leedra replied. "He only came that summer. He'd been there that other summer, but he was older and could come and go as he pleased. That particular summer, he'd been there just a couple of weeks. I don't remember seeing him on that night, either. I only know that he had an after-school job. Oh, and he said he hated it in Virginia. I think his mom had died or something and he had been sent to live there with his aunt. I really don't know, though. I guess his aunt was my foster dad's wife? She was in on the entire thing. She used to make us pretty for the camera. She would comb our hair and spray us with this sweet floral perfume. I do remember the boy saying that he was gonna go back to California and be a military police officer."

"He did?" Dexter said.

"Something to do with the police, I don't know. Wear a badge around his neck and stick it in people's faces and tell them what to do."

Leedra shrugged her shoulders. "I wish I could remember his name, Daniel something. Danny Mandel . . ."

When Clay heard the name his mouth went dry. He carefully reviewed what she said.

Military police aspirations—only the man in question now dogged the military because he couldn't make the cut. From California. Moved to Virginia to live with his mom's sister . . .

Clay shook his head. It could not be possible that Danny Mandel could be Danny Manning, obsessed with this case and always looking through Clay's notes.

Leedra shrugged her shoulders. "Danny something, I can't remember. His name didn't match his aunt's. I didn't know her maiden name."

When Clay's phone rang, he stood up abruptly. He looked down at the table and picked it up, closing his folder of notes as he listened to the other end. He nodded and hung up.

"Is it time to go?" Leedra questioned, as Clay moved to the door.

"No, no . . . I—one sec," Clay said over his shoulder. He flipped his phone again and dialed another detective he could trust. If he was wrong this one time, it could have repercussions that could ruin the legitimacy of his entire career—not that it even mattered. Clay spoke quietly for a moment and he averted his eyes as Leedra and Dexter whispered inaudibly and exchanged nervous glances.

Clay hung up the phone and returned to stand by the table. He gathered up the other documents as his mind raced to put together all the missing pieces. "Mr. Parker, that uh, was the police chief's assistant. Your father has taken a turn and is on his way to the hospital."

As Leedra was about to ask more questions, Cashell popped her head around the door. "We're ready."

As they stood, Dexter moved to take Leedra's hand but she turned to him purposefully.

"Listen to me, this may be the last time you see your father." She laid her hands on his chest and moved closer. "Please go tell him that you believe him. It's probably the only opportunity you'll have left."

Dexter shook his head sadly. "It's too late."

"It's not. It's *not* too late."

Clay made for the door with his folder under his arm, noting the impatience on Cashell's face.

"You will never forgive yourself if you don't go see your father one last time. Please?"

Dexter sighed, then reluctantly followed Clay to the door. His hand kept her by his side. "Keep your eye on her, please, Detective Clay. Escort her to the Parker house after the conference, or call me. I should be able to be back not long after it's over. I won't stay gone long, okay?" He looked back at Leedra.

Clay nodded.

Cashell beckoned them a second time to come with her, more impatiently this time.

Leedra and Dexter had no time for a hug, but he did kiss her and then leave the room. Leedra knew he didn't want to and, truth be told, she didn't want him to leave, but he'd never forgive himself if his father died and he didn't say goodbye. It was more than she'd had with Renee.

She looked at Clay who seemed closed off since the discussion and the details about that night had stopped coming. But she walked down the hall and took the elevator, even as her nerves grew over the silence. Dexter would hold her hand, encourage her and remind her that everything was going to be all right. She pulled her arm away with a start when Clay touched her elbow. She turned and apologized to him.

He smiled but didn't comment. "I'm going to just say that since I mentioned the boy's name, or what I think is his name, you seem a little less talkative." Leedra said.

Clay nodded. The doors opened and they moved down the hall. "I think the person has been under my nose."

"What do you mean?

"My former partner—his name is Danny Manning."

Forced to face forward, the tension creeped to new heights and Leedra had no time to process what Clay was telling her or the impact that it made on everything she was about to share. Even though he couldn't know the reality of what he said, she began to strongly dislike him for keeping that, especially now that Dexter was not here with her. She didn't know if she could continue to trust him and was annoyed at herself for sending Dexter away. She wanted to ask him to explain as question after question began to press on her mind.

She couldn't think straight. She thought she'd faint as all the press people in the room, the camera operators with all equipment mounted on their shoulders turned and pointed toward her as she took her place among all the men in uniform. She and Cashell were the only females and she hated it. The flashing lights began to hurt her occipital lobe and to think, her nightmare was really only starting. Her autonomy would be gone for a very long time and her life would never be the same.

CHAPTER THIRTY-ONE:
PUBLIC STATEMENTS

STANDING AT THE FRONT OF the room, Leedra took a deep breath as she watched the throngs of people entering the room. She didn't know why she had assumed there would be a place she could sit down. She should have asked Cashell about that . . . but it was too late now.

When she pictured a press conference, she now realized she had been imagining the fun and glamorous kinds. NBA or NFL events, for example, where all the stars sat behind some elegant table with a microphone at every seat; or some curative event, perhaps, where they announced some major medical breakthrough and took non-threatening, nuanced questions about it from the press.

This wasn't that kind of press conference.

"Ladies and gentlemen, we have invited you here today to make public the information that Ms. Leedra Henderson and Evie Carter are one and the same person. Ms. Henderson was one of the little girls from the local murder case two decades ago. She changed her identity after bearing witness to the tragedy for personal protection and in order to resume a normal life. Our federal investigators are working with Ms. Henderson and her family to uncover more information about this case. Retired Detective Philip Clay is with us to contribute his experience as one of the first investigators called to that horrific scene back in the early nineties. Ms. Henderson asks for privacy at this time in order to let justice be realized. Thank you for coming. I'll take a few questions at this time."

A hand in the middle row shot up and a tall man in a sport coat stood. "Jackson White, *Daily News*. Does the slow progress on Ms. Henderson's case have anything to do with the most recent spate of kidnappings? Those are also moving slowly with little new information."

Cashell was unruffled. "We believe that if there is an internal slowdown of processing evidence, the department is aware of it and is handling it. As I mentioned, Detective Clay is partnering with us as an independent special consultant. He brings a wealth of knowledge and unique historical perspective, as far as the details of this case are concerned. His sole interest is the truth. Next question, please."

"Erica Leigh-Moncook, *Morning Report*. Will you confirm that Ms. Henderson is romantically involved with Doctor Dexter Parker? Wasn't he implicated in an awful incident three years ago where his wife was killed?"

Leedra shot daggers at the woman who posed the question. She disliked all of these people instantly. Vultures. She looked dead-on when any of them caught her eye. Again, Cashell fielded the question without hesitation.

"Dr. Parker was never charged with anything relating to his wife's death. His personal relationships are of no concern to anyone, least of all to this investigation."

Leedra watched the rapid-fire exchanges, her mind whirling as she grew increasingly uncomfortable. These questions, the very ones she'd dreaded, vindicated her decision that Dexter should not to be present. These were personal attacks and she was relieved he was not there. She hoped her face appeared coolly engaged, rather than betraying her intimidation in the face of these aggressive questions and Cashell's lightning-quick responses. Now, Cashell was addressing the room again.

"Detective Clay will now speak briefly about some case-specific details."

"We have some new evidence and we will be pursuing those leads," Clay spoke up. "We also have several witnesses whose stories we are following up. If we uncover any new information, we will make those details public when they are appropriate—so long as they pose no danger to the delicate aspects of this case. Thank you."

Leedra had a headache. The event was finally over. Clay stuck close to her as she was ushered out of the room. She was relieved that all she had to do was show her face. While painful, she hadn't had to say anything.

Her uneasiness at his earlier revelation did not put her at ease. Soon, they were directed to return to the small conference room further down the hall where they would await further instructions and the press's exit. Although she had told Dexter to go see his father, she now wished he'd hurry and return.

The Chief entered the room, closing the door behind him, and sat down. "Chief Washington," he said, by way of introduction. He shook Leedra's hand and then Clay's. The two men sat down and Leedra, realizing they weren't leaving yet, followed suit.

"Ms. Henderson, you did well out there. First, I want to apologize for the lengthy delay in getting all this information together on your case. We now have the address of the home you were in as a child. It had been removed from the records, so we've only been able to locate it recently. We will be sending some deputies over there very soon with a warrant to search the premises. We'd like to do some digging and see what we can find."

Leedra sat up, amazed to hear the first genuinely new information that had come up during this entire ordeal. "Do you have reason to believe Renee is buried there?" she asked quickly.

"We are unsure about that part, but we do have a bit more news as well. One of our detectives currently resides at this same place. Ms. Henderson, does the name Danny Manning ring any bells? We are waiting for an age-progression photo of the boy in the photo you provided."

"That sounds familiar . . . I, I just told Detective Clay that it sounded like his name was Daniel something. I don't remember the woman's name—that would be Daniel's aunt?"

The Chief nodded.

Leedra exhaled. "How did my foster father die?"

"Drug overdose, but we don't know for sure if it was self-administered or if someone might have helped it along."

"Who do you suspect would have helped?"

"The boy in the photo."

"Daniel? But I thought he was only sixteen."

"It's not impossible," Clay interjected.

"But what about—you said he works for the department?" She shook her head and could not believe what she was hearing. The Chief continued, "Do you remember if your foster father asked any of you to, ah, prepare anything for him?"

"I made things often. I cooked for them, ensured the girls ate. I was the oldest."

"I mean, did you prepare any drugs for him?"

Leedra was somewhat taken aback. "No, I never did that. I would bring him a glass of water so he could take pills, but I didn't actually dispense the drugs. There were loose drugs around the place, small bags of powder, and then there were lots of prescription bottles and pills . . . packed into different boxes."

Leedra sat back when there was a pause in the questions. She was relieved to finally be making progress. All the information she'd given the other detectives had come to naught, after she'd sat there for hours answering the same questions over and over. She wanted it all to be out in the open, but at the same time she was irritated at being forced to relive something that should have been recorded correctly the first time. She really wished Dexter were there. It was even harder going through all this without him and she was exhausted.

She turned to Clay. While he had initially exuded a reassuring calmness, he now seemed nervous and on edge.

"I'd like to go now, please. Can we go? What are we waiting for?" she asked.

"All right, that's fine. Uh, let's go." Clay stood, pushing open the door for her.

In the hallway, Leedra spotted Cashell and tried to warm a friendly smile.

"You did good!"

Leedra shook her head. "I didn't do anything. *You* did great I just stood there dumbfounded by the entire thing. Thank you, Cashell. Thank you for your help. Dexter and I will be in touch with you. I hope we don't have to do this again, but if we ever do, can we call on you?"

"Sure. It's good to have consistency," Cashell replied. "Uh, Leedra?"

Leedra stopped and looked at Cashell. For the first time since they'd met, the striking woman before her wasn't press commander-in-chief. They were just two women concerned about the same man.

"Take care of Dexter, will you—please?"

"I will. I love him so much."

"Gee, I know that."

Leedra laughed and hugged her. She waved goodbye and let Detective Clay lead her into the elevator that took them several floors before opening up to the parking garage. Relief flooded over her at the thought of getting out of there as the two of them walked to the car. Leedra still felt jittery. She was thankful no members of the press were in sight.

Although Clay moved purposefully, as if he knew exactly where his car was, she wondered if he might have forgotten where he parked. She didn't question him and stayed steadily at his side. The garage was somewhat dim, though it was only late afternoon. Cracks of sunlight helped to otherwise illuminate the dark garage.

The next moment, she heard the screeching of tires. A black car rounded the corner, tires skidding and bright piercing lights headed straight toward them. The noise of the car's engine roared, only made more deafening as it bounced off the walls of the cavernous building. Before she could react, Clay pushed her from its path and she fell to the ground hard, her head narrowly missing a car's bumper. She lifted her head just in time to see the black car pick up speed and hit Clay from behind. It sent him flying and he landed on another car, crushing the roof and not moving. Leedra stood on wobbly legs. Her knees, skinned bare, were oozing blood. Before she knew what was happening, she started off at a run, first wanting to help Clay, but the car was moving back toward her. Stunned, she took off for the elevator. The car suddenly stopped, a door was flung open she heard the heavy footsteps thud closer to her.

She ran blindly, trying desperately to think of an escape, even as the door to the elevator would never open fast enough for her to escape and the only thing she could think of was to scream. She grabbed her phone from her purse and shoved it down her cleavage before flinging the bag deliberately to the ground, in the vain hope that he hadn't seen her take anything from it. She looked back and caught a fleeting glimpse of a man, but his face was covered. She saw a black gloved hand before something blunt hit her in the head, knocking her to the ground where everything went dark.

CHAPTER THIRTY-TWO:
CRYSTALS CLEAR

"WAKE UP, LITTLE EVIE, WAKE up!" Danny sang. You like the song I made up for you? How's it going, girl? Look at you, all grown now! But you didn't learn any lessons. You're still stirring up all sorts of trouble and stuff."

Head throbbing, Leedra's eyes adjusted to the darkness.

"Please." Her throat was sore, likely from her screaming. She felt dizzy, but was lucid enough to see the man before her.

"You left these the last time you were here."

He moved to put a pair of slightly bent glasses on her face, but she shook her head away from him. When she tried to sit up, she fell backwards. Her arms, she realized, were bound at her back. "I can see, thank you. I got some contacts."

"Oh! Well, aren't you fancy?"

"Are you Daniel? Weren't you my former foster brother?" Leedra tried to keep her voice steady.

"Something like that. I told you I was going to become a cop, didn't I? Nothing was going to stop me. Not even you and your little boyfriend. You two had your goals, and I had mine."

"Why did you even concern yourself with us? We didn't do anything to you."

"That's where you're wrong. I was stuck in this stupid hellhole with my aunt's stupid husband and all you stupid, stupid kids. You made my life such a drag. Then there was him. Always drinking and carrying on and partying—all the drugs . . . And I didn't kill him, by the way: he overdosed. I just provided a little more than usual and let nature take its course. You shouldn't mix drugs and he was ordering from different places—you don't know what you're getting when you do that. Those people are liable to give you anything."

Leedra was appalled as well as sad. She wasn't being told all of his past deeds so she could make an accurate statement to the officials. She knew that. She also knew she might never see Dexter again. She wanted to cry.

"Why did you kill the other girls?"

"Well, the head of the house was dead, and then my stupid aunt went batty and she took the drugs too. And then I was like, well what's a couple more? I started a porno ring of my own. Only then there were too many people to split it with, so they had to go too. I couldn't sell the girls in that porn ring: I was too young. They didn't trust me at first, so I had to go build my credentials. I did that in California after I got rid of those girls. I stepped up into the role my uncle was too strung-out to fill. I continued the ring—*I* kept it afloat. As a police officer, I had all sorts of access to the kids that kept getting in trouble—the vulnerable ones, you know. Even though I hated Virginia, I did like being this close to the capital. There really is too much shooting in some of those other places, but this is a nice area where lots of kids have too much money and not enough discipline. A job right in D.C., our nation's capital? Who wouldn't jump at that chance? Except for Santa Claus—you know he just had to interrupt the process."

Leedra listened in shock as the man before her ranted and babbled. Although she'd known him before, albeit briefly, she had no idea he was this crazy. She'd never met anyone as mentally ill as this. The truly chilling part was that he told her everything as if he were relaying the latest weather report. His reasoning for his actions and career aspirations was so detached and matter-of-fact as to almost sound logical. Murderers and porn dealers had goals too, she supposed.

"Look, I got my life together now, okay?" Danny continued brightly. "I haven't killed a single person since then. That's pretty good, isn't it?

Oh, except for Clay earlier today. Stupid cop. He couldn't solve *Who Framed Roger Rabbit* . . . Twenty-five years I put up with that dufus. That was just a way to get out of the mess."

He sat Indian-style across from her, twirling a pocketknife in his fingers. All of her knowledge of tactical psychology went out the window and suddenly she was hard-pressed to remember ways to get a person to keep talking. The few police shows she'd ever watched just ended with the victim being killed, which wasn't comforting. And how much more information was there to be had, anyway? He'd spilled all the beans the moment she woke up. It was like he couldn't wait to tell her.

Leedra looked down. She couldn't throw in the towel: not now. Finally, finally, she had the truth: that was what she sought. Now that she had it at last, she realized with a chill, that it didn't make her feel any better.

"Where is Renee buried?" she asked numbly.

"Oh, she's around here somewhere. Why? You want to be next to her? Well, I can't really do that darlin'. I put a big shed right on top of her. They didn't even look back there. Investigators are so lazy, so horrified by the scene, their stomachs couldn't take it." He mocked. "I would have buried all of you, but I couldn't afford this rundown house, had to wait until it went up for sale again which didn't take long once the story about what happened here got out. Sent value way down. Good for me. The shed is not far from here, though."

Leedra looked at him. Her anger made her ill, and she wanted to throw up. She swallowed several times, the saliva diluting the acid in the back of her throat. "Why did you kill them?"

"I told you—people were dead and those little girls were crying. It was stressing me out. I hated them. I hated you! I didn't have any milk or cereal, or anything because of all of you. You all took everything away from me and you weren't even of any blood relation. I got the girls out of people's hair once and for all. No more whining. I was almost done, was just getting to you when Santa came back in. He was high as a kite. Dummy."

"I tried to stretch the girl's food. I put water in their cereal so everyone would have some. I tried," Leedra found herself saying apologetically.

"Yeah well, that sounds disgusting. Who does that? Water? Yuck. And people think I'm weird."

Leedra stopped talking, defeated. This is what the truth had gotten her: bound up in the basement with a crazy man. *No, thank you.*

She needed encouragement. Resolve. *Think of something positive.* What encouraged her right then was thinking about Dexter and Kira and the hope of building a family. She wanted to see Allontis's baby. She wanted to take care of them all and to be a part of something wonderful, however she could.

"So . . . y-you would have killed me if it weren't for him, Mr. Johnson-Santa Claus . . . coming back . . . that night?" she whispered.

He looked at her as if exasperated by her slowness in putting it all together. "Yeah, Santa Claus, the dummy. High as a kite that night, I gave him some boxes and told him to leave us alone, but he wouldn't. He hid you from me so I couldn't find you. I would have buried everyone, if I had more time or just set the place on fire and ran away . . . and you know what, he was actually helping me before he sobered up . . . stupid fool? So, yes, yes," he spat. Leedra reared back crushing her wrist and fingers as he lunged in her face.

"The plan was, and still is, to kill you. As soon as I get done doing that, I'm gonna kill your stupid little, meddlin' boyfriend, too."

CHAPTER THIRTY-THREE:
MISSING 2.0

DEXTER SAT BY HIS FATHER'S bedside with his phone in one hand and his father's hand in the other. His father's voice was low and gravelly. No matter how many times Dexter saw someone close to death—and in his profession, he saw it weekly—he never got used to it.

"I couldn't be sure if that boy had done it or not. I didn't see him much. I wouldn't believe he'd do something like that . . . he begged me to help him, and I didn't want to cast accusations, if it turned out he didn't do it. I could have ruined his whole life, and I just wasn't a hundred percent sure. Later, he told me he'd made it to California, that he was a cop—that he'd escaped that awful life. I believed him. I thought he deserved a second chance. I didn't know."

Dexter nodded. He tried to show his father patience in these final moments. It wasn't in his nature to be unkind, no matter how wrong his father had been. He had Leedra back now, after all these years of time, distance, life's hurdles and roadblocks: that was all that mattered. If his father was or wasn't actually a sex offender, what difference did it make now? It wouldn't give either of them back the time they had lost. It might have convinced Dexter to let the old man see his grand-daughter—which he was considering doing in these final hours—. He was only here because Leedra had told him to visit, he reminded himself. He had to forgive, and dredging up the past solved nothing.

"Dad, I'm gonna see if I can get Kira here to say goodbye to you, okay?"

"That would be nice, but I know you want to protect her, son. You're a good father—you're a good boy."

"You were a good dad. Why didn't you ever tell me you were playing Santa Claus in that house?"

"Oh, I couldn't tell you. Them nice church people would have gotten in trouble for letting me do it—but that way I got to see you, didn't I? I thought that was pretty clever, huh?" Garrison attempted a weak smile.

Dexter nodded, fighting tears. When his father started to cough, he handed him the water and helped him sip through the straw. When he finished, his father patted his hand.

"Thanks. My time is drawing near, son. I love you."

Dexter nodded. "I love you, too," he spoke quietly. His father closed his eyes calmly, his breathing now even and unhindered. Dexter stepped from the room, his eyes adjusting to the brighter lights overhead. This was a different hospital, D.C.'s George Washington University Medical Center, closer to the federal facility his father had been held at. As such, everything around him was unfamiliar, and he was easily turned around. Eventually, down the hall, he stumbled upon the waiting area and stopped. It was dead quiet and all eyes were riveted to the television mounted in the corner, so he looked up at it too.

The bottom fell out of his world when a snippet of grainy surveillance footage showed Clay and Leedra. He watched in horror as a car hit Clay at breakneck speed and sent him flying, before the driver appeared to chase Leedra down on foot. Then, the camera flicked automatically to another angle, showing nothing except the same car speeding out of the garage. The pictured flipped to earlier footage of the news conference and Dexter felt fear consume him.

Search for Missing Evie Carter, again? The perpetual news ticker scrolled at the bottom of the screen.

Dexter ran out of the hospital and leapt into his SUV. He could be home in about twenty minutes if there was no traffic, but that was never the case. As he clicked his seat belt belatedly, he put his phone in the holder on the dash and instructed for it to call Cole. When nobody picked up, he called the Chief of Police.

Leedra awoke again, still in darkness. She suspected that she had only been alone for a few hours, but of course when one was bound up in the dark, it felt like forever. It had to be dinnertime right about now because thoughts of Dexter's omelets and a pot of hot buttered grits had her mind, despite everything else whirling inside at that moment. *Kill your meddling boyfriend too.*

The words Danny had said played over and over, and her heart quickened with renewed determination. She looked around and managed to scoot herself back far enough to lean against something before passing out. When she came to again, she saw her old glasses glinting nearby in the sliver of weak sunlight filtering into the gloom. Most of the day must've passed.

She'd seen enough television to catch a few episodes of MacGyver as a child. Taking a leaf from the show, she bent down to retrieve the glasses with her teeth, but stopped when she realized she could just scoot around and grab them with her bound hands. Working mostly by feel, she bent the wire frame, popped out the lenses and snapped them, sucking in her breath as she felt a sharp glass shard scrape her skin. She turned the shard over and began a small but steady sawing motion back and forth between the zip tie cables. When her hand seized up from the repetition, she rested and started again, trying to keep her sawing concentrated on the same small section with increasing pressure. She was relieved to feel the ties loosen slightly, and at last the restraints broke and slipped off her raw wrists.

She remembered that her phone was still in her bosom. It was likely off, because in the press conference she hadn't wanted it to start beeping. That seemed like a million years ago. Swiftly, she reached into her top. Rather than risk making the noise of a phone call, she texted 9-1-1: a handy tip she'd learned from the abused women at the

Anchored Center. She hit send and put the phone quickly behind her just as the door opened.

Danny came down the steps with a bottle of water. She put her hands behind her and scooted back against the wall, hoping he couldn't see the light from the phone or her unbound hands. For once, she was actually grateful for the coverage of her plump derriere.

He held the bottle to her lips and she gulped it, some of the water spilling down her shirt as she exaggerated the pretense of still being immobilized. She couldn't be sure something wasn't in the water, even though he'd opened it in front of her, but she thanked him nonetheless.

When he pulled out a small compact, she looked at him.   She hadn't expected he would kill her with an overdose but she should have guessed: it was less messy. He was too cowardly to deal with any blood and gore, she was certain. He didn't have it in him to butcher, nor to shoot.

"Let's see, the blue pill mixed with this white pill will make your heart accelerate," the deranged man said. "You'll be dehydrated, but you should pass out pretty quickly. Now, these are nasty tasting and you have to take like 100 of them according to the online reviews, but I can pop them in your mouth for you. I brought you something to wash it down."

He held out a can with the word "Margarita" on it.

"Who knew margaritas came in cans these days? So clever."

Danny turned to put the compact full of pills on the floor. As he turned back to her, Leedra reared up on her knees and managed to shove the thin wire frame, as hard as she could into his side. He staggered back, stunned, with a look of disbelief and puzzlement.

Wasting no time, Leedra sprang up the steps—but the door was locked and wouldn't budge for all her shoving. She kicked and screamed, then looked in vain for something hard to beat it down with. She must have hit a main artery: Danny wasn't getting up. Blood was starting to wet the front of his shirt, and he was coughing.

She didn't want to watch him die or be stuck there with him until help arrived. She wanted to see if she could pick the lock with any part of the broken glasses, a piece of wire or something. To do that, though, she'd have to go back over to his slumped form. Warily, she picked up a broom and moved down the steps. He lunged for her with what little power he had left, but she dodged. It sounded as if he were gasping for breath as he wheezed.

"I should have killed you in your sleep. I should have killed you when you and that girl were here months ago," Danny growled, wincing in pain. Leedra looked at him with contempt. She looked around, trying to remember if they had been there or somewhere else entirely. The glasses had to mean she was there. She dismissed it—it didn't matter since she wasn't going to be there much longer, and she'd never be coming back.

"You're just a coward. You hide behind the law. Isn't that why no one could find the kidnappers—because *you* did it? Right under everyone's noses? Moving evidence, rewriting information so that it led in circles, creating wild goose chases . . . How many other children have been forever lost because you hindered their progress at every turn?"

Leedra wanted to scream. "I'll spend the rest of my life untangling your messes," she said. "and I'll get justice for all the families you've grieved." She understood all of it now. He probably had a ring of people, inside and out of the police force. It almost certainly didn't stop with him: it was likely a system-wide affair. Taking down one person in something like that was like putting out the fire in just one room of a burning house. She felt sick.

She gripped the broom more tightly, marched over to him and without hesitation swung it hard against his leg. He cried out in pain. She lifted it and swung it against his other leg before seizing her phone, calling 9-1-1 this time. She saw something shiny Danny had been holding skitter across the floor: the key! She reached for it as Danny howled and tried to reach out to massage his injured legs. As wicked and crazed as he was, his cries brought her no satisfaction.

Finally, *finally*, she heard sirens in the distance. Once she wrenched open the door, she tore up yet more stairs and through the house, the place that had claimed the lives of her sister and the other girls. Tears blinded her, but she kept running, her only mission to leave that terrible place for the very last time.

With a sudden burst of superhuman strength, Leedra wrenched all four locks off the rotting front door to shove her way through it, tumbling straight through the screen door to the ground. She picked herself up and, when she saw Dexter running to meet her, scrambled up and into his arms.

CHAPTER THIRTY-FOUR:
LETTING GO

INSIDE THE AMBULANCE, DEXTER HELPED the paramedic attend to Leedra's injuries. Picking shards of glass out of her arm, he looked with concern into her glazed eyes. "I'm worried about shock," he told the paramedic who was applying salve to the cuts she'd sustained from her exit through the fiberglass screen door. Despite the minor injuries, Dexter saw with a flood of relief that Leedra was going to be okay, although he didn't know what had happened in the house. He couldn't believe the place had been occupied by anyone.

Leedra sat in the ambulance, coherent but in shock.

"Is your father still . . .? How is Detective Clay?"

"Clay is, uh, pretty banged up, but he . . . should be all right," Dexter lied, avoiding her gaze. He didn't want to cause her any more stress by telling her that the detective had suffered a broken leg and that even with rehabilitation for his physical injuries, he'd also sustained a neck and brain injury. He could understand her concern about Detective Clay, but he was appalled that she would ask about Garrison after all that had transpired. Leedra noticed his hesitation.

"You have to forgive him, Dex. He's not the awful person you think. He made a mistake. It's eating me alive."

Dexter kept rubbing her back, motioning to the paramedic to pass him the bedpan on a nearby shelf. He was encouraging her to let go of what she was holding onto both physically and figuratively. The medic's purple-gloved fingers fumbled with the plastic packaging and barely got it out before she grabbed it from him and threw up into it.

"I'm sorry—I'm sorry," she gasped.

"It's okay. It happens a lot," the paramedic said shrugging. He disposed of it and put on fresh gloves, opened another one and set it on her lap. "Just in case," he said. Leedra nodded and leaned back, drained.

Dexter wiped her mouth and nose. "You feel better now?" He smirked, realizing that sounded a little silly, but she managed to nod.

"I have to tell you something," she breathed.

"It can wait."

"No, it can't," she insisted.

"Are we ready to go?" Another paramedic stood just outside, nodded and slammed the door. The vehicle started, and they belted Leedra onto the stretcher as they began moving. Dexter remained standing beside her, holding her hand. He leaned against the gurney and grabbed one of the rails as the vehicle jostled them around.

"What about the . . . other guy in the basement?" Leedra asked the paramedic.

The man simply shrugged. "He had a bunch of pills beside him. They're calling the coroner. He'd already taken most of them by the time we got to him, from what it looked like . . ." Dexter shook his head as the paramedic looked him.

"What about the stab wound? I stabbed him," Leedra blurted out.

"Ma'am, I saw a small wound to his abdomen, but that wouldn't have been enough to kill him. It probably hurt a lot because it looked like it was near one of his lungs. It even rendered him immobile, maybe, but it didn't kill him. He was foaming at the . . ."

"Ahem," Dexter said in warning.

"Oh, uh, sorry man. You didn't kill him, ma'am. He took the drugs, by himself."

Leedra nodded and lay back on the gurney. Dexter held her a little tighter. His mouth hovered above her ear as he spoke softly: "You didn't kill him, okay. He did it—he did all of this to himself. You understand? And even if you had killed him, you would have been absolutely justified."

A part of Dexter wanted to have been the one to make Danny pay.

However wrong and un-Christian that feeling was, it was undeniable. He'd lost so much. She'd lost so much—and for what? For the crazed killer to escape the justice he deserved? None of his victims could be brought back to life—and then there were all the broken homes, lives, other people, even Detective Clay. The man should have paid dearly for all the irreparable loss he had caused, both now and then.

"Dexter, I have a headache."

"Do you want some aspirin?"

She shook her head.

"Don't talk. We can talk later. Just rest."

"I want you to really forgive him, Dex—for you."

Dexter nodded. He knew that answering with a glib "okay" or "fine" wouldn't appease her. After thinking about everything so hard over the last few days, he knew deep down that she was right.

"Your father? He's still alive, and he wants you to forgive him so badly. You have to forgive Danny, even. He lost something too—he lost his foundation. All this is eating at you, Dex, like it did me. It's like a canker sore. I have the answers I sought, and I'm not any better."

Leedra started to cry and Dexter wrapped his arms around her. Her pain hurt his heart and brought tears to his own eyes. "He told me Renee was buried under the shed, so they will find her remains—but no one will be any better. I won't be better," she repeated, sobbing.

"But you made sure it ended," Dexter reminded her softly. "He can't hurt any more children, and the investigation continues; they'll probably find more of his operatives, and that's really good ..."

"But I don't *feel* any better. All the anger and hurt I feel is stifling. It's kept me from living, from loving you."

Dexter held her tighter. There wasn't anything that could be done, and he was deeply saddened by that.

The longer he held her and really listened to what she was saying, the clearer he understood what she was telling him to do.

It was hard to forgive, so he was resisting it. His brain hurt just thinking about it. Anyone could have gone through the motions of taking care of his father, he ruminated. Paying his bills and ensuring he had the things he needed were all just little things that made Dexter feel better about himself. It hadn't been about his father at all; it wasn't real love. It was obligation.

Dexter was loath to admit the mistake he'd made—that his father just had a real drug problem, maybe even curable with real love and time. Maybe he wasn't the perverted monster he'd believed him to be for so long. He failure to distinguish Garrison Johnson from his associates had cost his father a relationship with his precious granddaughter. He'd simply come in to get his drugs and got tangled in a horrible mess of much bigger proportions. He'd suspected the terrible thing that Danny had done, but he'd wanted to give a struggling sixteen-year-old a chance.

At heart, Dexter knew it had been easier for him to lump them all together because that meant he didn't have to dig deeper for the good in his father, or in anyone for that matter. And no one had ever asked him to, until now. His father had saved one little girl that fateful night, even when he couldn't save the others. *He saved her.* Despite everything else, Dexter had to remember that. If it hadn't been for Garrison Johnson, Leedra would be dead too. He squeezed his eyes shut at the thoughts.

A little tired himself, Dexter moved Leedra over just a bit to cradle her more securely in his arms and to prop his hip on the bed.

He simply listened as she talked and held her while she cried, absorbing all the information so he could shield her from the police when they came later with their inevitable, redundant questions. She knew what happened now, so she might finally be able to enjoy real rest in the freedom of the truth.

Would Dexter rest when his father died, or would he be eternally angry over the lost opportunities? He kissed her forehead and whispered how much he loved her, assuring her that he'd be there for her forever and take care of her. Meanwhile, he began to search every repressed nook of his soul that might hold even a small amount of love for his father. He prayed hard, asking for God's strength to find the right words to bring peace and comfort to Garrison as he passed on—if he was still around when Dexter got to him. For once, Dexter actually wanted more time with him, and that had to mean something.

CHAPTER THIRTY-FIVE:
PARTING FAREWELL

SEVERAL DAYS LATER, GARRISON JOHNSON passed on. In that short span of time before he left, Leedra got along without Dexter as he tried to build a relationship that was almost forty years overdue, with his father. Regardless of the short amount of time left to do so, his effort made her smile.

Leedra herself had spent a little time chatting with the old man and was glad she'd had the chance to know more about him. Most of all, she was elated that Dexter finally let his father meet Kira. As if Garrison had been holding on just for the opportunity to meet her, he went to be with the Lord just hours after the little girl left his bedside. Once he'd had those first precious moments with his granddaughter, it seemed, he was free.

For now, Leedra worked on her grief daily. With Dexter's urging, she had regular appointments with a counselor and was working through her stages: the delayed grief, the mostly distant anger that still reared its head daily, and the occasional desire just to tune out and wallow in the overwhelming sadness and pain of her loss. Every step of the way, however, Dexter was there. He held her hand and comforted her, and she hoped she was doing an equally good job in comforting him over his father's passing. Life had to go on.

Back at Dexter's house, the family had come together to watch football. Leedra was listening to Kira, who was sitting on the floor at her feet. She smiled and gave the little girl her attention while taking in just how fast she was growing. Allontis was getting stronger with child and was free to move around their home without being confined to her own home and her bedroom.

Allontis made her tea and wordlessly hugged Leedra at regularly, nervous and unsure about what to say or do. Leedra began to look on her more fondly, and enjoyed having another female so attentive and close by.

"He's the number fourteen," Kira continued excitedly. "The quarterback! ESPN says he has a really good arm and that he's been flying under the radar . . ."

Leedra smiled down at the child who sat at her feet. She tried to listen as Kira ran on about her Uncle James, Dexter's youngest adopted brother, who Leedra had yet to meet.

"Kira, baby?" Dexter said softly.

When Kira got the hint to stop talking, she smiled sheepishly and scooted back around to the blanket with the other children and focused her attention on the television. She made eye contact with Leedra and pulled a funny face. Their silent communication continued every day, and they made funny little mime-messages when Dexter wasn't looking.

Leedra's eyes met Dexter's in silent thanks for knowing she needed rescue. Although Kira's babbling got to be a little much at times, she appreciated the child's willingness to engage her by telling her stories and keep her mind off her personal woes.

She continued to stare at Dexter until he winked at her, at which point she pretended to look back down at the open book in her lap. Having yet to read a single word, she stared unseeing at blur of text in front of her eyes.

Dexter held his nephew, Jacoby, in his arms. Although he was also trying to watch the game, he looked back at her, as he did often, silently checking in to make sure she was all right. She smiled at him assuredly. His love, time and energy had been the only things that had gotten her through the last few months. He'd given her a life to participate in and a family to care about. An anchor. They went to church together and did activities with Kira over the weekend.

Leedra liked their version of family so much, she was starting to hope that she could be a permanent fixture.

Dexter's other adopted brother, Adrian, was sprawled on another sofa in front of the television with his girlfriend. The kids—Hannah, Kira and Adrian's girlfriend's son—were playing on a blanket. Everyone was well fed and snacks and soda were passed around as they enjoyed the game.

Leedra sat back in contentment. Cole had made Sunday evening dinner for everyone just a few hours ago, and Leedra had enjoyed the calm and the quiet.

Eventually, on some random weeknight, in the not-too-distant future she looked forward to cooking for Dexter and Kira and enjoying just the three of them together like a family.

Leedra knew Allontis would be ecstatic to hear that Leedra's heart was moving forward to embrace the notion of a forever kind of family and permanence. It amazed her to think about no more running and making things work with these people in this very special house, just like Allontis had begged her to think about several months ago.

You wanna be a wife.

Her back went ramrod straight at the silent thought and the book she'd been holding sprang off her lap and onto the floor. She would have laughed out loud at that, but she didn't want to alarm anyone: she was actually feeling pretty good of late. *Wifely* was another realm altogether, though, and it would take time to think about that moniker as one of her many titles.

"Just gonna sit on the back porch for a bit," she whispered to Dexter. She stood, retrieving the book and placing it in the chair. Dexter's hand shot out and touched her hip as she passed him. That was another thing she was getting used to, and even liked: the intimate touches and caresses. Not pushy or suggestive, just there to hold, support, massage. She liked that part a lot. She smiled down at him as she passed and touched the baby's head, who wriggled away from her hand, laughing at this fun game. When Dexter began to hand the child over to his brother, ready to get up and join her, she shook her head gently and put a hand on his arm. "I'm fine. Just going outside.

I'll be back." She indicated the door to reassure him that it wasn't far and that she would be all right.

Outside, the evening fall sky was darkening even earlier than just the night before. Four o'clock felt more like six, and the skyline dimmed with every passing moment.

Leedra looked out at the vast yard of Dexter Parker's home, where she'd been almost every day for the last month. She was "coming along." That was the only phrase she had to describe how she felt. Shortly after Danny Manning's death, they'd found the remains of her sister in the back yard of that dreadful house. They'd planned a small service for Renee, which had been sparsely attended but quiet, serene and peaceful: a final gesture that comforted Leedra immeasurably. At last, her sister was at peace.

When Dexter's father had passed, everyone had said their own private goodbyes and Leedra had been there to witness the way Dexter finally let it all go. She smiled at the memory of Kira lying on her grandfather's chest during their short, first and consequently, last visit. From where Leedra stood, it looked like that was all the old man had been waiting for: to see his only grandchild before he left the earth. It was that single thing, that tender image, that gave her the comfort she needed.

She was moving along with her life. She still needed occasional moments away from all the happiness one could stand inside those sweet walls, but she was slowly integrating herself into the family life she hadn't realized she longed for. Dexter didn't rush her. The past would always be in the back of her mind, but finally she was getting closer to real happiness.

She had the truth, and out of that crazy experience, she'd also gotten a wonderful man. The love he exhibited for her continued to surprise and somewhat terrify her. He was attentive and made sure everything she needed was taken care of. She was relieved that she didn't have to be in charge of anything. The media attention had died down and Leedra was moving on.

Now she had to decide what to do with herself and her life. She wanted purpose. She loved the staff and the women at the shelter, but she couldn't shake the temptation to quit. She didn't want to be ungrateful to Allontis, although she knew Allontis likely wouldn't think that. Leedra was also wary of moving too fast, for fear she might make a move too quickly. Whatever her choices, she wanted them to be made for the right reasons. Even in the last weeks, it had cost her some willpower not to run back to Africa, ask for her old job back and rejoin the Mercy Ship she'd left earlier that year. The thought of the salt air and the sea had her feeling nauseous, though, so she quickly squashed that notion. More to the point, she'd be leaving the man she loved and his precious daughter. Her heart had found a home. She was still adjusting to the attention, but she was resolute that she wanted her new life to start there. She had to be patient— that's what she kept telling herself, as all her wounds continued to heal and as she showed the man she loved that she truly wanted to be with him and his whole family.

At her back, she heard the door open and close and felt a pair of arms wrap around her. She knew instantly who had come to see her.

"I told you I'm all right," she said, laughing. "You don't believe me?"

"I believe everything you say," Dexter answered. "It's just that 'I'm all right' can mean all sorts of different things, and they all have the word Dexter on the end. I'm all right, but I need a hug, Dexter. I'm all right, but I need a kiss, Dexter. I'm all right, but I want you, Dexter."

"Have you always been so sure of yourself?" she retorted, smiling. She did like it when he came to check on her. He kissed her and hugged her at all the right times, and she savored every "Leedra-break" he took.

"Never," he responded, his eyes serious. "You make me uncertain all the time. I want to impress upon you, but I don't want to press you."

Leedra turned from looking out on the evening sky, "I'm fine. Thank you for being so patient. I don't want to come off as too needy or anything."

"You come off however you'd like. I *want* you to need me."

"I do need you, so much . . . But you know what I mean—needing you, rather than a kind of stifling dependence on you."

"Can I depend on you?" Dexter asked sternly.

"Of course you can. I would—"

"Do whatever you could to help me?" Dexter finished.

Leedra smiled and bit her lip. "Very funny."

"I like that phrase—'stifling dependence,'" echoed Dexter. "Sounds like a self-help book you should write."

"Funny you should say that. I'd love to write a book someday. Writing is so wonderful and cathartic. The psychologist seems to think that the journaling is really helping my progress. Lately, though, I've been thinking about what I really want to do in the nine-to-five department—once Allontis has the baby and returns to the office."

"I was thinking about that too."

"Really? Why would you be thinking about that? Don't you have enough to worry about as it is?"

"You and Ms. Kira are my top priorities. There is nothing else to think about."

Leedra leaned back into him further. She turned in his arms, and her hands went up around his neck.

"I've been thinking that perhaps you'd like to work more closely with families? Something around child psychology would suit you, if you feel it wouldn't be too emotionally taxing."

Leedra paused. That sounded like fun. She hadn't really thought about that as an option per se, but she had been contemplating the fact that working at the Center didn't give her a connection to the women and their children on the more essential levels. She was, in essence, just ensuring that they had somewhere to stay, that the doors remained open, the board met and had oversight, and the staff were paid fairly and arrived on time to do their jobs. All of that was important, of course—without her work there would be no place to house them at all—but recently she'd just felt as though she wasn't *helping* them in the truest sense of the word. She didn't listen to them as they worked through their deepest and most personal issues and overcame their individual tragedies. She actually felt sort of perked up by the suggestion alone.

"How do you discern things so well?" she asked him with a grin. His insight truly amazed her.

"When you want to know someone intimately, you want to find out everything you possibly can about what they want, like and need."

The idea he had mentioned appealed to her. She was touched by him noticing that her current job somehow wasn't as heart-stirring as it should have been.

"How much you want to know scares me. How much you *already* know renders me speechless."

"You don't have to work," Dexter said, out of the blue. "You do know that, don't you? Lord knows the psychologist that saw Kira costs a pretty penny, but working doesn't have to be a priority for you, nor is it a requirement. I want to make that clear."

Dexter leaned back and held her eyes. His hand traveled up her arm, took her hand and placed it on his chest.

Leedra smiled, scrutinizing him closely. This mention of new possibilities was already pushing the woes she'd brought outside with her, to the back of her mind.

"But I don't want to ask you to move too fast." Dexter's face was serious.

She nodded reflectively. Allontis and all the women at the shelter were truly wonderful, but Allontis would be returning to work after the baby came and she didn't really need Leedra, except perhaps for peace of mind. The Center was Allontis's passion and it showed.

"You know I want to work, I mean..."

"And that's fine. I just want you know that you don't *have* to. Hey, I heard that some places are even using that new app Pokémon Go to search for missing children now. They're doing some really innovative and exciting things in the field. Perhaps you'd like to work on something like that instead?"

"I do—that sounds exciting. But I don't want to tell Allontis I'm quitting. I think she believes I'll stay on there with her long after she returns. That we might . . . might save our little corner of the world for women—you know, together."

Dexter nodded. "You need to get one thing straight, Leedra: Allontis doesn't hold grudges, especially not against her close friends and family. She wants you to be happy—to find love."

"I found it, and it's overwhelming. It scares me."

"Doctors recommend small doses until you get used to it," Dexter smiled.

"I don't want to hurt her feelings. I love her."

"I have a plan," Dexter said mischievously. He led Leedra over to an old chair that creaked when he sat down in it and pulled her onto his lap. She snuggled in, getting comfy.

"You always have a plan. That's disconcerting," she laughed.

"This is a good one. At least, I'm hoping you like it."

He took a deep breath and continued.

"Every time we say good night on the phone, I get to thinking it would be so much easier—I would be so much happier—if you were lying next to me. I could kiss you awake, tuck you in at night."

"That's sweet. You already talk me to sleep every single night on the phone."

"Yes, but that hasn't been enough for me."

She nuzzled into his chest. "I've been around the world and after all that, everything I've wanted is here. The world wasn't enough. All I needed in the end was peace, a small house and you. Took me so long."

"Sometimes our GPS can be a little off."

"Like, a whole other continent off? That's pretty bad."

"You didn't know how irresistible I'd be, or you'd have come back sooner."

Leedra laughed. "I had no idea about any of this . . . how *right* all of this is." She stared out past Dexter's head to the back yard, envisaging hot summers, backyard barbeques, family life. *Wifey.* A peace came over her unlike anything else she'd felt. "So long to get here, Dexter . . ." she repeated dreamily.

If only she could have avoided everything in between.

She looked back to Dexter and smiled, in spite of herself, as sounds of cheering burst forth from the living room. They shared a laugh.

"Maybe we should go back inside?" Leedra suggested.

"I can send them home if you want some alone time," Dexter replied.

Leedra shook her head. She liked the company; in time, she'd be fine. She'd get used to it.

"It's okay. Of course they are excited. It's James's season opener. What's James like, anyway? Will he come by some time so I can meet him?" Leedra asked about Dexter's youngest, adopted brother, James.

"I figure we can go to one of his games sometime: maybe take a road trip. He's a good kid."

Leedra nodded. "That would be so cool. I'd love a road trip, so long as there are absolutely no boats and no water involved. I have a bucket list of things I want to see and do, but they're mostly local."

"And with me of course?"

"Yes, of course. Nobody but you. I love you."

"I love you too." Even though he'd started to kiss her, she pulled back again momentarily, remembering what they'd been discussing. "Oh yeah—what was the idea you had about telling Allontis I'm quitting?"

"Oh, well, I was just thinking that perhaps we'd tell Allontis that you quit, and then tell her that we're getting married. Sound like a fair trade-off?"

"What?" Leedra hadn't noticed him pull a ring from his shirt pocket. He placed it on her finger and she stared at it, tears clouding her eyes before spilling down her cheeks.

"Will you marry me, Evie Leedra Carter Henderson?"

Momentarily speechless, Leedra held the stone up, almost afraid that it would disappear off her finger if she stared at it for too long. Even in the weak light from the one bare bulb by the door, the round diamond sparkled. It was flanked by a cluster of tiny diamonds, as if they were protecting it, adorning it, caring for it, helping it shine. What a perfect analogy for how she felt: so cherished and protected by him and his wonderful daughter.

She leaned against his chest and cried her eyes out, but not before getting out the words he waited so patiently for: "Yes. I will marry you, Dexter. It would be the second-best move I've ever made."

"Oh yeah, what was the first?"

"Coming home," she whispered, meaning that for the first time since she'd arrived.

They sat in silence together a little longer. This night on the old back porch was likely the first of many in their long shared years to come. She couldn't believe it. Deep down, she'd been wanting exactly this, yearning for it—and now it was here. Hers for the taking. She thanked God for blessing her and keeping her safe to get her to this very day. She couldn't believe it.

When the encroaching chill chased them back inside, they re-entered the warm house hand in hand. When Dexter announced their news, cheers erupted again and it wasn't because of anything they saw on television.

THE END

DEAR READER,

The following words—yes, even from a writer—really and truly cannot express how happy I am to be able to share another story with you. I'm delighted that you've spent time getting to know Leedra, Dexter and the Parker family, as well as visiting with Cole and Allontis, many of whom you'll hopefully remember from my last novel, *Anchored Hearts*.

I hope you enjoyed this carefree and clean romance. My goals are to entertain, to inspire and to allow you a moment to escape from your regular life. I aim to write inspiring stories that spark hope by depicting people who overcome adversity and obstacles.

Please consider writing an honest review on Amazon, Barnes and Noble or Goodreads.

I'd also love to hear from you directly. You can connect with me by:
Visiting my website and dropping me a line via e-mail
Signing up for my Newsletter.
Friending me on Facebook
Following me on Twitter

Teegarner@aol.com

Until next time, may God richly bless you.

ABOUT THE AUTHOR

TRACEE LYDIA GARNER IS A bestselling, award-winning author who writes stories full of complex heroes and heroines, relationships and families that experience tough but realistic life challenges in their quest for love. Born and raised in a Virginia suburb of the DC metro area, Tracee has a degree in Communications, works in health and human services by day and is a speaker-advocate for people with disabilities. Find Tracee on the web at www.teegarner.com or connect with her on Facebook and Twitter.

www.ingramcontent.com/pod-product-compliance
Lightning Source LLC
Chambersburg PA
CBHW050519260626
47157CB00004B/1396